THE AL

O L

Mandana Hendessi (OBE) has spent over thirty years working on women's rights and empowerment in some of the world's most fragile places. Between 2008 and 2016, she lived and worked in Kabul, often visiting Afghanistan's largest women's prison – a place of dimly lit cells, whispered confidences, and *bolani* frying on makeshift stoves. Over countless glasses of tea, she listened to stories of injustice and defiance that would inspire *The Almond Garden of Kabul*. Her debut novel carries the voices of those women – raw, courageous, and unforgettable. Mandana is also the author of *The Kurds: The Struggle for National Identity and Statehood* (Agenda Publishing, 2024) and co-author of *The Elgar Companion to Gender and Global Migration: Beyond Western Research* (Edward Elgar Publishing, 2023). Her article on the criminalisation of Afghan women's sexuality, written as a prelude to *The Almond Garden of Kabul*, appeared in Missing Perspectives in 2023.

'An astonishing book. Wonderfully written, stories beautifully told. In the darkest of places, there is also light and love, defiance and dignity. You will not forget the remarkable women of Badam Bagh prison. And you shouldn't – because their story is true.'
—**Lyse Doucet**, CM OBE, BBC's Chief International Correspondent, author of *The Finest Hotel in Kabul*

'As searing and unforgettable as *Shawshank Redemption* – a shocking story of women's oppression and resilience against the "democratic" Afghanistan. A story of female love, friendship and endurance. A must read for everyone who wants to understand the failures of Westernisation of this country through the eyes of its primary victims: women.'
—**Dr Loretta Napoleoni**, Economist and award-winning author of *Technocapitalism*

'Mandana Hendessi's novel is based on the lived reality of the most oppressed Afghan women in 21st century. She powerfully raises the voice of the voiceless. As we read through this beautifully written novel, we become aware of women's agency seeking empowerment – refusing to be the passive victims. We also read how some women survive by enforcing patriarchal norms; choosing to be on the side of the powerful rather than focusing on gender justice. This novel is different from other books on Afghan women. It's an important source of Afghanistan's oral history based on gripping narratives. It's a great contribution to literature. Furthermore, it's an important contribution to our knowledge as academics, advocacy groups and policy makers.'
—**Dr Elaheh Rostami-Povey**, retired academic, University of London, author of *Afghan Women: Identity and Invasion*

The Almond Garden of Kabul

Mandana Hendessi

Afsana Press
London - Folkestone

First published in 2025
by Afsana Press Ltd, London
www.afsana-press.com

The Almond Garden of Kabul is a work of fiction. Although the story is based on real events, all the characters and events are the products of the author's imagination, and while certain organisations and institutions are mentioned, the characters involved are wholly imaginary. Any resemblance to actual persons, living or dead, is purely coincidental, except for the well-known persons. Places and times may have been rearranged to suit the purposes of the book. The opinions expressed are those of the characters, and should not be confused with the author's.

Typeset by Afsana Press Ltd
Printed and bound in Great Britain by Clays Ltd, Elcograf S.p.A.

A CIP catalogue record for this book is available from the British Library

ISBN: 978-1-0684958-0-9

MIX
Paper | Supporting responsible forestry
FSC® C018072

A Note from the Author

I first walked through the gates of Badam Bagh – Kabul's central prison for women – in the bitter winter of 2010. At the time, I was working for a women's charity in Afghanistan, leading programmes focused on women's rights, gender justice and civil society in conflict-affected regions.

For several months, I visited the prison regularly. What I witnessed there shaped me irrevocably.

The women of Badam Bagh had been accused of crimes – some real, many imagined. They were imprisoned not just for defying laws, but for rebelling against the systems behind them: systems that punished dissent, independence, and often, survival itself. For four months, every weekend, I drank tea, listened to stories, and sat in dimly lit, overcrowded cells, with women whose lives had been broken and buried long before they ever reached trial. And yet, what I found was not only despair, but defiance, wit, creativity and fire.

This novel is fiction, but it is rooted in truths I was never able to forget. *The Almond Garden of Kabul* is for those women – those who spoke, and those who never had the chance. It is a story of fire, resistance, and memory. Of what happens when women who were meant to disappear, begin to speak.

Prologue

They called it Badam Bagh. The Almond Garden. A name soft on the tongue, conjuring winter blossoms and spring rain. But behind the gates, there was no garden. No mercy. Only concrete, barred windows, silence, and the rusted machinery of punishment. It was Kabul's central prison for women – those accused of defiance, disobedience, dishonour. Many had been caged for love. Others, for leaving. Some, simply for surviving.

There was no light in the corridors. But the fire burned quietly. Inside them.

In Afghanistan, fire was once sacred – a symbol of life, truth, and divine power in the old Zoroastrian and Buddhist traditions. In Zoroastrian temples it burned as divine witness. But in Badam Bagh, fire took on another form: it flickered in grief, in memory, in the rage that could not be spoken aloud.

When Niloofar, a teenage inmate, set herself on fire, it was not just a cry. It was an ignition. She did not create the fire. She released it – the fire that had always burned within her, and within many other victims of injustice. The flames blackened her body, but not the truth. The silence that followed screamed louder than the blaze.

Two women began to listen. Sultan, who walked like a man and had once killed one – her abusive husband. She ruled the prison like a tribal chief: part protector, part tyrant, carved from the same stone that had scarred her. And Setara, a teacher and artist, who carried charcoal and *bolani* flour beneath her fingernails and saw what others refused to see. Her fire burned through portraits – images that exposed what silence could not.

Between them, a strange alliance was formed not of friendship, but of shared fury. As they began to uncover the truth behind Niloofar's self-immolation, a deeper rot revealed itself. One that reached far beyond the prison walls onto the hands of those who used power to traffic women, erase them, and bury the evidence.

This is the story of what happens when women remember.

When silence becomes witness.

When the fire within refuses to die, and the imagined garden begins to burn.

Burning Daybreak

That early morning, Sultan awoke with a jolt. A low, persistent buzzing filled her ear, drilling into the edges of her sleep. She shook her head, swatting at what she assumed was an insect. But the sound lingered, vibrating inside her skull. With a scowl, she sat up, pressing her temples hard with both hands as if she could squeeze the noise out. Slowly, grudgingly, it faded.

'I'm getting old,' she muttered. At thirty-three, she felt ancient among women ten, sometimes fifteen years younger. Seema and Humaira – her wives – were both, or at least seemed to be, a decade her junior. But in Afghanistan, where births were seldom registered, none of them knew their exact age. She envied their limber ease, the way they sprang out of bed while her own movements grew sluggish, her joints stiff from years spent on a prison mattress. Yet it wasn't just the mattress. The pain in her spine ran deeper, lodged in the bone and sinew – a relic of her teenage years, when she endured torture at the hands of the husband she had later stabbed to death, twenty-six times. Those nights of agony had left their mark, etched into the very marrow of her being. These days, the ache in her lower back greeted her like an old adversary, making the first steps of the morning a struggle.

She peeled herself from the warmth of the cot she'd shared with Seema the night before – her wives took turns in her bed – and walked barefoot to the door. Stooping, she peered through the hatch, searching for the guard on duty. But the corridor lay empty, swallowed in darkness. Not a flicker of movement. No distant footsteps, no jingle of keys. A frown settled on her brow. *Isn't it prayer time already? Where the hell is she?* Turning, she cast a wary glance at the barred window, searching the sky beyond the grimy mesh for a hint of dawn. But the heavens remained an unbroken canvas of deep indigo – no echo of morning light, no shift in the stars. *Strange.*

She rummaged through bundles of plastic bags and old shoes, searching for her phone – a contraband every inmate owned. Finally, her fingers closed around it in the pocket of her grey trousers. She pressed the button. Nothing. The battery was dead. And their shared charger? Nowhere in sight.

Normally, the guard would have knocked by now, rousing them for the *Fajr* prayer. The absence of that routine – the small, rigid predictability of prison life – made her uneasy. A strange restlessness prickled at her skin, whispering of something wrong.

Seema stirred, lifting her head just enough to grumble, 'What is it? Come back to bed. Let me sleep, for God's sake.' She yawned, burying her face back into the pillow.

'The guard isn't here,' Sultan murmured. 'Something's wrong.'

Seema groaned and rolled onto her side, facing the wall. 'Maybe she's late. Who cares?'

Sultan exhaled sharply but said nothing. Instead, she made her way to the corner of the cell where a cramped bathroom stood behind a flimsy, corrugated metal door. She turned on the tap for ablution, bracing for the icy bite of water against her skin. But just as she raised her hands to begin, something stopped her – something outside.

A soundless jolt of movement. A flicker of orange against the dark. Sultan turned. Her breath stilled. A plume of black smoke curled against the sky, swelling from the prison yard. She stumbled forward, pressing her face to the mesh-glass window, her pulse hammering in her ears.

'*Ya Allah!*' she cried, her voice fracturing the silence. 'Fire! Someone's on fire!'

Seema shot upright, her mouth parting in a silent gasp before she found her voice – a bloodcurdling scream. Humaira stood frozen, arms crossed tight over her chest, eyes wide with dread.

Below, in the yard, a woman stood engulfed in flames. Her arms were stretched out like a crucifix, her back rigid, her face tilted towards the sky. Her long hair, once dark, burned bright – an eerie halo of fire licking at her scalp.

Sultan lurched towards the door, slamming her fists against the cold blue metal. 'Fire! Fire!' she bellowed, her voice raw, hoarse and desperate. Seema and Humaira clung to each other, their eyes locked on the inferno below, horror stretching their features. From cell to cell, cries of alarm erupted – women pounding their doors, screaming for help.

'The guards are here!' Seema yelled, pointing towards the yard, her voice hoarse and grating. She yanked up her scarf, pressing it over her nose and mouth.

Sultan spun back to the window. The acrid stench of kerosene and burning flesh clawed at her throat, sharp and thick. She doubled over, heaving between coughs. Following Seema's gaze, she locked her eyes on a cluster of female guards hurling grey blankets over the burning woman. The fire hissed. Flames lashed back, defiant. Their frantic movements cast jagged shadows against the walls, wild and frenzied in the flickering light. Soot settled over the blankets and darkened their hands and faces.

Moments later, an ambulance tore into the yard, its sirens ripping through the dawn. The flashing lights painted the scene in sharp, blinding pulses – white, red, white, red. A final, desperate gasp of smoke curled into the air as the flames died. The woman was nothing but a motionless bundle of grey, charred and twisted.

A hush settled over the yard. Soot rose in ghostly tendrils, vanishing into the emerging pale strands of morning light. Then, from the minaret of Badam Bagh Mosque, the first notes of the *Fajr azan* rang out – loud, slow, solemn. The call to prayer filled the silence, settling over the smouldering remains of the fire's victim – charred pieces of cloth, singed balls of hair floating over blistering earth.

The Flames Within

The day at Badam Bagh prison rose beneath a cloud of bewilderment, shock, and grief. The air in the cellblocks was thick with unspoken questions, blank stares, and muted dread. Not even the prison's oldest inmate could recall a day like this in the short, troubled history of this jail – or its predecessors, the women's wing at Pol-e-Charkhi and Welayat.

'No one has ever set herself on fire in a Kabul jail. No one...' Fahema remarked, leaning against the wall in Sultan's cell. Her faintly hennaed index finger absently traced a shallow crack running in the wall, her voice wavered, tailing off before hanging in the thick, suffocating air. At fifty, with a sharp memory honed by over a decade behind bars for murdering her mother-in-law, Fahema had witnessed more of prison life than most. Her release was approaching – six months from now, just in time for Nowruz, the Afghan New Year. After sixteen years of silent counting, only six more months, and yet, there was nowhere to go.

Her gaze drifted over the cell, unfocused. There was no spark of joy in them, no glimmer of hope or enthusiasm in her voice. The future loomed as bleak and murky as the grimy, grease-smeared prison walls. She had no home to return to, no family waiting to celebrate. Her embittered, vengeful husband had divorced her the moment she was arrested, and her four grown children and their families had long since severed all ties. Fahema could no longer even picture their faces; they had become mere shadows of a life lost.

The inmates had been kept indoors since early morning while the cleaners worked to erase all traces of the fire from the yard – the space where they exercised, socialised, sometimes played volleyball, and watched their children on the swings and roundabout. Outside, the fierce and bitter *Jadi* wind swept through, sharp enough to drain the colour from lips and cheeks in an instant. Despite the cramped and heavy atmosphere inside, the warmth offered a welcome reprieve from the biting cold.

Only a few inmates had glimpsed the eerie shape of ash and melted asphalt from their windows after the burnt woman was taken to the hospital. Its twisted, unnatural form sent a chill down their spines. Some whispered it looked like 'the devil, its horns and hooves etched into the scorched ground'. Others muttered *'Astaghfirullah'* under their breath before turning away from the window, repulsed.

Rumours about the identity of the burnt woman spread like wildfire. A coterie of inmates, notorious for their love of gossip, lingered near Sultan's cell, eager for answers. Some claimed she was a drug smuggler from Iran, while others swore they had seen her on *Afghan Star* as a hopeful singing contestant. All of them were keen to know what Sultan knew, convinced – as always – that she held more information than they did.

Sultan was no ordinary inmate; she was the chief – a Colossus among them. She wasn't just any female villain either. She had butchered her abusive husband, proudly confessed it to the police, the prosecutor, and the trial judge without a flicker of remorse. She dressed, spoke, and carried herself like a man, boldly declaring that she was a man trapped in a woman's body. She had long since rejected everything feminine. Ruthless and unforgiving, she was carved from the same rock that built Afghanistan's patriarchy. It was no surprise, then, that the other inmates saw her as a father figure. She had vowed to protect them – to fight for their cause whenever they were unjustifiably victimised by prison officials. But she also abused them at will, exercised her power without limit, and punished them mercilessly when they disobeyed. Not unlike her own father. Or her late husband. A cataclysmic personality, Sultan simmered beneath her cold exterior like seismic waves gathering force – ready to hurl her rage upon the world.

Born into a family of three daughters, Sultan had spent the first twelve years of her life as a *bacha posh* – a girl dressed as a boy – A practice that had been common in Afghanistan for generations. Officially, it was meant to spare her mother the dishonour and crushing shame of the *dokhtar za* label – she who brings only daughters. But deep down, Sultan believed she had been destined to be a boy, that God had made a small mistake at the last moment, an error she now knew could be corrected through surgery.

She had been quietly stashing away every dollar and Afghani she could for the surgery – Her only hope of becoming who she truly was. The plan was to undergo the operation in Iran after her release, still thirteen long years away. So far, she had scraped together the equivalent of two hundred dollars – still eighteen hundred short. It felt like an impossible mountain to climb, but every bit brought her a step closer.

She scammed for every cent: extorting protection fees from terrified newcomers, the same ones she had personally intimidated upon their arrival, swiping gifts from visitors, and dealing drugs within the prison walls. It didn't matter how dirty the money was or how far she had to go to get it, every desperate deal brought her closer to her ultimate goal.

The years she had lived as a boy were the happiest of her life – Forever etched in her memory as the most vibrant and carefree. During those years, she roamed freely through the dusty streets of Kabul's Dehmazang, dressed in her white *pirhan tunban* – a long cotton shirt and baggy trousers – taking part in all the thrilling activities boys did. She played marbles with fierce determination, rolled hoops alongside her rivals, and hunted sparrows with a slingshot.

But all that joyful freedom had come to a cruel end with a *baad* marriage – a transactional affair – at the tender age of twelve to the crooked Sharif, a wealthy 'businessman'. She could never understand why they called such a dreadful union *baad;* the name fell miserably short of capturing the bondage, anguish, and pain this marriage – arranged by her father to repay a loan – had inflicted on her.

'The burnt victim,' Sultan told the curious crowd gathered at her cell, 'is called Niloofar.' One of the many erotic names Persian poets and playwrights bestowed upon their idols, muses, or obelisks. It was Farzana, the toothless prison guard, who had quietly revealed the woman's identity to Sultan, teetering on high heels at breakfast. 'A Herati,' she had whispered with a knowing nod and wink. 'But *alhamdulillah,* she is alive,' Farzana had added, glancing upwards, her hands raised in a praying gesture.

Bewildered, Sultan clicked her tongue and shook her head, lost in the meaning of the name Niloofar, the water lily. She imagined the glorious white flowers that floated briefly on her family's pond every spring – Sacred and untouchable. Her mother had always scolded her for daring to touch their delicate petals.

Sultan closed her eyes, cringing at the thought of the poor woman shrivelled in pain on a hospital bed, all alone just as she herself had once been. She recalled the despair she had felt in that Peshawar hospital, recovering from her own suicide attempt. But why had Niloofar wanted to end her life? And in such a cruel way? Why did so many Afghan women resort to suicide to escape their unbearable lives?

God had rarely smiled on Afghanistan, Sultan thought. For thirty years, Afghans had endured relentless war, but for Afghan women life had been especially harrowing. They were brutalised not only by the ravages of conflict but by their own men – Men who had grown doubly vicious since the wars began, asserting their dominance with venomous cruelty. Sultan knew this all too well from her own experience. She understood why women were driven to suicide when life became an existence devoid of hope, filled only with fear and anguish. She had lived as a slave to others' power, tasted the excruciating pain of a bleak life – The sallow complexion, the hollow eyes, the empty, distant stare that came with that life.

She remembered waking up groggy and grief-stricken in a hospital ward, cursing Aziza, Sharif's maid, for finding her in the basement – The place she had chosen as her grave after swallowing countless amphetamines. She had lain on the cold concrete floor among crates of rice and chickpeas, longing for the darkness to consume her.

Unbeknownst to her family when they married, her husband had made his fortune by trafficking young Afghan women and men into sex slavery across neighbouring countries. The same fate awaited her as she sat at the *nikah* ceremony, helplessly watching her father sign her life away with a single stroke of his pen. What followed that fateful day were years of brutal sex slavery in Peshawar, Pakistan, where in a cruel twist of fate, she and other unfortunate women had sought refuge from the civil war in Afghanistan.

Sullen and stolid as ever, Sultan wasn't in the mood for talking with other inmates. She kept her gaze lowered, tuning out the hot air filled with chatter – The swirl of dreams and nightmares the inmates swapped, each competing for her attention. Yet whispers of eerie premonitions rippled through the prison, too strange to ignore.

Zahra, a twenty-year-old mother of a newborn, jailed for theft and deception, claimed to see her cell window swarming with crows, their beaks furiously pecking at the sill. Samira, a convict charged with *zina* – forbidden sex – had spotted a broken mirror on the floor of the meeting room where she'd last met her social worker.

But the strangest tale of all came from Parwin Chapool, a cross-eyed pathological thief, known to everyone as 'the Prison Snitch'. Short and chubby with arms and fingers scarred and disfigured from a childhood burning accident, Parwin recounted a dream of cockroaches crawling backwards in a chaotic swarm. 'That,' she declared matter-of-factly, 'means death by fire.'

The dream was so bizarre that even the toothless guard who rarely smiled, burst into laughter.

'But she's alive, isn't she?' Sultan quipped, shooing Parwin away with a swift flick of her hand.

Yet a thought lingered. Wasn't that incessant buzz she'd heard in her ears – a sound she had dismissed as a mosquito's whine – also a premonition?

After the inmates dissipated, Farzana confided that Niloofar, a *zina* convict, had been transferred to Badam Bagh just a week ago from Herat prison due to overcrowding. The number of women convicted of *zina* had soared beyond the provincial prison's capacity – An unprecedented surge in both Herat's and Afghanistan's history. These women now made up the majority of female prisoners.

Prison authorities attributed this rise to Afghan returnees from Iran, claiming they had picked up 'bad manners and perversion' from the Iranians. The belief was so deeply entrenched that Afghanistan's Islamic Guidance Council had publicly warned young people during Friday prayers against migrating to the Islamic Republic of Iran. Adding to the crisis, Herat had seen a sharp increase in cases of self-immolation, particularly among women. This, too, was blamed on the returnees from Iran.

An impulse stirred inside Sultan, nudging her towards the mystery of Niloofar. Instantly, she thought of Setara, who was also from Herat. Setara must have crossed paths with Niloofar and would likely know enough to shed more light on her. It was common for people from the same province to seek each other out when in Kabul, offering companionship and guidance on how to navigate the unfamiliar territory.

Besides, Setara was the prison scribe – one of the few inmates who could read and write. Because of this, she was held in high esteem and affectionately called 'Madam Teacher'. Inmates trusted her with their most intimate secrets. Before being sentenced to life in prison for conspiring with her lover to murder her husband, Setara had been a teacher. Now, she wrote letters for the inmates and read aloud those they received, even those from secret lovers and suitors. These love letters, often crafted in exquisite calligraphy by scribes in the bazaar, were the inmates' most treasured possessions. Carefully tied with red or orange ribbons taken from the tailoring workshops and delicately perfumed with rose water or dried rose petals from cookery classes, they were kept in neat, cherished piles.

Setara knew everyone's secrets – Everyone's except Sultan's. No one knew Sultan's secrets. Not even her wives, who had been closer to her than anyone else.

Sultan thought long and hard about how to approach Setara, uncertain of whether she would be well received. She even rehearsed their potential conversation several times. After all, Setara was a *khanum* – a lady – Nothing like her wives or Parwin Chapool. She was educated and respectable. That meant every word had to be courteous and respectful – No swear words.

They had rarely spoken to each other. Setara was a Herati, a Tajik, and a native Persian speaker, while Sultan was a Pashtun from Kabul. Their two ethnic groups hardly mixed anymore. Animosities between them – and with other ethnicities like the Hazaras and Uzbeks – had become insurmountable since the civil war, with atrocities committed on all sides. The Pashtun-supremacist Taliban regime, which had ruled with brutal force for five years until their downfall a decade ago, had only fuelled these tensions further.

The divisions were so intensely vindictive and venomous that each group had erected metaphorical walls, isolating themselves from the others in a desperate bid for survival. Kabul had become a city divided by ethnicity: Hazaras lived secluded lives in the southwest, Tajiks in the northwest, and Pashtuns in the eastern districts. Meanwhile, the newcomers – Americans and Europeans – had taken over the central and affluent areas, building their own fortified enclaves with tall blast walls, sandbags, and razor wire. Kabul was no longer the city of Sultan's childhood; it had turned into a garrisoned town.

Driven by insatiable curiosity, Sultan tried to suppress her doubts and break the ice with Setara. Sporting a crew cut and dressed in her new pair of jeans – the ones she'd forcibly taken from Geisha, the bonkers Kimono-clad Hazara inmate – and a freshly ironed blue shirt acquired from Dina Charsi in exchange for a small lump of *chars*, she sauntered down the corridor with tense shoulders and her hands buried deep in her pockets. Her clunky, uncertain gait echoed sharply on the cold concrete floor as she made her way to Setara's cell at the end of the corridor. Her heart hammered in her chest.

Cautiously, she knocked on the heavy blue door and was relieved to find Setara alone, engrossed in a book. It seemed as though her three cellmates were away at some morning workshop, and their four small children at playschool.

'*Sobh bakhayr,* Setara *jaan,*' Sultan said softly, her voice barely audible as she stood at the threshold, pressing her sweaty palms against the doorknob.

Draped in a worn, threadbare cream-coloured kaftan, Setara glanced up and met Sultan's gaze.

'*Sobh bakhayr, jaan.*' At forty, Setara was seven years older than her, yet she looked much younger with her glowing skin and slim frame. Without pausing, she added tersely, a frown forming on her brow, 'I'm not writing letters today. Not in the mood.' She turned away, eyes drifting towards the shadows gathering at the edge of the cell.

Taken aback, Sultan swallowed hard and forced a thin smile. No one in the prison had ever dared speak to her so brusquely. But this time, she decided to let it go.

'No, *jaan*... I'm not here for that,' she said, clearing her throat. 'I have no one to write letters to anyway.' She offered a smirk. 'I came to ask about the woman who set herself on fire early this morning. I was wondering if you knew her.'

'Akh, Niloofar...' Setara let out a heavy sigh and gestured for Sultan to come in and take a seat on the floor opposite her. Adjusting her voluminous scarf, which she wore with a regal grace like an Ottoman turban, Setara turned her head to the side and rested her hand under her chin as she stared into space.

Her profile reminded Sultan of a drawing she'd seen years ago in Peshawar – A portrait of Nefertiti, the ancient Egyptian queen, which once hung above the bed she shared with Shaista, the love of her life. 'Do you know her?' Shaista had asked, her eyes curious as she pointed at the picture. She hadn't been the least surprised when Sultan shook her head. Sultan had never been to school, whereas Shaista had been privately tutored at home. Her mother, Nasrin, had amassed a fortune running a high-class brothel frequented by Pakistan's elite – The same men who had made millions off the arms trade during the Afghan wars.

Setara's eyes welled up with tears. She stared back at Sultan. 'Poor child... barely nineteen.'

A blaring silence ensued.

Setara's cell smelled of home – warm, and rich with the aroma of freshly fried food and tea, an unfamiliar blend that stirred something deep within Sultan. The walls, though stained in places with greasy fingerprints, were mostly clean and bare, and shelves bowed under the weight of books – A sharp contrast to Sultan's cell where Bollywood movie posters of her icons Salman Khan and Shah Rukh Khan, adorned every inch. The posters which captured the stars in dramatic dance and battle poses. These were her only mementoes from Peshawar, the only things she'd brought with her to prison besides the brightly coloured Kuchi dress she'd been wearing at the time of her arrest. They were gifts from Shaista, her only source of hope during that dark chapter of her life as a child prostitute. It was Shaista who had introduced her to modern Indian cinema, inspiring Sultan to dream big, to become a Bollywood star when she grew up. A dream that real life had swiftly and painfully suffocated.

She recalled those precious moments with fondness, the times they'd cuddled up on Shaista's bed, watching videos of Shah Rukh Khan in his various heroic roles.

Those cherished moments of togetherness, before the inflow of clients. The evening onslaught. Something to distract them from the daily grind and the immense weight of shame they bore for having to please repulsive, pot-bellied, middle-aged men reeking of alcohol and tobacco.

'Have you seen Indian movies?' seventeen-year-old Shaista had asked one autumn afternoon.

'Yes, I saw some in Kabul,' Sultan replied proudly. '*Sangam* with Raj Kumar and *Sholay* with Amitabh Bachchan.'

'No!' Shaista burst into a loud guffaw. 'Not those dead-and-buried old films, *yaar!* I mean Bollywood.'

Roaring with laughter, they both jumped up and danced to the tune of Salman Khan's latest song blaring from the speakers.

The memory tugged at Sultan's lips, her smile faint but fleeting. She barely noticed Setara pouring two cups of sweetened black tea from the flask by her side until the aroma broke through her thoughts, rich and soothing. Sultan accepted the cup gratefully, the warmth anchoring her to the present.

Setara rose and fetched some *bolani* – fried flatbread stuffed with potatoes and leeks – which she made daily to sell in prison for a meagre income. The routine comfort of tea and *bolani* felt like a fragile thread pulling Sultan back from the swirling memories of a livelier time.

The offer of *bolani* was a welcome surprise; Setara's *bolani* had become a famous treat in Badam Bagh, with everyone raving about it. Sultan was chuffed by Setara's warmth and hospitality – So unthinkable, so unexpected. They quietly savoured the mouth-watering pieces of *bolani* dipped in yoghurt, washing it down with generous sips of the scented tea.

'This isn't prison tea, is it?' Sultan remarked, raising her thick eyebrows that arched over striking green eyes. She wiped away the beads of sweat forming on her deeply lined forehead with the sleeve of her shirt. Running her index finger over the soft fluff of hair above her upper lip, her gaze met Setara's.

'No!' Setara smiled shyly, shaking her head. 'It's from Iran. I bought it from Farzana a few days ago. She'd been on vacation in Tehran. With the money I earn from *bolani*, I treat myself to books and good tea – my lifelong companions.'

Sultan was at a loss for words. She glanced down at her teacup, squinting slightly as she pursed her lips. She and Setara couldn't have been more different – like two people from parallel universes. Setara reminded her of her mother – righteous and compassionate, earning her keep through honourable means unlike herself, who had always got what she wanted in prison through force and intimidation. But then again, she was the *baashi*, the chief inmate. That's what everyone expected of the boss. There was no other way she could have attained her status.

'Poor Niloofar…' Setara sighed, rocking gently from side to side. 'She's a lost soul. Lost in sadness and rage from one betrayal or another. I saw her twice. She asked me to write letters for her. One to her husband in Pol-e-Charkhi prison and another to her mother in Herat. She was literate. She could have written them herself, but she said she was too muddled, couldn't think straight. Both letters reeked of remorse for her past mistakes, pleading for forgiveness. She spoke of the shame and fury consuming her. "The flames within," she called them. And then something happened.'

'What?' Sultan enquired.

'I don't know. She didn't say. Maybe she got disturbing news about someone,' Setara said, sipping her tea. 'Whatever it was, it made her restless and irritable. She was in a cell all by herself, so there's no cellmate to shed light on what happened in the hours before the fire.'

'How did she get hold of kerosene?' Sultan's voice dropped. 'I've been in this prison for two years, and before that, in Pol-e-Charkhi for five, and I've never known where they keep the food and fuel supplies.'

'No one knows,' Setara concluded. 'Not even the guards. Or maybe they know and just don't want to tell us the truth… I really don't know. It's all a big mystery to me.'

Setara

Setara described herself as a 'war child'. Born in 1970 in the oasis city of Herat to a family of two boys and one girl, she knew only a fleeting period of relative peace – when Herat was celebrated as Afghanistan's cultural jewel. Back then, the city's weavers tenderly crafted exquisitely designed carpets, intricate as fine-art tapestries, while its people were enraptured by the poetry of Rumi, Saadi, and Hafez. The narrow, sunlit alleys – divided by rows of sparsely planted trees and partially shaded by domes and minarets – bustled with life, the air thick with the scent of rose gardens and the sound of children's laughter.

But those golden days vanished like a mirage when the horrors of war descended on Herat as Setara turned ten. The poetry and carpets – the symbols of the city's grandeur – became ghostly relics of a past that now felt as distant and unreal as fairy tales. Herat's glory years were swept away, replaced by the relentless rhythm of artillery fire and the anguished cries of families torn apart.

Setara's childhood also coincided with a brief chapter of Afghanistan's own renaissance. The country, rebuilding itself as a modern nation, flaunted a democratic constitution with a king at its helm. During this fragile period of hope, Setara's love of literature became her sanctuary, a fortress against the madness engulfing her world.

As the youngest child of a mother nearing the end of her childbearing years, Setara was the apple of her parents' eye and received all the encouragement she needed to thrive in her studies. While her siblings, especially Naseema – a stoic and altruistic girl – handled the household chores and shopping, Setara immersed herself in books and poured her heart into poetry. By the age of eleven, with her long ponytail swaying and her school uniform crisp and starched, she had already mastered the works of Dostoevsky and Tolstoy. Her teachers, recognizing her rare talent, often awarded her for her exceptional knowledge of Afghan and Russian history.

This period coincided with the fragile reign of Afghanistan's communist government, propped up by Russian firepower. At the regime's behest, schools interwove Afghan history with Russian, filling classrooms with sombre portraits of Lenin, Marx, and whoever was at the helm of Afghanistan's communist party at the time – Each figure briefly topping the other in a brutal power struggle. Yet, amid this ideological onslaught, Setara found solace in Russian classics – A strange comfort in a world unravelling at the seams.

She fondly recalled her early teens as a time of intense love for poetry, particularly the lesser-known and taboo. Her passion led her to the works of Rabia Balkhi and Forough Farrokhzad, poets who spoke with courage, tenderness, and poetic eloquence about love and women's desires. Though separated by centuries – Rabia from tenth-century Afghanistan and Forough a modern-day Iranian – they spoke in unison, unveiling the passionate love affairs of women whose feelings had been suffocated by archaic traditions.

Setara's love for poetry deepened further through her acquaintance with an erudite family who ran a small bookshop not far from her home. The shop offered a rich selection of risqué literature smuggled from Iran, available only to a few trusted clients. The bookshop owners restricted distribution not out of fear of the state, but because of the rapidly growing number of Islamists who terrified them. Extremists had begun attacking cinemas, bookshops, and unveiled female students. Heeding her mother's advice, Setara always erred on the side of caution, wearing a scarf when walking to and from school.

Soon, the drums of war began to beat, and Herat became embroiled in fierce battles between government forces and the Mujaheddin – Islamist-led rural elites – who opposed the Soviet invasion and rejected state policies of co-education and women's employment. Their vision of liberation would have seen women confined to their homes as subservient housewives. This wasn't the future Setara's family wanted for her or her sister. To escape the surrounding gloom, Setara sought solace in books. Her family called her 'Madam Philosopher', a satirical nickname for spending countless hours at home, her nose buried in one book or another.

As the battles between the government forces and the Mujaheddin grew more frequent and fiercer, Setara retreated deeper into her own cocoon. The once-vibrant sounds of Herat faded; she no longer heard the morning chants of birds or saw the delicate rose petals blooming along the city's boulevards. Butterflies no longer fluttered in the gardens. The air, thick with the stench of rockets and gunpowder, reverberated with the crack of gunfire.

When her favourite bookshop was reduced to rubble in a night rocket attack, and its owners were forced into hiding, Setara was one of the fortunate few to salvage some of the precious books. She carefully unearthed them from the debris and hid them in the basement of her home, tucking them beneath sacks of rice and behind rows of jam and pickle jars her mother had stored in case of an Islamist attack.

Pursuing her childhood dream of teaching Persian literature, Setara enrolled in Herat's teacher training college when she was eighteen. But shortly after, unimaginable events intervened. Suitors began flooding their home, each competing for her hand in marriage. Not only was she intelligent, she had also blossomed into a beautiful young woman with long, jet-black hair and dark eyes made even more captivating with Afghan kohl.

Her siblings had already settled into family lives of their own and moved to Kabul in search of work. With Setara being the only child left at home, her parents were eager to see her wedded to a man of distinction and eloquence. The Soviet army had just withdrawn from Afghanistan, and the nation dared to hope for peace. But these hopes were swiftly dashed when the Mujaheddin intensified their attacks on the cities.

In the midst of the mayhem and bloodshed, Izzuddin entered her life, embellishing it with his magnetic charm. He stole her heart with his smile and bewitching eyes – dark and mysterious, like the eyes of a mystic. A skilled craftsman, he created exquisite pieces of furniture and wooden sculptures. He gave her a small, polished carving – A robed female figure carrying a jug of water on her head. It was a gift she cherished so deeply that she kept it in sight at all times. The wooden figure sat on her desk, watching over her as she penned poems for Izzuddin – The enigmatic marauder of her heart.

Her parents hurried them into marriage to quell any idle gossip in the neighbourhood. Izzuddin, who had been orphaned as an infant in Taloqan, northern Afghanistan, moved in, bringing with him all his magnificent creations that adorned their sparsely furnished home. Suddenly, it felt homely again. Their front room, where they entertained guests, now had an ornate dresser skilfully carved with Nuristani motifs, topped with a delicately carved wooden bowl filled with jasmine – Setara's favourite flower.

Also, Izzuddin gave Setara and her parents each a chest made of aromatic cedar wood to keep the ravenous moths away. But finer than those was the gift he had set aside for his beloved: a slender dressing table with an intricately carved mirror. To the envy of her siblings, their parents doted on Izzuddin, convinced that Setara couldn't have found a better husband.

Buoyed by their approval, Izzuddin worked tirelessly to bring in much-needed cash to support the impoverished household. But the money was eventually drained by mounting medical expenses, until Setara's mother succumbed to heart disease and her father to cancer shortly after.

Soon after she buried her parents, Setara's daughter Yasmin was born. Her arrival transformed Setara's world overnight. Her and Izzuddin's home became overrun with handmade baby outfits in a riot of colours and stacks of nappies. While Yasmin's birth brought immense joy, it also drained Setara's energy. She no longer had the strength, nor the time, to browse through the heaps of books that adorned the beautifully varnished walnut shelves in their lounge. As the baby suckled at her breast, she would gaze longingly at the bookshelves, yearning for those quiet moments when she could lose herself in the world of words – A world more familiar and comforting to her than family life.

By then, Setara was working part-time as a secondary school teacher and found juggling her roles as a mother, wife and educator increasingly cumbersome. Thankfully, Somaya, her selfless and kind-hearted sister-in-law, came to her rescue. Somaya moved in to help with childcare and housework, providing much-needed support. Already in her forties, Somaya had never married, as she had a limp from childhood polio and a face pocked by smallpox scars. No family in Herat wanted their son to marry a disabled woman, regardless of her gentle nature and radiant soul.

Yet, this harsh rebuff had not tarnished Somaya's positive view of life. Her words were always filled with praise for the little joys that brightened their war-torn existence, and she ended most of her sentences with *'Subhan Allah.'* With her abundance of love and tenderness, she filled the void left by Setara's parents, becoming a pillar of support and a beacon of warmth in their home.

Yasmin's sister, Raha, was born two years later. They named her Raha – meaning 'free' – because her birth coincided with jubilant crowds of Heratis celebrating the arrival of a new governor. Following the crushing defeat of the communists and the establishment of the new Mujaheddin government in Kabul, Ismail Khan, the revered son of Herat, was crowned its governor, having risen from its blessed soil.

However, the much-coveted freedom was tragically short-lived. The Pakistan-sponsored Taliban – followers of the strict Salafi Islamic sect – stormed Herat, driving Ismail Khan and his 8,000-strong militia into neighbouring Iran. Under the Taliban's rule, Setara's life turned into a living nightmare. Schools were ordered to shut their doors to girls, and women were forbidden from working. The Taliban also banned women from leaving home without a *mahram* and *burqa*. Neither Setara nor Somaya had ever worn the all-enveloping blue garment. They felt suffocated within its folds, forced to see the world through its tiny mesh grill.

Confined to the house with Somaya and the girls, Setara sought refuge once again in her books. She began with Tolstoy's *War and Peace*, finding solace in the character of Princess Marya Bolkonskaya, who had survived her father's cruelty by embracing spirituality and a deep love of God while secretly yearning for more earthly, passionate love.

Back in her bubble of literature and poetry, Setara tried to mentally escape the grim realities of life under the Taliban. Poetry became her lifeline, a vehicle for expressing the anguish and yearning of life in captivity – The caged bird longing for the open sky. The serenade trapped in the throat of a silenced troubadour. The forlorn, arid alley craving the invigorating sound of chatter and haggling that once reverberated off its mud-brick walls.

Izzuddin, who had to work around the clock to support the family, was forced to send his apprentice, Matin, to escort Setara and Somaya when they went shopping in the bazaar. The girls, meanwhile, had to be educated at home. Setara taught them to read and write, while Somaya covered maths.

Not long after, Setara began hearing from her former colleagues about secret girls' schools springing up across Herat. She and Somaya were thrilled to join the clandestine network which became known as the 'sewing circles'. Masquerading as sewing classes, these gatherings taught girls – hidden beneath their *burqas* to conceal their identities – everything from basic literacy and numeracy to classical Persian poetry by Hafez, Khayyam, and Rumi. They persisted in these secret lessons until the US invasion of Afghanistan and the fall of the Taliban five years later.

When the guns finally fell silent, birds returned to the beleaguered Herati sky; their morning chorus greeted Setara each day as she awoke for *Fajr* prayer. With the arrival of spring and Nowruz, the hillsides were strewn with aromatic narcissi and vibrant red and yellow tulips. Life had returned to the ancient city once more.

Schools reopened. Setara went back to teaching and the girls were finally in proper classrooms. Yasmin started secondary school, while Raha – who had never stepped foot in a real school – happily settled into the fourth grade.

The sweetness did not endure. It soon curdled into bitterness. It happened in the middle of a typical, blistering Herati summer, where the scorching sun ruthlessly withered the honeysuckle and geranium saplings Setara had lovingly planted in their small garden. Keeping cool was impossible without an electric fan; electricity was always in short supply. Tempers flared, and Izzuddin complained bitterly and incessantly about their dwindling fortunes. He was no longer the kind and caring husband and father Setara had once known. The harsh years of war and the Taliban's barbaric rule had transformed him into a bitter, irritable man who seized any excuse to shout obscenities at his wife and sister.

One day, he stunned Setara by announcing that he had found a suitable husband for twelve-year-old Yasmin and was already negotiating with the groom-to-be's family over the terms of marriage – the dowry, bride price, and wedding expenses.

'What? Yasmin? Are you out of your mind?'

'I can't afford to support this family anymore,' he snapped, staring furiously into Setara's eyes. 'I can't even keep Matin. And your wages aren't enough.'

'I won't let that happen. Yasmin is too young for marriage.' Setara met his gaze, unflinching, and let it linger in the suffocating air between them.

Izzuddin stormed out of the room in a violent rage, slamming the door behind him.

Their arguments became a daily occurrence, and Setara dreaded waking up each morning to the sight of his sour face. Somaya, who had quietly endured the endless squabbles between husband and wife, finally broke her silence. She pleaded with her brother to see reason and consider other ways to boost the family income. She even volunteered to help out by taking in people's washing and ironing. But nothing swayed Izzuddin. 'No one in my family will ever be a servant to others,' he barked. His mind was made up, he said, and he wasn't backing down. Their home became cloaked in a thick fog of gloom and despair. Setara, however, wasn't backing down either.

One day, after yet another nasty and bitter row, Izzuddin declared that he was divorcing her. He shouted the word *talaq* three times in the midst of an angry outburst and demanded that she pack her belongings and move to her aunt's house on the outskirts of Herat. Setara, however, dug in her heels and refused to leave. She sat in stony silence in the kitchen, peering down at a large tray of rice, methodically picking out stones and grit. Izzuddin glanced at her through the gap in the kitchen door, then stormed out of the house, slamming the door behind him.

The shouting matches continued for an entire week, both of them screaming and hurling insults, neither willing to relent. By the end of that week, Izzuddin's anger grew even more intense, swelling into a hurricane that tore through their lives, leaving nothing but devastation in its wake.

'That's it!' he roared, his eyes bulging like those of a wounded beast. 'I've had enough of you and your foolish stubbornness. Get out of my sight!' He stood with his shoulders stiffened, towering over her, his voice trembling with rage as he stared her down.

She didn't utter a word in response. Nor did she move or even blink. She sat quietly on one of his hand-crafted chairs, her gaze fixed on her hands, which were clasped over her lap. She remained steadfast in her opposition to the arranged marriage.

But as time went by, Izzuddin's mood miraculously softened. Little by little, his characteristic tenderness began to resurface. Setara could see it all in his eyes – how his menacing glare had transformed into affectionate glances. He became more helpful with household chores, friendlier with his sister, and took a greater interest in the girls' homework. The Izzuddin she'd once known and loved had returned, bringing back his inherently alluring charm.

One day, he finally opened his heart to her. 'I'm not perfect, I know… I lost my parents in childhood and was sent, along with Somaya, from Taloqan to Kabul to live with my uncle and his family. Sometimes the nightmares of my past come back to haunt me.' His eyes welled up as he gazed into Setara's.

She clasped his craggy hands in both of hers and gently raised them to her lips, kissing them softly.

'Forgive me!' he sobbed. It was a raw, painful lament, and the first time she had ever seen him weep. She, too, began to weep. She knew then that beneath those rocks of anger and bitterness lay an abundance of affection, longing to resurface. But then he spoke of their divorce. He confessed that he deeply regretted having triple-divorced her and wanted them to remarry. 'And that,' he added, 'has to happen soon because we are currently living in sin.'

Setara furrowed her brow, staring at her husband with wide eyes. She had never imagined that uttering the word 'divorce' three times could have such drastic implications. Izzuddin said he would consult the local imam and seek his guidance on how to resolve their predicament.

That evening, he came home beaming, his eyes alight with

excitement. 'I've found a way to release us from the grip of triple divorce!' he announced. The mullah had advised him to find a single, virgin man and arrange a *halala* marriage to dissolve the divorce.

'What? What is a *halala* marriage?' Setara asked, her voice tinged with disbelief as she searched his eyes for answers.

'It means you marry someone for one night only. That's all.'

'Are you out of your mind? I won't do that! Never!' she exclaimed, leaning back in her chair and folding her arms tightly across her chest. 'Have you consulted your sister about this? I guess not. Because if you had, she would've scolded you for coming up with such an outrageous plan.'

'It's none of her business or anyone else's. This will be our secret, right? And let's not have another row... This is what the imam recommended. It's Hanafi jurisprudence, a formality, really. The one-night marriage will dissolve the triple divorce, which is exactly what we want. Right?'

Izzuddin's voice brimmed with conviction, making it difficult for Setara to refuse even though the entire idea sounded bizarre and deeply unsettling.

He went on to say that the imam knew someone suitable and had agreed to conduct the *nikah* ceremony.

'His name is Aziz. He is twenty-four or twenty-five. A vegetable vendor in the bazaar. *Imam sahib* said he would persuade Aziz to do it as a *sawab*, for the love of God, and the *Ummat al-muslimin*.'

The wedding had to wait until the snow and ice melted in Aziz's village, where the *nikah* and the party would be held. Aziz, who lived with his elderly widowed mother in a small mud-brick house, took care of all the arrangements – right down to the bride's bouquet. It finally happened when the village trees were heavy with blossoms, and the air was sweet with the scents of spring.

Setara and Aziz had never met before their wedding night. Even then, they only saw each other briefly, late in the evening, after the gender-segregated wedding party came to an end. For the first time, bride and groom exchanged glances as they padded towards the waiting car. Aziz, tall and handsome with a thin moustache, wore a smart navy suit and tie. Setara, head down and lips pressed tightly together, was dressed in a white frilly gown adorned with a twin set of pearls, and a long, lacy veil covered her face. Her hair, neatly gathered in a bun at the back of her head, was secured tightly to the veil.

During the short journey to Aziz's house, she couldn't help but wonder if the wedding feast had been unnecessarily lavish for a one-night marriage. The tables had overflown with food and fruit – enough to feed the entire village. It all felt strange, overly generous.

They arrived at Aziz's modest mud-brick home in the dead of night, the courtyard bathed in shimmering moonlight. A light breeze brushed against Setara's cheeks, gently lifting the edge of her veil as they walked in silence through the small courtyard. No sooner had she entered his room than he lunged at her. His feverish hands tore at her veil and necklace, sending pearl beads scattering like drops of rain across the floor. The veil fluttered down in shreds as Setara, losing her balance under his weight, tumbled onto the ground amidst the scattered pearls. Her hair cascaded loose from the ruined veil, spilling out across the floor.

As he glided his searing lips over the tender skin of her face and neck, his feverish gaze burned through her, his bloodshot eyes reflecting a wild, primal intensity – a foreboding sense of allure. He ripped open her dress and ravished her with the most intoxicating passion she had ever known. Never in her fourteen years of marriage to Izzuddin had she experienced anything remotely as spirited. Sex with Izzuddin had always been a fully clothed affair under a blanket – No cuddling, no kissing, and no seeing each other in the nude. Their encounters were distant and mechanical, utterly devoid of intimacy.

But with Aziz, Setara felt invigorated, her senses alive with desire. She could hear his heartbeat, feel the soft brush of his skin against hers, and savour the sensation of his lips caressing her neck and breasts. Every touch, every glance, every whisper made her heart race. Never had she known sex to be an expression of such intense affection and passion. It made her feel cherished, wanted, and alive.

The next day, she woke to the clink of teacups and the warm, inviting smell of freshly baked bread. Aziz had risen early to prepare a lavish breakfast of fresh cheese, yogurt, *qaimaq*, honey, and dates. They spoke for the first time at the breakfast table. It was Setara who broke the silence, stirring sugar into her ruby-coloured tea.

'You have to divorce me today,' she murmured, looking down at the steaming glass of tea cupped between her slender fingers.

'Divorce? Nonsense!' he scoffed, biting into a plump date and savouring its sweetness. 'You are now mine and forever.'

Setara's jaw dropped. Bewildered, she stared into his eyes and urged him to act sensibly. Although she had grown fond of this strange young man, they had to stick to their agreement. He had to divorce her so she could remarry her husband. He was lost in thought. He only snapped back to reality when the phone rang. It was Izzuddin. He said he was on his way to collect his wife. Aziz curtly dismissed him and hung up the phone. Without a word, he walked out into the blinding sunlight over the blossoming fruit trees, leaving Setara alone, her heart heavy with apprehension.

When Izzuddin arrived he immediately asked for Aziz and was stunned to learn that he wasn't there to complete the deal. He and Setara waited, each minute stretching into what felt like hours, but Aziz never showed up. Izzuddin dialled Aziz's mobile number repeatedly, the ringing echoing through the tense silence, but there was no response. Eventually, they drove back to Herat, a heavy silence filling the car. The absence of any word from Aziz left them bewildered, a gnawing anxiety creeping in as they wondered what could possibly be going through his mind. To Setara, it felt like the calm before the storm – an unsettling quiet that made her skin prickle with unease.

It didn't take long for everything to unravel.

One evening, a dour-faced Aziz appeared at their doorstep. Setara and the girls glanced out of the window, curious to see who would be knocking so late at night. Izzuddin opened the door and Aziz stepped forward, declaring with a chilling calmness that he'd come to take his wife home.

Brimming with rage, Izzuddin seized him by the collar and shoved him out into the dark alley. The air crackled with tension as Izzuddin hurled obscenities at Aziz, his voice reverberating off the narrow walls. Suddenly, with a swift, terrifying motion, Aziz forced his way back in, brandishing a knife that gleamed ominously in the dim light.

Before anyone could react, he lunged at Izzuddin, plunging the blade into him over and over. Izzuddin's screams shattered the night, drawing Setara and the girls to the yard. There, they found him sprawled in a spreading pool of blood and Aziz clutching the blood-soaked knife. Setara's world spun as she gripped the wall for support. Yasmin and Raha clung to her arms, screaming in terror. Somaya left the stew simmering on the stove and rushed outside, her eyes wide with horror as she took in the harrowing sight of her beloved brother butchered by a stranger.

Neighbours began spilling out of their homes. Someone frantically called for an ambulance and the police, their voices barely audible over the chaos that gripped the yard.

Izzuddin died on the way to the hospital. The police arrived shortly after the ambulance had left and arrested both Aziz and Setara. He was charged with murder, and she as his accomplice. The detectives dismissed Setara's account of the events. They accused her of being Aziz's lover all along and of secretly plotting Izzuddin's murder alongside him.

Setara pleaded with them, swearing on the holy Quran that it had been a *halala* arrangement gone wrong, but they refused to believe her. Before her trial, the prosecutor demanded a two-thousand-dollar bribe to drop the charges. When she explained that she had no such money, he lowered it to one thousand. She had never held that much money in her life and couldn't pay. As a result, she stood trial without a defence lawyer at the local primary court. She was convicted of the crime and sentenced to death – a sentence that was later commuted to life imprisonment through the intervention of the human rights commission.

It was her daughters' testimony against her that sealed her fate. Under the coercive and manipulative tactics of the prosecutor, they yielded to the police's narrative. During the trial, they avoided their mother's eyes while recounting instances where she supposedly flirted with Aziz in the bazaar, their voices soft and strained.

Yasmin and Raha disowned her. So did Somaya – The once compassionate and caring friend who had stood by her through so many hardships. Now, with Setara in prison, Somaya took on the role of caregiver for the girls, poisoning their hearts with words against their mother – Sentences that no longer ended with *Subhan Allah*.

Sometimes, when alone in her *bolani*-infused cell – brimming with books and dirty nappies – Setara thought back on the poetry she'd written during the dark years of Taliban rule about life in captivity. Was she still the caged bird yearning for freedom? Yet, the meaning of freedom had changed so drastically over time.

Blossoming Almond Trees

A month or so after the self-immolation incident, an intriguing text message arrived on Sultan's mobile phone. She couldn't read it, nor could she recognise the number. Neither could Seema or Humaira, as they, like her, were illiterate. That's when she thought of Madam Teacher. Setara could read the text and might even recognise the number, Sultan reasoned, since she knew many current and former inmates – women for whom she had written and read letters to.

It was late afternoon on a Friday. The prison's school, playgroup and all literacy and crafts workshops were closed. Most inmates, especially those with babies, stayed indoors to keep warm. For a private chat, Sultan thought of the secluded almond trees tucked away at the back of the prison yard, their blossoms just beginning to show. She grabbed a couple of long shawls and a threadbare old blanket before heading down the corridor towards Setara's cell. The air was heavy with the comforting smell of chicken broth wafting up from the kitchen on the ground floor. She found Setara sitting cross-legged on the floor, surrounded by screaming babies, a book open on her lap. The pungent stench of dirty nappies filled the air in the cell. Sultan, in her usual rose-scented, lightly-starched shirt and jeans, wrinkled her nose, and gestured for Setara, sporting her everyday Nefertiti look complete with a heavy woollen cardigan, to come out.

'I need your help with something,' she whispered in Setara's ears. Taking Setara's hand, which faintly carried the aroma of grease and *bolani*, Sultan led Setara down the stairs to the row of almond trees. She loved this spot. It was quiet and secluded from the rest of the prison. A good distance away from the swings and roundabout, used by no one only a few boisterous kids who couldn't settle for indoor games.

Once upon a time, the trees had been part of a larger almond orchard hidden behind tall walls, from which the area had derived its name. Even now, the sight of the almond trees blossoming in the dead of winter, exuding their honey-sweet fragrance, brought a smile to Sultan's usually hardened face. She admired the courage of these trees, daring to bloom at a time when no other fruit tree would challenge the brutal Kabul winters. The punishing cold winds lashed at their branches, and icicles froze the life out of young stems, but still, they blossomed.

Her mind drifted to the glorious almond orchard in her native Dehmazang, where the brutish owner would chase out prying kids with his tall stick, mercilessly beating them if they dared to sneak in. She still recoiled at the memory, feeling the lingering sting of pain on the back of her thighs.

Her father, an erudite man, who believed the Pashtuns were descendants of the Greek colonisers who settled in Afghanistan following Alexander the Great's conquest, had been an avid reader. He would often recite a couplet of a Greek poem whenever the trees bloomed in the neighbour's orchard: 'I said to the almond tree, "Sister, speak to me of God," and the almond tree blossomed.'

Sultan unfolded the blanket and spread it on the concrete ground, under the almond trees. The sun was slowly fading in the sky, and the February air was turning colder and less hospitable. Snow was expected any moment. Wrapping shawls around their shoulders, her and Setara sat side by side on the blanket, facing the prison's outer walls.

'Setara *jaan*, I need your help.' Sultan tilted her head to the side, and glanced into Setara's narrowed eyes, her warm breath forming a cloud in the crisp air. Rarely did Sultan use '*jaan*' as a term of endearment – not even for her wives, whom she wouldn't even call by their names. For them, a hand gesture or subtle eye and brow movement sufficed. She even felt awkward and out of place saying the word. But Setara was different. Setara held a higher position in Sultan's life than anyone else. She was no ordinary inmate. Sultan had even sung Setara's praises to her wives, provoking envy or perhaps admiration. 'She is a lady. A *bibi* in the truest sense, as saintly as the Prophet's wives, peace be upon him.'

Sultan glanced around to make sure no one was watching.

She then partially uncovered the mobile's screen, which had been carefully wrapped in an old duster. 'What does this say? Do you know this number?'

Setara squinted and fixed her gaze on the screen, discreetly cradling the mobile under the corner of her shawl.

'It says, "*salaam,* I'm Nazia. When is a good time to ring you?"'

'Who's Nazia? I don't know anyone by that name. Do you?' Sultan asked, furrowing her brow, her index finger pressed against her lips.

'I don't know,' Setara replied, looking up into the distance with her hand under her chin. 'The only Nazia I know of is Niloofar's mother. I wrote a letter for her, remember? I addressed the envelope, too… It was for Mrs. Nazia Sadiqi. The blue door, Four Gardens Street, opposite Nasiragha Chaikhana, Herat, if I recall correctly. Not far from where I lived.' She gazed into the distance and pulled the shawl tighter around her.

'Ask her if she is Niloofar's mother,' Sultan said, searching Setara's hazel eyes that had caught the glint of winter sun. 'If she says yes, ask her to call me in the evening after the lockdown. Will you write the text for me, Setara *jaan*?'

Setara, her curiosity visibly piqued, nodded without hesitation. 'Fine. I'll help you. But let's go back inside. It's too cold out here. We can go to your cell. It should be quieter than mine.'

As they climbed the stairs to the second floor, they stumbled across Parwin Chapool. She wore a scruffy brown cardigan over a loosely fitted floral dress, and was mopping the stairs, her gnarled fingers struggling to hold the mop handle steady. Parwin looked up to greet them, adjusting her pink scarf and giving off a stale waft of sweat mixed with the sharp tang of disinfectant. Sultan and Setara nodded politely in response and continued on their way.

'Oh, I nearly forgot,' Parwin called out, her voice raised, a wide grin spreading across her face.

Sultan and Setara paused on the step above her, glancing back in her direction.

'*Baashi Sahib, Raees Sahib,* wants to see you,' Parwin said, looking up at Sultan with her wonky eyes.

Scowling in her typical fashion, Sultan dismissed Parwin's words with a sharp shooing gesture. Then pointing her two fingers dangerously close to Parwin's eyes – as if she were about to gouge them out – she yelled, the corners of her mouth frothing, 'I don't need a messenger. She can tell me that herself. And don't you dare raise your ugly voice at me!' Her fingers hovered so menacingly near to Parwin's face that, bending backwards to dodge them, Parwin lost her balance and bumped her head on the banister.

'Akh!' Parwin let out an anguished cry, clutching the back of her head.

'Another one of your fibs, no doubt,' Sultan shouted, staring down at her.

Whimpering pitifully, Parwin sat down, eyes squeezed shut in pain. 'I heard it from the guard. Honest! I swear to God and the holy Quran. I'm not lying,' she pleaded between sobs, her eyes brimming with tears and her eyebrows knotted with fear.

Sultan narrowed her green eyes and stooped lower. Then she spat – A thick glob landed so close to Parwin's legs it narrowly missed them. Parwin gasped and shrank back. Sultan straightened up slowly, pulling down her sleeves, her gaze never leaving Parwin. Turning her back on her, Sultan cursed through her gritted teeth, '*Kussi... Harami*. Shouting at me? You will get my belt next time.'

Setara fixed her eyes on the stairs as she and Sultan climbed in silence. She pulled the shawl tighter around her shoulders, her face drained of colour, and walked with quick, deliberate steps, as if wishing to put as much distance as possible between herself and the unsettling scene below.

Back in Sultan's cell, saturated with Bollywood posters and reeking of the scent of rose water, Setara sat cross-legged on the floor, typing the text message on the mobile's keys. 'Are you Niloofar's mother? Call me at 6 pm,' in response to the obscure sender and pressed the send button.

Her eyes widened with amazement at the colourful images of Sultan's favourite Bollywood actors in dance or fighting moves, as she followed the rows of posters around the cell.

Seema and Humaira walked in with bowls of chicken broth,

yoghurt and stale flat bread, left over from yesterday's dinner.

'Dinner time,' Seema shouted melodiously, bending down to place the tray of food on the floor.

'Ahhh... Stale bread again... It gives me indigestion. They will kill us with their disgusting food,' Humaira said, wrinkling her nose.

'Bakeries are closed on Friday. Remember?' Sultan shot her a stern look.

'Forgive me, I forgot,' Humaira said, looking sheepish as she cupped her hand over her mouth. She then pulled the cell's kerosene heater closer to the bowls of broth, covering them with plates to keep them warm. The sweet and appetising smell of parsley and coriander filled the air.

'Be our guest today. Have dinner with us, Setara *jaan*,' Seema said in her sweet Kunduzi accent.

No sooner had Setara accepted the invitation than Seema and Humaira rushed out of the cell to get another bowl of soup and yoghurt. Suddenly, Sultan's mobile vibrated, and Sultan and Setara heard the ping of a text message. Setara picked up the mobile from the floor and squinted to read the text.

'It says, "Yes, I am Niloofar's mother. Can I call you now?"'

'Tell her, yes. Now is a good time. We have a few minutes before Seema and Humaira get back.'

Immediately after Setara sent the 'yes' text message, the phone rang. Sultan answered, turning on the phone's loudspeaker. Out came a low-pitch resonant voice.

'Sultan *jaan*? *Salaam.*' The voice uncannily resembled that of Maryam, Sultan's *anbagh,* Sharif's other wife. The Ahmadzai-clan female with hennaed hands that always smelt of fried onions. The woman who had cared for her like an older sister, when she was a scrawny and confused twelve-year-old baad bride sold into sex and domestic slavery. The woman who had helped her survive those tumultuous, dark years.

'*Salaam*. Sorry, I only have a couple of minutes to speak to you... How is your daughter?'

'*Alhamdulillah*. She is... alive. Her face, arms, hands and chest have been badly burnt, worse than the other parts of her body.

She is bandaged up from head to toe. She can't speak, so she tries hard to write what she wants to say, but only a couple of words at a time. She is on strong painkillers. But *Shukr-e-khuda,* she is alive.' After a short pause, she continued, 'I'm coming to meet *Raees Sahib* tomorrow afternoon. Niloofar eventually managed to write your name and number from memory. It's remarkable that her memory has remained intact. Until I received your text message, I wasn't sure I had the correct number for you. Can I see you after the meeting with *Raees Sahib?* It's crucial to hear your account of Niloofar's state of mind before the incident.'

Sultan and Setara exchanged glances.

'Say, yes,' Setara whispered, looking intently into Sultan's eyes.

Sultan looked down and took a deep breath. She glanced back at Setara and saw her nodding.

'Yes, see you tomorrow afternoon. *Khoda hafez.*' She hung up, shoulders stiffening. 'How did Niloofar get my number? Until a month ago, I didn't even know her.' Sultan pondered.

'You never know who does and knows what in a prison.' Setara shrugged.

'Does Nazia think I have something to do with her daughter's attempted suicide? If so, she has another think coming.' Sultan sat back, leaning against the bed and folding her arms across her chest.

'Give her a chance,' Setara said, placing her hand on Sultan's shoulder. 'She sounds like a nice woman. Cultured and well-spoken. She wants to have the picture of her daughter's circumstances here, more than *Raees Sahib* could provide.'

'She can be the Queen of Sheba for all I care! I don't know her. I don't trust her,' Sultan said, biting hard on her bottom lip. Then, with a sudden spark in her eyes, she looked up. 'I will go on one condition… that you come with me.'

Setara shook her head, vigorously. 'No, no, no! She hasn't asked for me. It's disrespectful, if I come uninvited.'

'You are the prison's scribe! You wrote letters for Niloofar before the incident. You know more about her than I do. Besides, I want a witness there because I don't trust this woman.'

They squabbled over this until Setara succumbed. She then

sent another text to Nazia on behalf of Sultan, asking her if 'Setara the prison scribe' could join the meeting given her closeness with Niloofar. Nazia welcomed the idea in her reply.

The next day, Farzana, boasting her new red patent high-heeled shoes, teetered in Sultan's cell at breakfast time. Humaira was the first to spot the new shoes. Mopping the bathroom floor, she popped her head out. '*Maqbool*,' she said sarcastically, pointing at the shoes. 'Like a pair of *banjan rumi*.' The three cackled.

Farzana's shoulders slumped. She looked down at her shoes and feigned a toothless smile before standing upright again. She cleared her throat, and looked in Sultan's direction. '*Raees Sahib* has instructed me to tell you that Niloofar's mother is coming to see you and Setara this afternoon. *Raees Sahib* wants to see you now.'

Sultan stood up. She took the last sip of her black tea, and smoothed the creases on the legs of her jeans and shirt sleeves. Seema got up promptly and brushed the fluff off Sultan's shoulders, while Humaira crawled under the bunk bed to get Sultan's trainers. Sultan then forced her broad feet into the trainers, before Humaira pulled and tied their laces, brushing the dust off them. After a short walk along the corridor, Sultan and Farzana stopped by a dark brown door next to the meeting room at the centre of the second floor, boasting a large gold plaque with the inscription '*Raees*'. Farzana knocked on the door and walked in immediately after hearing the word 'Enter,' leaving Sultan behind. A few minutes later, she popped her head out, nodding to Sultan to enter.

Shahla Mousavi, a tall, attractive police lieutenant with a slender frame, dark silky bobbed hair and high cheekbones, had been in the prison manager position since last autumn. She had succeeded Lieutenant Meena Nuristani, who tragically lost her life while travelling to a training workshop organised by the American embassy in Kabul. The incident had left three young children orphaned, and now cared for by relatives. Their father, also a police officer, had been killed in an earlier Taliban attack on a Kabul guest house frequently visited by Indian intelligence officials. Shahla, a Hazara, was among the very few of her ethnic group to be promoted to a higher rank. The police service was dominated by Pashtuns, who held a dim view of Hazaras – A throwback to centuries of Pashtun kings enslaving Hazaras and forcibly displacing them from their strongholds in Bamiyan and its neighbouring central provinces. Many Pashtuns watched with resentment and envy as a new generation of university-educated Hazaras – returnees from Iran and Pakistan – broke out of the traditional servitude roles in the new democratic Afghanistan, and attained professional status.

Eyes cast down, Sultan stood next to Farzana, facing the Lieutenant with her hands clasped in front of her. Shahla's office, carrying the waft of 'spring blossom' room spray, her favourite scent, was hardly big enough for her massive desk, which bore the imposing Afghan flag adopted eight years ago, two years after the US invasion and the fall of the Taliban regime. The flag's centrepiece, a mosque and sheaves of wheat against a background of black, red and green stripes, was topped by an Arabic inscription incomprehensible to most Afghans.

Shoulders tensed, Sultan fixed her eyes on her clasped hands. *Has she forgiven me? Hopefully she won't go on lecturing me again about loyalty and morality.* There had been bad blood between Sultan and Shahla since the prison riot last autumn. Sultan had led that uprising in opposition to Shahla's ban on smoking in prison, a policy Shahla adopted two weeks into the job. Although the policy was scrapped the day after the riot, Shahla had shunned Sultan ever since. A punishment Sultan considered worse than 'the dungeon' – dark, solitary cells in the basement reserved for wrongdoers. Perhaps shunning her was Shahla's admission of defeat, Sultan had often wondered self-righteously.

Shahla broke the unsettling silence, leaning back in her swivel chair and twirling a stylish gold pen around her fingers. 'I'm so pleased you're going to meet Mrs. Sadiqi today. She is a desperate mother, curious to know what might have happened to her daughter during the two fateful weeks she was here.' Shifting in the leather chair, which made a harsh squeaky noise, she tilted her head to the side. 'I've authorised Setara to join you in the meeting this afternoon. She is a learned and articulate woman. Only God knows why she ruined her life and that of her family by giving in to evil temptations.'

As the meeting came to an end but before Farzana and Sultan left the room, Shahla, looking in Sultan's direction, said in a louder voice, 'My door is always open, whenever you want to inform me about the prison's goings-on. I have all the confidence in you as a *baashi* to nip trouble in the bud.'

Sultan turned around to face her, smiling and nodding politely in response. *The bitch knows she needs me. She knows they cannot run this prison without me. But I have my own rules and expectations, too. It's never been a one-way street.*

Sultan and Setara sat next to each other at a table near a kerosene heater, facing the entrance of the visitors' hall. They had been waiting for Nazia's arrival for almost an hour. The sun gazed through the murky barred window. The air was thick with the stale smell of tobacco and disinfectant.

'Where is she?' Sultan fidgeted in her seat, her eyes fixed on the clock on the hall's tobacco-stained wall. 'She's not coming. Let's go back,' she said, frowning, gesturing for Setara to get up and leave.

Just as they were getting ready to leave, the door flung open and in strode Farzana followed by an elegant and stylish lady. She wore a smart dark navy blazer suit and brown leather boots, a little mud on the toes and heels. An intoxicating aroma followed her, nothing like the traditional Afghan rose water Sultan used to freshen her shirts. No, this scent was foreign, reeking of opulence. A large purple and green scarf in Herati silk covered her slender shoulders. Her dark hair was neatly pinned back in a bun and her eyes were carefully made up with black eyeliner – not the customary Afghan kohl – mascara, and a light dust of sparkling blue eyeshadow that added a distinct spark to her brown eyes. Smirking to herself, Sultan thought that it was just as well this meeting hadn't fallen on a normal visitors' day. No way such a delicate and pampered creature could survive the chaos, noise, and sharp, pungent smells of destitution sitting next to inmates' relatives from downtown Kabul or the neighbouring provinces. The very people she would casually toss a few coins at while covering her nose and mouth, unable to hide her disgust.

Wide-eyed, Setara stood up and moved closer to Nazia to greet her, shaking hands warmly and enthusiastically like Heratis usually do. Farzana retreated to the door, where she stood upright with her hands clasped in front of her, gazing into space.

'Khosh amadi,' Setara, wearing her customary kaftan and scarf wound in the usual voluminous turban, said in a slightly raised, excited voice that echoed in the desolate and sparingly furnished room.

Sultan, remaining behind the table, raised slightly from her seat, and extended her arm just far enough to touch Nazia lightly on her fingers. Nazia smiled, revealing a neat set of white, polished teeth that dazzled like diamonds. Her resemblance to Maryam, Sultan thought, stopped at the voice. Maryam, although beautiful with long hair reaching her waist, shapely eyebrows and long eyelashes, would never dress so stylishly or behave so sophisticatedly and urbane. Maryam's mind never grew larger than Gardez, the province she came from in the southeast Pashtun belt. However, her heart was as large as the universe, and her kindness unlimited.

Tilting her head slightly to the side, Nazia offered no apology and said nothing about her late arrival. She held her gaze on Setara for a moment, as if recognising someone familiar. Then, she shifted her eyes to Sultan who was standing with her feet wide apart and arms folded across her chest, staring into space. When they were all seated at the table, Nazia was the first to speak. 'My daughter has had a tragic life,' she said, dabbing her eyes and nose with a tissue. 'I need to tell you this so you can understand her mindset. I divorced her father, a brutal and violent man, when Niloofar was only ten. I married an Iranian and moved to Tehran when she was twelve. I couldn't take her with me. Her father had sole custody. At the age of fifteen her father forced her into marriage with a wealthy, albeit already-married man, in order to keep her away from the petty trader she was so desperately in love with: Sohrab.'

Nazia paused a little to clear her throat, then took a sip of water from a small plastic bottle she pulled out of her bag. 'I stayed in touch with her through my mother and sister,' she continued, tapping her fingers on the table. 'She and Sohrab eloped and settled in Mashad, masquerading as a married couple. Unbeknownst to her, Sohrab was a drug smuggler. He left her one day on the pretence that he was taking cargo to Herat and would be back in a week. He never came back and abandoned her there with nothing. She had to return to Herat, having no one to turn to.' Nazia paused, her trembling hand wiping away the tears that streamed relentlessly down her cheeks. Her quiet sobs echoed softly in the heavy silence of the room, the tension thick as Sultan and Setara exchanged uneasy glances.

Setara rose and walked around the table, her eyes welling up with tears. She embraced Nazia from the side, placing her head on Nazia's shoulder close to her delicately-hewn neck. Nazia, gazing tenderly at Setara, lightly tapped on her hand, holding the tissue firmly on her nose and mouth.

Sultan leaned back in her seat with arms folded across her chest, watching Setara endearing herself to Nazia. All the feminine traits she had discarded years ago: hugs, kisses, alluring games, whining, tears, all the trappings of intimate vulnerability. It was after that frenzied attack on Sharif, the man who had become a loathed figure in her life, that another Sultan had emerged, free and irreproachable, like a phoenix from the ashes. Her mind drifted to this exact moment – when she was drenched in Sharif's blood, collapsed on the floor, staring at his stomach which she'd ripped apart with her 26th stab of the knife. A sudden burst of radiant energy had engulfed her body like a rebirth. She remembered the warmth of the blood, the metallic smell filling her nostrils, and the sharp, exhilarating sensation of power and liberation running through her veins.

After another sip of water, Nazia gained composure and continued, 'Returning to Herat, Niloofar roamed the streets in a *burqa*. She was arrested for loitering and charged and convicted of *zina*. She was later sentenced to ten years.' She let out a short gasp, shaking her head. 'It was there that she found out that Sohrab had been jailed for drug smuggling. That destroyed her… my poor Niloofar.'

'And you think that's why she attempted suicide?' Sultan's voice cut sharply through the air, her frown deepening as her words hung between them. 'Don't you think it was because she had been abandoned by her family all her life?' Sultan's chest tightened, her mind spiralling to a familiar ache. Abandoned by her mother, discarded by her sisters – those who should have shielded her, should have held her hand through the tender years. A bitter lump rose in her throat.

Nazia shifted in her seat. She crossed one leg over the other and shot a glare at Sultan, her lips curling downwards. Without a word, she lowered her gaze to her jacket, brushing off flecks of tissue from her sleeve with quick, distracted motions. Discreetly, she pulled out an envelope folded in four and rolled it into a small bundle the size of her thumb. 'I don't blame you for thinking that. That's my sin, I know, and I will take that with me to the next world, leaving the judgment to *Allah,'* she said softly, moving slightly forward, slipping the bundle gingerly to Sultan under the table. Sultan grabbed the little bundle and shoved it into her jeans pocket.

Holding a straight face, Nazia turned to Setara. 'Did you notice anything unusual about Niloofar when she was here?'

Setara thought a little while eyeing Farzana who was now gesturing that the visiting time had come to an end.

'Only on the day before the incident did I notice she was restless, pacing up and down her cell. She said she hadn't slept the night before. I didn't know she was literate because she asked me to write letters for her. One to you and another to Sohrab in prison. Did you receive the letter?'

'Yes, I did. She knew I was back in Herat, staying with my elderly mother. We had spoken on the phone.' Heeding Farzana who had just loudly announced the end of her visiting time, Nazia stood up, and straightened the creases on her trousers. They quickly said their goodbyes and Nazia left the room, her enticing aroma lingering.

Outside, the air was sharp with frost, and a thin veil of snow blanketed the ground, crunching softly under Sultan's feet. Sultan stood waiting for Setara under the almond trees, her large woollen shawl draped tightly around her shoulders, the cold biting at her cheeks. The envelope that Nazia had secretly passed on to her rested in her hands, its edges crumpled from being folded many times and passed in haste.

Her fingers hovered over the seal, torn between waiting for Setara who had to rush back to her cell to grab her shawl, and giving in to the gnawing curiosity.

Finally, with a quick glance around, she pried it open. Inside was a folded letter, the paper smudged slightly with streaks of black ink, as if brushed by rain. As she unfolded it, a crisp twenty-dollar bill slipped free. Sultan snatched it from the air, her breath catching for a moment. She slid the money into her pocket, her heartbeat quickening. Another step closer, she thought, her secret stash steadily growing. The surgery she'd dreamed of for years suddenly felt just a little less distant. She tucked the letter back into the envelope and tightened her shawl around her.

Draped in a large grey shawl with red flowers embroidered along its edges, Setara wove her way through rows of screaming kids, each waiting their turn for the swings. She reached Sultan at their usual spot beneath the almond trees and sank down beside her on the old, scruffy blanket. The frosty air carried the faint, sweet scent of blossoms. Without a word, Sultan handed Setara Nazia's letter. The elegant, calligraphic handwriting immediately drew her in.

In a hushed tone, Setara started reading the letter. "Dear Sultan and Setara. Here is a little gift as a show of gratitude for your efforts." She stopped, turning her head sharply towards Sultan. 'What gift? Where is it?'

'I don't know. I didn't see any… I don't know. Swear to God.' Sultan shrugged, blinking her eyes a few times.

'Check the envelope.'

Sultan opened the envelope, stretching its sides. She shook her head. 'Nothing.'

'That's disgusting.' Scowling, Setara clicked her tongue several times.

'What is? What do you mean?' Sultan grimaced, glaring at Setara, worried if she had suspected her of taking the money.

'Nazia lying to us. What do you think it is? A goodwill gesture?' Setara clicked her tongue, shaking her head.

'You never know.' Sultan let out a sigh of relief for seemingly having been let off the hook. 'She might have forgotten to enclose whatever it was,' she continued in an unusually gentle tone. 'Come on, read the rest. What else does it say?'

Setara sighed, staring intently at Sultan. 'You can't trust anyone these days.' She shook her head in despair. 'Everyone tries to con you.'

Sultan felt a sudden choking sensation in her throat, convinced that she hadn't been let off the hook after all and Setara had instinctively known she'd taken the money. Had she seen her pocketing the money from her cell window? Unlikely, she thought. From that height and angle, only the tops of the almond trees were visible. She coughed a few times and maintained a straight face.

Setara began reading the rest of the letter. "Niloofar can't speak or write much. I've been trying to find out what had triggered her to set fire to herself. She managed to write just one word: Diba, in response to my question. Do you know anyone there or in Herat prison by that name? Also, Niloofar had a mobile phone with her in prison but no one has handed it over to me. I asked *Raees Sahib* but she just said inmates were forbidden to use mobile phones, though I know everyone has one. So did Niloofar. She once phoned me from her cell. The phone would likely throw light on who this Diba is. Send me a text message if you find the phone or if you find Diba. Respectfully, Nazia Sadiqi."

The women glanced at each other. Setara, holding her index finger over her lips, shook her head after a short pause. 'I don't know any one by that name. Not here, nor anywhere else. How about you?'

'I know a Dina but not a Diba.'

'Well...' Setara said thoughtfully, 'Niloofar might have wanted to write Dina. Poor thing, confused and in pain, probably made a simple error.' She then glanced back at Sultan. 'Who is this Dina, anyway?'

'She's the inmate in the cell above ours. A Pashtun Kuchi known as Dina Charsi,' Sultan said. 'Convicted for abducting and killing a child... and eating bits of her flesh. She spends her days high on *chars*. She shares the cell with Geisha. Do you know her? The mad Hazara who wears a yellow kimono? Completely insane. Nothing she says ever makes sense. Her other cellmates are Bibi Gul and her little daughter, Shirin, the serial killer from Jalalabad.'

'What a bunch!' Setara laughed, her voice ringing out louder than she intended. 'The batty, the cannibal addict, and the mass murderer.'

Sultan's eyes narrowed as she leaned forward. 'I wonder what they call us. Savage husband killers? Callous family wreckers?' Her words cut through the air like shards of glass.

Setara swallowed hard. A flush crept up her cheeks as she quickly averted her gaze, her fingers fumbling with the edges of Nazia's letter. Her smile faded into a taut, uneasy line as she stared down at Nazia's letter.

'What about Niloofar's phone? Where was her cell?' Sultan asked after a tense pause.

'On our floor,' Setara replied meekly.

'It's been a long time since the incident, though. It'll be impossible to find the phone. Phones are gold dust here.'

'Besides, whoever's got it has certainly wiped out everything on it to hide the identity of its real owner.'

A Journey Across Continents

It was nearly lunchtime. Setara stopped by the kitchen to check the lunch menu. She wrinkled her nose in distaste at the sight of haricot beans in tomato sauce. Her tummy had been troubling her since early morning and she knew the beans would likely exacerbate the discomfort. She asked one of the cooks to replace the beans with yoghurt and bread.

'Do you want rice too?' the stout cook asked, glancing up from an enormous rice pan. She wiped her thick, oily hands on her stained white uniform, the fabric blotched with streaks of grease and a brownish substance. Her wide eyes were fixed on Setara, who responded with a polite nod.

The creak of the kitchen door broke the brief exchange as two tall African women entered. Setara turned her head towards the sound, catching the cook's muttered complaint under her breath: *'Ya Allah!* It's those beastly women again.' The words dripping with disdain as she grunted in displeasure.

Setara shot a disapproving frown at the cook, and turned her gaze onto the newcomers as they approached the counter. One wore faded jeans and a T-shirt, her hair styled in neat braids, while the other was draped in a glamorous blue robe adorned with a large, white motif on the front and back. A matching blue turban crowned her head, strikingly similar to Setara's own Nefertiti headdress.

A faint 'hello' escaped Setara's lips as she attempted to strike up a conversation.

'Oh!' gasped the woman in jeans, her grin lighting up her face. 'You speak English!'

'Only a little,' Setara replied, her tone modest as she glanced coyly ahead. 'I studied English at university.'

'Nice to meet you. My name is Hope, and this is my friend Mary. We are from Nigeria.'

'Hope? That's a beautiful name,' Setara said warmly. 'Happy to meet you, Miss Hope and Miss Mary. My name is Setara. It means "star" in our language.'

Her smile faltered as her eyes flicked to the cook's face, catching the ugly smirk etched across it. Quickly turning away from the woman, Setara refocused on her new acquaintances. 'Would you like to join me for tea in my cell?' she offered, shifting her glance between Mary and Hope, her voice steady despite the tension lingering in the air.

The Nigerian friends threw glances at each other. 'Thanks for your kind invitation,' Hope replied. 'We will come to see you one of these days. We are new here and not yet used to the surroundings.'

After Setara left the kitchen, carrying her tray of food, Mary shot Hope an admonishing look, lowering her voice. 'I'm not sure visiting this lady is a good idea.'

Hope shrugged, unbothered, and passed Mary a tray of rice and beans.

Mary hesitated before taking it, watching Hope's face for a flicker of doubt, but there was none.

'Look, we are strangers here, right?' Hope's tone was light, but her gaze held steady, locking onto Mary's.

Mary hated when she did this, when she climbed onto her pedestal and started preaching. It was Hope slipping back into her teacher mode, as if they were back in Benin City, in the life they had left behind. 'We should make friends with the others. What did Jesus say?' Hope tilted her head, blinking a few times, as if the answer was obvious. Mary braced herself for the inevitable. 'Love thy neighbour!'

Mary glanced towards the cook who was still watching them with hawkish eyes in case they stole the few pieces of flat bread resting on a glass plate on the counter.

'Did you see how the cook was looking at us?' Hope continued. 'The displeasure, the suspicion in her eyes? This is just fear of the unknown. I'm sure many have never seen an African before. So, let's banish their fear with love.'

Mary pressed her lips together. Hope had a way of saying things that sounded so simple.

Hope exhaled deeply, letting her words dissolve into the silence. Her eyes widened with that same unwavering conviction when she flashed her toothy grin – the one that always made Mary feel she was so damn self-righteous.

As they carried the trays of food upstairs for themselves and their Ugandan cellmates, Esther and Hazel – all of them recently convicted of drug smuggling – Hope's voice broke through Mary's thoughts.

'Libyan slippers! How did you manage to liberate them, sister?'

Mary glanced down at her feet, a ghost of a smile flickering across her face. 'I squeezed them into the lining of the small backpack I carried on the boat,' she murmured, her fingers pressing against the edges of the tray. 'I like them, despite their connection with that awful country. They are soft and very comfortable. They've been a loyal companion, staying with me through thick and thin.'

The words hung in the air, her voice softer now, wistful. The memories came unbidden, crashing over her like the sea she once believed would swallow her whole.

Three years. Three years since the Libyan 'safe house' nightmare. Since the suffocating heat of the rooms without windows. Since the cries of women who didn't make it – whose names she never learned – began to haunt her. Since the boat, and the fear, and the moment she stopped praying because she thought God had turned away from her.

Surviving the entire odyssey – from southern Nigeria through the Niger Sahara, to Libya, and later to Turin and Milan – felt like a miracle.

And yet, here she was. In another prison. In another limbo.

Back in Benin City, her hometown in Edo State, southern Nigeria, she, like her peers, had fallen prey to Nigerian and Libyan traffickers. Criminals who deceitfully lured them, promising a prosperous future but delivering a fate worse than death. The Libyan experience had been anything but pleasant. After a long and arduous trek through the unpredictable Niger Sahara, their minibus had finally arrived at Sabha, an oasis city in southwestern Libya. There, the women were separated from the men. The women were taken to a house managed by black-robed and masked Libyan women, while the men were sent to a detention centre notorious for its cramped and equally deplorable conditions.

The safe house was heaving with African women, several of them pregnant. The Libyan women, who bore an uncanny resemblance to medieval executioners, handed out thin blankets for them to sleep on. As more women arrived, however, these blankets were not replenished. Consequently, the new arrivals, some of them pregnant, had to sleep on the wooden floor. The air was thick with the acrid smells of urine, sweat and stale garbage while flies and rodents hovered around them day and night.

After weeks of uncertainty, Mary and five other women were awakened early one morning for yet another long journey, this time to the coast. Their other companions were left behind because their *maman,* female Nigerian pimp, hadn't paid for them. It was a distressing moment, having to leave their fellow travellers behind, women Mary had become closely akin to. Arriving at Tripoli, they were taken to a deserted coast. Mary's heart raced as she glanced at the dinghy they were about to board. She swallowed hard, quickly averting her gaze, fixing it on the ridgelines of the hills in the hazy distance where the coast curved to the left. At gunpoint, they were forced to join a large group of other Africans lined up near the flimsy vessel powered by a small and noisy motor. None had the option of turning back and those who protested were beaten. They were ordered to take off their shoes and leave them on the shore. Mary, however, managed to hide her favourite slippers in her backpack, away from the hawkish eyes of the Libyan traffickers.

As the boat sailed on for several hours, Mary felt her feet burning. She gasped when she realised they were soaked in fuel which was flooding the base of the dinghy. Desperate to save her feet from the corrosive substance, she shifted positions, causing the entire raft to twist and bend slightly. It was evident that the boat was too feeble to carry the weight of so many passengers through the rough waters. Crying out in pain, Mary was overwhelmed by fear as she watched the Libyan shore disappear behind them. Panic and a foreboding fear of death had besieged the entire boat. People around her were vomiting, urinating, and defecating. Soon, the engine ran out of fuel, and they began to drift in the open sea. Some of the women standing in the middle of the dinghy were hysterical, crying inconsolably. The scene resembled what Mary had always imagined the apocalypse to be like – chaos, fear, rage, and unrelenting pain and suffering.

Clasping the edge of the dinghy, Mary closed her eyes and prayed. She was certain they would sink to the bottom of the sea. As the sun began to set, she thought she saw the silhouette of a large boat on the horizon. At first, she thought it was a mirage and blinked a few times. But it was a real boat. With a yelp, she raised her hands, followed by the women standing behind her. Shortly after, they were spotted by the Italian Coast Guards, who promptly rescued them. Each person was checked for injuries and burns and then wrapped in a blanket. Those who had vomited on the dinghy were administered drips to rehydrate them. Everyone was provided with water, biscuits, and apples. Upon disembarking from the rescue boat onto the island of Lampedusa, they were directed to a couple of large tents equipped with army cots for rest. Their names and places of origin were recorded, and they were assigned identification numbers. After a brief period, they were provided with shoes and organised into groups before being escorted towards buses parked outside the tents.

The camp she had been allocated to in Lampedusa was the largest on the island, primarily inhabited by Africans from Ghana and Nigeria. Much of her memory of the camp had faded with time, but what remained vivid were its appalling conditions. It was rat-infested, overcrowded, with an unbearable stench of rotting rubbish strewn all around. There was just one thing she could never forget, one thing that still made her shudder with fear: the shrill cries of a woman who was gang-raped at night by traffickers, cries that everyone heard but ignored.

It would have been impossible to forget the young woman's stooping figure the next day as she staggered out of her room. Her pretty face was marred by a bloody knife scar and her clothes were torn. Mary could never forget the haunting look on the woman's face when their glances met – a look imbued with shame, remorse and agony. Mary recalled sitting among a small group of Nigerian women later that day who whispered about the incident, looking around nervously to ensure no one else heard their hushed voices. 'You know what happened to Winni? That's what they do if you refuse their orders,' one of them murmured, her wide, bulging eyes betraying her deep fear. Two years later, in Turin, she crossed paths with the same young woman – unmistakably pretty. The dark scar slashed across her cheek only sharpened the memory. Mary recognised her at once: Winni, the girl from Edo. But Winni, catching sight of her, turned away – eyes cold, unreadable.

In Lampedusa, Mary finally found out that she wasn't there to train and work as a hairdresser as she'd been promised back in Benin City; instead, her role involved roaming the streets, rain or shine, giving pleasure to men in cars, behind park bushes, or in deserted alleyways, for which she received no payment. Shortly after the horrifying rape incident at the refugee camp, Mary was relocated from there to Turin, where she resided in various overcrowded slum housing for approximately two years, walking the streets looking for punters.

Dina

Dina looked up with blood shot eyes when Sultan walked into her cell. Wearing a colourful Kuchi nomadic dress and baggy trousers, she was sitting under the window, her knees pressed against her chest, and her skinny arms wrapped around her legs. She greeted Sultan with a faint *salaam* and rested her head on her knees. Bibi Gul was reading a book for Shirin, her five-year-old daughter. They both looked up from the open book and smiled at Sultan, holding her gaze for a while. Geisha, in an old yellow kimono with her hair pinned back loosely, was in the adjacent bathroom washing up tea glasses. Poking her head out slightly, she asked if Sultan wanted tea.

The cell was filled with the sour odour of stale tobacco and a hint of *chars* mingled with the sweet smell of freshly brewed tea. Sultan declined the offer with a swift hand movement and sat cross-legged on the floor next to Dina whose breath carried a waft of cannabis. Turning her gaze to Bibi Gul and Shirin, and then to Geisha, Sultan made a swift gesture with her head and said, 'Move!'

In a flash, all three put their shoes on and left the cell.

Seated on the floor, Sultan placed a hand gently on Dina's shoulder. Switching to Pashto, her voice softened. 'Did you know Niloofar?'

Dina lifted her head, her eyes drifting somewhere far away. 'The Herati girl?' she murmured, brows knitting together.

'Yes. The one who set herself on fire.'

A flicker of recognition passed over Dina's face. 'I met her. She showed up one day after lunch. She looked shaken. Asked me for a smoke.'

Sultan leaned in slightly, her tone sharpening. 'What did she say to you?'

'Not much. She smoked a little and left. Poor thing was crying.' Dina frowned, as if trying to pull something from the fog in her mind.

'Is that it? Did she say why?'

'I don't remember.' Dina dropped her gaze, resting her chin on her hands.

Sultan's grip on her shoulder firmed. 'Try. It matters. She must have said something, mentioned someone.'

Dina's eyes grew distant again. After a pause, her voice came, low and slurred. 'She mentioned a place. Somewhere in Kabul.' Dina reached for her cigarette pack and lit one with trembling fingers. 'Dunya Khana. Something like that.'

'Dunya Khana?' Sultan repeated, eyes narrowing. 'Never heard of it.'

Dina exhaled slowly, blowing rings into the stale air. Her gaze met Sultan's, steady and unblinking.

'Doctor says I have leukaemia. I'm dying, *Baashi Sahib.*' She flicked ash onto the floor. 'I can't remember everything. Not anymore.'

Sultan stared at her with a furrowed brow before turning her glance away. With her head hung, she hurriedly left the cell.

Dina glanced sardonically as Sultan walked out in quick steps. She then got up on her spindly legs, holding on to the windowsill, and stared out of the grubby window at the dark clouds slowly concealing the blue sky.

What did the Herati girl say? She thought. *She said something about someone at this Dunya Khana place. Or was it Dunya Khana Street? That sad, lonely girl. She was hysterical. She needed chars to calm her down. Did she mention a man in a black car? God knows! At least she was generous enough to give me her phone as payment for the chars. The phone marked with a squiggle in an irremovable red nail varnish.*

One thing etched into her memory was Niloofar's horror-struck eyes when she discovered that Dina was serving a life sentence for allegedly killing a child and eating bits of her flesh. Niloofar had run out of her cell quickly, not waiting long enough to hear Dina's full story. How the police, the prosecutor and the judge had stitched her up for a crime she had not committed. How child witnesses, including Faiza, her own daughter, had been manipulated to lie under oath during the trial. How cunningly they had failed to inform her about her right to have a defence attorney.

Dina was perpetually haunted by her memories of that fateful day in Deh Sabz, the surly and arid neighbourhood in Kabul province. She and Faiza, alongside other Kuchis, had set up a camp there in the heat of summer to sell *churis,* the bangles and bracelets she'd part purchased and part pinched from a shop in Jalalabad. A *churi* seller, Dina only camped in one area for the duration of holidays – Eids and Nowruz – usually for a week or ten days. The demand for *churis* was always high among women during these holidays but for some unknown reason it didn't appear so then in Deh Sabz. Some of her fellow Kuchis were urging her to leave, arguing that the neighbourhood was unsafe and controlled by criminal gangs. They were also worried about the likelihood of police harassment had they stayed longer than a week. Moreover, local people generally resented them and viewed them with disdain. Anything that went missing was always blamed on Kuchis. People would even hide their children when Kuchis were around. But Dina, against her better judgement, decided to stay and try her luck for another day.

As she strolled from door to door with Faiza in tow, their hands weighed down by the *churis,* they entered a narrow and deserted blind alley. The air was thick with the pervasive stink of refuse and the irritating buzz of black flies. Stray cats were climbing up the mountains of garbage, searching for morsels of food. It was getting close to the mid-day azan with most people indoors for pre-prayer ablutions. The only sounds were coming from distant chatter and water flowing from hoses and courtyard taps. In a corner, a ragged little girl with a snotty nose and matted hair sat crying for her mother. When Dina bent down and asked about her home, the girl pointed in a vague direction to their left.

Using the corner of her scarf, Dina tenderly wiped the girl's nose and watery eyes. In the process, her scarf slipped off her head, revealing the thinning strands of her hair. A mischievous little boy standing across the alley cackled and taunted, *'Kachal! Kachal!'*

Dina scowled and hastily pulled her scarf back over her head. 'You, rascal!' she shouted, brandishing a clenched fist. *'Bacha be-adab!'*

The boy, suddenly sheepish, averted his eyes and began to retreat slowly.

Dina turned, watching him with a stern expression as he

slinked away.

Dina rang a few doorbells, searching for the girl's mother, but no one recognised the little girl. Eventually, she stumbled across a man named Akbar by a butcher shop who claimed to be the girl's uncle. He came close and touched the girl on her cheek. The little girl averted his gaze and pushed his hand away.

'Shaima *jaan*, don't you remember Uncle Akbar? Where have you been? Your mother has been looking for you,' he said, coaxing the child with a gentle and pleading look. He then turned his glance to Dina. 'You can leave her with me. Thank you for finding her. Her mother will be delighted to see her,' he said, holding Dina's gaze.

Pleased to have found someone to take custody of the child, Dina left the tearful girl with Uncle Akbar, and went back to the Kuchi camp to prepare lunch for herself and her daughter. A few days later, the police raided the camp, handcuffing everyone and taking them to the police station for questioning. The detective said they'd found the dead body of a little girl on a rubbish dump with bits of flesh chewed away from her arms and bones protruding from her wounds. They showed a picture of the girl's body to the Kuchis who looked horrified and aghast. Dina immediately recognised the girl and recounted to the detective the entire event that had unfolded in that blind alley and later outside the butcher shop.

As the detective wrote down her words on a piece of paper, he occasionally gave Dina sideways glances. After finishing writing, the detective, with eyes reeking of contempt, looked in her direction and slid the piece of paper across the table to her. 'Thumb-mark this,' he commanded, throwing her an ink pad. He then motioned for a policewoman to help Dina with thumb-signing.

The policewoman, stern in uniform, held her nose as she approached Dina. Stretching back her head and turning her face to the side, she took hold of Dina's thumb, dabbed it on the ink pad, and pressed it firmly onto a spot at the bottom of the page as she muttered, *'Lochak!'* She held her nose, as she hastily walked away.

The detective then snatched the statement from Dina, fanning himself with his notebook.

'You, disgusting liar,' he scolded her, his eyes narrowing into accusatory slits. 'We have witnesses in the area who testified to your guilt. They said they'd seen a *churi* seller with a bald patch forcibly taking a lost little girl. Take off your scarf, you scum.'

Dina's throat tightened. She closed her eyes, trying to suppress the lump rising within. The room blurred as her eyes filled with tears. Removing her scarf in front of non-*mahram* men felt like stripping herself of her faith, her dignity.

'Take off your scarf!' the detective shouted again, his voice ricocheting off the stark whitewashed walls.

Dina's trembling fingers reached for the knot beneath her chin, fumbling as if her hands refused to obey. At last, the scarf slipped down to her shoulders, exposing the thinning strands of her hair.

'Look!' The detective's sneer deepened, his finger jabbing in her direction. He scanned the row of policemen, a sardonic smirk playing on his lips. With a sharp gesture he summoned the guard who stepped forward and clasped Dina's wrists in handcuffs. The metallic click resonated through the tense air.

Faiza, clutching the folds of Dina's dress, burst into sobs, her tiny frame shaking uncontrollably. A policewoman stepped forward, her expression softening as she knelt beside the child. From her pocket she retrieved a red boiled sweet, unwrapping it with deliberate care.

'Here,' she whispered, her voice gentle as she moved Faiza away from her mother, cradling her close. The girl hesitated before taking the candy, her tears slowing as she sucked on the sugary comfort.

'Where is your guardian? The detective demanded, his voice cutting through the moment of tenderness. 'Husband? Father? Brother?' His eyes bore into Dina, daring her to defy him.

Dina straightened, knotting the scarf firmly back under her chin. 'My husband died of an illness a year after Faiza was born,' she replied, her voice trembling but steady. 'All I have in this world is my daughter.' Her gaze flickered to Faiza, who whimpered softly in the policewoman's arms, the red sweet glinting in her mouth.

'We'll take her to an orphanage. She'll have a better life there, square meals and a proper bed to sleep on,' the detective uttered through clenched teeth. He gestured for a policewoman to lead Dina to the cells. Faiza's eyes widened with fear upon witnessing her mother being taken away. She screamed, kicked, and threw her arms around, attempting to break free from the policewoman's grasp. Her small body trembled with the effort, but the tight grip on her shoulders and chest only intensified, a cruel restraint for a scrawny child caught in the turmoil.

Dina's fellow Kuchis moved by Faiza's pitiful screams, offered to look after her instead of her being sent to an orphanage where troubled children had been known to be mistreated by the staff.

The detective, glancing at them sideways, ordered them to leave. 'Move before I throw you in jail too!' he yelled, pointing at the glass-panelled exit door.

Eyes cast down, the Kuchis hurried out of the premises.

In police custody, Dina was ordered to undress. She cried bitterly when she was hosed down with cold water.

Holding her Kuchi dress and trousers up with two fingers, the policewoman, wrinkling her nose and screwing up her eyes, dropped them into a bucket filled with strong disinfectant. Her colleague combed Dina's hair so harshly that Dina began to weep from the agonising pain.

Wearing a mask over her nose and mouth, the same policewoman sprayed Dina's fine hair impetuously with pesticide, a lethal substance that would haunt Dina's throat and eyes for days to come. Forced to wear a huge, frumpy black dress and trousers made for a giant rather than someone with Dina's petite frame and plastic slippers twice the size of her feet, she was thrown into a putrid, urine-stained cell. The prison door slammed shut with a resounding clunk, its hefty chain reverberating through the air and echoing off the graffitied, grubby walls, creating a cacophony that seemed to linger in the stifling atmosphere.

From there, Dina, clad in her threadbare Kuchi dress and reeking of cheap disinfectant, was moved to the women's remand centre in an old and even more squalid facility in Kabul – Welayat. The pungent stench of Welayat's open sewers assaulted her senses as she stepped out of the prison van. Browbeaten and handcuffed, she was forcefully propelled through the decrepit wooden entrance by two policewomen. As the door's rusty hinges opened with a deafening screech, a wave of stale air carrying the musty scent of damp and mouldy walls was released. The prison's old and grey internal landscape felt grim and cold. In this harrowing place, she endured taunts and vile abuse from fellow inmates who, in unison, yelled 'slut', 'murderer', 'child eater', as she, with eyes cast down and slumped shoulders, walked through the path of shame towards a solitary cell.

She endured four punishing months there in a cold, windowless cell with the fetid stench of vomit and urine. In one corner a hole served as toilet. Throughout her trial, she kept her head down, attempting to avoid the scornful eyes of the judge and the prosecutor. Their voices were often muffled and hard to discern, or perhaps it was their arcane language that was difficult to grasp – cold and strange. The hawk-nosed prosecutor, clad in a dark suit, cast a dismal and contemptuous glance at Dina and announced in a loud screeching voice on the first day of trial that the missing infant had been found dead in a small box on the rubbish heap. A couple of *burqa*-clad women sitting in the first row of chairs snivelled as he presented a graphic description of the child's injuries. 'The child was found with bits of flesh bitten off her little arms.' He yelled, pointing his index finger at Dina, 'This is not a woman. It's a beast, like Zardad's dog. The cannibalistic human-dog the warlord Zardad used during the war to terrorise people at Kabul's Sarobi checkpoint, extracting money from them. The coroner has now verified that the bite marks on the girl's body matched the defendant's teeth.'

Next came the testimony of a child witness, Samir. He stood in his tiny frame, looking up at the bearded judge.

A chill ran up Dina's spine as she stood by the rain-streaked cell window, the memory of that fateful summer's day flooding back. Samir's slighting insults rang in her ears as clearly as if he were there. She gazed tearfully at the dark clouds above, her thoughts consumed by how the prosecutor had manipulated the boy, putting words into his mouth.

In his high-pitched voice and childlike vernacular, Samir had stated that he'd seen Dina and her daughter dragging a little girl, kicking and screaming, out of the alley. Prompted further, he claimed Dina's scarf had fallen off, exposing an unsightly bald patch on her head. At this, the prosecutor had nodded with a self-righteous grin, turning towards the *burqa*-clad women seated in the front row.

Though unwilling to order Dina to remove her scarf – an action that would have been considered sinful – the prosecutor revealed a large photograph taken while Dina was in police custody, displaying the back of her head for all to see.

Dina blinked. The chill of that moment lingered in her body. What came next, however, sealed her fate as a convict heading for a long jail sentence. The judge, with his predatory eyes, fixed his unblinking stare at Dina and read her daughter's statement. Faiza's words, delivered by a voice tainted with malice and denigration, fell upon Dina like a sharp and hefty axe breaking her into pieces. In her statement, Faiza expressed long-standing doubts about 'the skinny and swarthy' Dina being her real mother. She recalled her mother as voluptuous with softer and plumper skin and a lighter complexion.

'You see, the poor, pitiful girl the defendant claims to be her daughter is in truth an abductee.' The judge concluded the long tormenting session. 'This beast of a woman earns her living from abducting children and turning them into beggars, murdering those who fight back.'

Tears rolled down Dina's cheeks, looking back on that day and those vile words that continued to haunt her existence. Holding her mouth firmly with both hands, she imagined herself with horns, red devilish eyes, and a mouth agape wide to a silent scream – a scream which no one heard but one that tore her heart apart. She coughed and cried bitterly, collapsing on the floor.

Although Dina had eventually found peace within Badam Bagh's walls, surrounded by women who respected her and cared for her, she knew she didn't have long to live. Her days were numbered. Death held no fear for her; she had even cheered when informed that leukaemia was too advanced and incurable. All she wished for was to be buried under an almond tree in the yard rather than in a nameless grave in the cemetery adjacent to the prison. She would love the tree's white blossoms to shield her soil from the cruel winter months.

Women's Day

Farzana enthusiastically announced that the upcoming Monday, the 18th of Hoot, would be dedicated to celebrating Women's Day. The small group of inmates gathering around her exchanged curious glances; no one knew what she was talking about. They had never heard of Women's Day. She urged the group to contribute something special to the festivities be it a heartfelt poem, an intricately crafted embroidery or crochet, or a vivid drawing that captured the essence and virtues of womanhood. Farzana explained that representatives from the UN and an Italian organisation called *Azadi Baraye Zanane Afghan,* Freedom for Afghan Women, would be joining them to commemorate the day, bearing gifts. The word 'gifts' resonated with the small assembly, eliciting smiles and winks.

Farzana took a moment to emphasise the significance of the event, reminding the inmates that both organisations had played a crucial role in raising funds, including support from Italy, for the construction of Badam Bagh prison. This, she said, had marked a positive shift for the inmates, rescuing them from the horrors of the previous Pol-e-Charkhi and Welayat prisons. She then continued her speech, delving into popular subjects like the sanctity of marriage and motherhood. Sultan, casting a thoughtful glance at each woman gathered in the corridor, wondered what thoughts about womanhood lingered in their minds. Were they, like her, having visions of faces scarred from abuse and torture, dishevelled with matted hair, their bodies crippled by frequent beatings? Or were their minds conveniently focused on the gifts the foreign visitors were supposedly bringing?

Setara said she would make *bolani,* if the prison management paid for the extra flour, oil, and vegetables. It was close to lunchtime and everyone's mouth watered at the mention of *bolani.* Sultan stood in her towering silence a few steps away from everyone else with her feet apart and arms folded across her chest, observing one and all. She chuckled heartily when Parwin Chapool announced in her usual high-pitched voice that she would recite a poem about the sacrosanctity of motherhood. '*Gom shoo,*' Sultan said with a harsh, derisive laugh, flicking Parwin away with her hand. 'How many kids have you had?'

The group erupted in laughter, the sound echoing through the corridor, fuelled by the shared understanding of Parwin's penchant for self-aggrandisement.

Fahema hesitated for a moment before expressing with a hint of trepidation in her voice that she would draw a mother tenderly cradling her baby.

Everyone welcomed that, some clapping their hands. They had all seen and admired her drawings, which adorned every inch of the crafts workshop's walls. Charcoal on white sheets depicted women clad in white cloth – some saintly, others eerily ghostly, shrouded as if for burial. They sat alone or in groups; some gazed appreciatively at their reflections in mirrors, while others bent over skillets, stirring large pots of broth.

For Sultan, the images embodied the ideal mother, the virtuous female, nurturing, loving, docile, and accepting. A woman Sultan had never encountered in her lived experience. She, in her view, existed only in fairy tales. While she had witnessed plenty of docility and demureness in womenfolk, nurturing and acceptance had been scarce. Her own mother and elder sisters were the first group of females in her life who sacrificed Sultan's future for a comfortable life for themselves, heedless of her cries for help. However, Sultan recognised, though grudgingly, that the pious image of motherhood was an expectation ingrained in girls from infancy. Not all girls, of course. Having been brought up as a boy – a male in a female body – she was never taught the virtues of motherhood or expected to become a mother. Yet, she had been ruthlessly forced into marriage at a young age, all for the sake of money.

The visitor's hall was decorated with red and green balloons and paper chase running across. The decorations had transformed this dull, square space into a warm and cheerful environment. The air was now filled with the delicious and homely smell of freshly made *bolani.* Inmates, all looking cleaner and smarter than usual, were milling around chatting or serving juice and coke. Amidst the crowd, Sultan spotted Setara. Shining like a Bollywood star, Setara's eyes exuded glamour with kohl. She looked like a vision dressed in a dazzling dark red embroidered Herati tunic and black trousers. A matching scarf, elegantly wrapped around her head in her signature Nefertiti style, completed her stunning look, making her the undeniable star of the show. She was standing with her back to the make-shift stage, serving the front row audience the scrumptious fried snacks she'd been preparing since the *Fajr* prayers early in the morning.

Concealed behind a stack of chairs in the corner of the hall, Parwin Chapool, embellished in a new outfit – a red sequined Punjabi *Kamiz* and matching *Shalwar,* possibly on loan from Geisha – was immersed in quiet memorisation, likely preparing for the poem she was to recite. Wringing her hands, her feet tapped the floor anxiously as she soliloquised.

Sultan was greeted enthusiastically, though rather unexpectedly, by Shahla, who stood next to two foreign women close to the entrance. The foreigners beamed wide grins at Sultan as if they had encountered a long-lost friend.

Shahla motioned for Sultan to come forward and introduced her to the foreigners in both English and Persian as 'a model inmate', which surprised and amused Sultan immensely, prompting a quiet chuckle.

She's forgotten about the Autumn riot, it seems. Is she being her sarcastic self again? Joking at my expense, as usual?

The guests were then introduced to Sultan in Persian. The blonde and plump one, clad in an oversized floral dress with a name too hard to pronounce was presented as the head of the UN's crime and drugs agency.

She should come here more often to enhance her knowledge of the drugs we consume in Afghan prisons.

Next to her, the tall and slender younger woman dressed in a big jumper and skinny jeans, was introduced as Simona from *Azadi Baraye Zanane Afghan*. In a sudden move, Simona walked forward to hug Sultan, speaking rapidly in a foreign tongue.

Sultan jumped a few steps back, vigorously moving her hand from side to side.

Shahla, watching the scene with widened eyes, feigned a smile, attempting to assuage the unpleasantness. 'Sultan *jaan*,' she said with an unusual tenderness, as if consoling a crying child who had been injured in a fall. 'Simona *jaan* likes you. She called you her sister and wished you a happy Women's Day.' Then, with graceful ease, she held Simona, who appeared confused and bewildered, by the arm and directed her attention to a leaflet she claimed to have produced in collaboration with the Ministry of Women's Affairs.

In the midst of Shahla's discourse, Sultan discreetly slipped away, finding a seat in the front row next to Geisha, who, adorned in her faded yellow kimono, had her hair pinned back with a golden butterfly hairpin studded with blue stones. Holding Dina Charsi's hand, seated to her left, Geisha motioned for Sultan to take a seat next to Dina, as the middle seats had been reserved for the foreign guests. 'We're only here for the gifts,' Geisha whispered with a grin, prompting Sultan to chuckle loudly. Feeble and fragile, Dina grinned, displaying her few yellow and decaying teeth.

The programme kicked off with a scratchy rendition of the national anthem playing from an aged cassette player. Everyone rose and some sang along, their voices echoing in the hall.

Following this patriotic start, Shahla stepped forward to initiate the speeches. Speaking in Persian, she profusely expressed her gratitude to the UN and the Italian charity for their instrumental role in securing funds for the construction and furnishing of the prison two years prior. She then read passionately lengthy excerpts of a leaflet co-authored with the Minister for Women's Affairs, as if she were weaving an epic tale. She meticulously emphasised the prison's grand achievement – providing a clean and safe environment enriched with learning opportunities, and its daunting challenge – staff shortage due to lack of funds.

A rather sluggish and tiresome translation in English ensued after each sentence. It was delivered by a woman from the prison's administrative office who, clearly unsure of the accuracy of her translation, stretched the proceedings to at least an hour.

As the foreign speakers began their delivery, Dina fell into a deep sleep, audibly snoring. A vigilant guard escorted her out of the ceremony to avoid further disturbance and embarrassment.

Unbeknown to anyone but Sultan, Dina left something behind on her seat – a mobile phone.

In the hushed ambiance of the ceremony, Sultan's hawkish eyes honed in on the device. With a swift, almost choreographed move, she snatched the phone and deftly slipped it into her pocket. She was itching to take a closer look at the phone; her curiosity had peaked, mainly because she had never seen Dina using a phone, nor had she heard her mention it. The only way to escape the rest of this dull event, she thought, would be by feigning sickness. She initiated an unrelenting cough that gained volume with the passing of time.

Farzana hurried towards her with a bottle of water. 'Come on, take a sip,' she said, thrusting the bottle towards Sultan's mouth.

'My tummy is hurting. I'm getting sick,' Sultan whispered, pushing the bottle away. This was followed by a bout of coughs.

Farzana motioned for her to get up and follow her out of the hall. No sooner had Parwin Chapool started her poetry recital than Sultan and Farzana were out of the hall.

Back in the prison, Sultan rushed up the stairs, taking two or sometimes three steps at a time to Dina's cell, ignoring the pain in her lower back that had started to grow with each step.

Bursting into Dina's cell, the air of which was thick with the musky odour of cannabis, Sultan found Dina sprawled on the floor, her forehead almost touching an ashtray overflowing with cigarette butts. A half-lit cannabis pipe rested on top of it. Sultan's heart sank at the sight, a mix of concern and weariness tightening her chest.

'Dina… Dina.' Sultan nudged her, shaking her bony shoulder. 'Are you alright? Wake up! I've got your phone.'

After a few attempts, Dina half-opened her sleepy eyes and looked up at Sultan. 'Have you brought my gift?' she asked, expectingly.

'No. You will get that later.'

Looking disappointed, Dina sat up slowly with the help of her decimated arms.

'Your phone.' Sultan fished out the device from her pocket, and handed it over to Dina.

'*Baashi Sahib,* fetch me some water. I'm parched,' Dina said with a slur.

Sultan looked around the cell and spotted a half-full bottle tucked in the corner by Geisha's bottom bunk. She rushed up to her feet and fetched it for Dina, who took a massive gulp from it.

Leaving the bottle on the floor, Dina lit a cigarette. 'No one ever calls me, *Baashi Sahib.* My daughter doesn't want to talk to me. She says I'm not her mother. I have no one else in this world.' Her watery, bloodshot eyes roved uneasily, searching for Sultan's gaze.

'So, why do you have a phone? Have you stolen it?' Sultan locked gazes with her.

'No.' Dina scowled. 'How can you even think that? This phone was a gift from the Herati girl. See the red nail-polish mark on it?' She blew out the smoke with such a force that it made her cough deeply, spitting out phlegm into a jar by her side.

Filled by a rush of gusto, Sultan held the phone closer and saw the small scribble in the bottom corner.

'Take it, if you want it. It's no good to me.' Dina lay slowly back down on the floor, closing her eyes. A rush of footsteps in the corridor heralded the end of the Women's Day event. Sultan shoved the phone in her pocket and left Dina sleeping on the floor. She went down to the floor below, in search of Setara.

The air in the corridors was filled with the appetising smell of kebab. Rarely was kebab on the lunch or dinner menu but today was Women's Day and Shahla had decided to pamper the inmates.

On her way to Setara's cell, Sultan bumped into Farzana holding two large gift bags.

'A quick recovery, it seems!' Farzana remarked with a hint of sarcasm. 'Here, this will make you feel even better.' She handed over one of the gift bags to Sultan. 'This one,' she said, pointing at the other, 'is for Dina.' Then with a cheerful wave of her hand, she was gone.

When Sutan entered Setara's cell, Setara looked up from the trays of *doogh*, the salty yoghurt drink meant to accompany the kebab and rice that was on its way. Beaming, she greeted Sultan jubilantly. 'I love the scarf they've given us! And look, they've also included a sketchbook, charcoal, coloured pastels, a notebook, and writing pens!' With childlike exhilaration, she emptied the gift bag onto the floor, its contents scattering across the worn, permanently stained carpet. She picked up the large orange and red flowery scarf with gold fringes, holding it up in the hazy light streaming through the cell window. Admiring its vibrant colours, she glanced at Sultan and motioned for her to open her gift bag. 'What scarf did you get?' she asked eagerly.

Sultan shrugged, pulling out hers from the bag with lazy nonchalance. She unfolded the scarf and laid it on the floor.

'Be careful, it might get stained on the floor,' Setara said and picked it up cautiously. The green and blue flowers encircled by a silver fringe shimmered softly in the dim light. 'It's beautiful,' she murmured, her eyes dreamy.

'No good to me,' Sultan said, folding the scarf neatly and returning it to the bag. 'I never wear scarves. Do you want it? If not, I'll sell it.'

'I'm more interested in your sketchbook and stationery,' Setara remarked, pointing at Sultan's gift bag.

'You can have it all.' Sultan left her gift bag by Setara's bunk, then glanced back with a mischievous grin, pulling a phone out of her pocket. 'This is the real gift, my friend!' she said triumphantly and held up the phone, pointing to a scribble of red nail polish on one corner. 'Look at this,' she said.

Setara held the phone firmly, squinting at the mark. 'The English letter "N",' she pondered aloud. 'Niloofar's?' she muttered under her breath, her eyes widening with disbelief.

Sultan nodded, giving her a thumbs-up.

The phone, however, was out of charge. Setara plugged it into a charger near her bunk, hiding it carefully under her pillow.

'Tomorrow, at our usual spot,' Sultan whispered.

'We'll check the messages and write down the names and numbers of everyone she contacted before the incident,' Setara said.

'Absolutely no one can know about this,' Sultan commanded.

'Definitely!' Setara complied.

Spring had been aloof this year. The air was still cold and frosty and there had been occasional snow showers. The prison's yard remained covered under a thin layer of snow. The four almond trees, however, were in full bloom and pleasantly aromatic with a rich nutty undertone, towering over Sultan and Setara, who were sitting underneath them, wrapped up in thick woollen cardigans and shawls.

Squinting, Setara began clicking through the text messages on Niloofar's phone, while occasionally scanning her surroundings to make sure no prying eyes lingered. After some time searching, she spotted a trail of messages from a "Dunya Palace".

The name immediately resonated with Sultan, rejigging her memory of the earlier conversation with Dina, where she had mentioned something sounding like 'Dunya Khana'.

'Yes,' she said, snapping her fingers. 'The name is very close to the one Dina vaguely remembered Niloofar telling her the day before the incident.'

Setara turned to Sultan, her eyes wide and mouth agape. 'Listen to this,' she said in a hushed tone, glancing at Sultan. 'This guy called Abdullah is telling her to meet him at Dunya Palace. That's probably a shop, don't you think so?'

Sultan nodded. 'I think so. Thinking back, I know a clothing shop by the same name in Dehmazang.'

'Listen to this,' Setara added, thrilled. Her eyes gleaming. 'He is saying that he's very friendly with appeal court judges, as they are all his *andiwal* and that he will make sure Niloofar's appeal will be successful so she can be released soon.'

Sultan, equally taken aback, released a sharp gasp. 'Who is this Abdullah? How does he know Niloofar? Who's taking her there?' She quickly lowered her voice, spotting a guard standing near the steps to the main entrance.

Setara stared into the cold air, immersed in thought. 'Let me see,' she said, pursing her lips. 'He mentions a contact by the name of Rina, whom he says will bring Niloofar to the location. Do you know anyone called Rina?' she asked, a hint of concern in her voice.

Sultan shook her head, puzzled. 'Maybe a mutual acquaintance from Herat?'

'A mutual acquaintance from Herat in this prison? No, I don't think so!' Setara shook her head. 'I know all the Herati inmates in this prison and none are called Rina. In any case, this Rina must be a guard or cleaner. Someone who can enter and exit the prison.'

Setara paused. Something shifted in her expression. 'Nazia!' she called out.

The name sent Sultan back to their meeting with Niloofar's mother a month ago. It was Nazia who had first alerted them to Niloofar's missing phone, asking them to let her know if they ever found it.

'Shall we tell Nazia we've found the phone? And about Abdullah?' Setara asked in hushed tone of voice.

'No!' Sultan replied, raising her voice slightly. 'No way! I don't like that woman and don't trust her.' After some hard thinking, she came up with a plan. 'Let's buy some phone credits from Geisha and you call Abdullah. Use that classy voice of yours. Pretend to be a potential customer. Charm him into revealing more about himself and his business. We need to find out who this Rina is.'

The Curse of Unmarked Graves

Piercing screams reverberated down the second-floor corridor. Sultan waded urgently through the crowd of women and children emerging from workshops and school. She spotted Farzana standing frozen at the door of Cell 74. Her eyes widened in shock, as she covered her mouth with both hands as if to muffle a scream.

'What's happened?' Sultan yelled at Farzana, her voice cutting through the chaotic air.

Farzana remained motionless, her gaze fixed on a scene unfolding inside the cell.

Sultan leaped into the room, finding Roya, Fahema's cell mate, kneeling beside Fahema's bunk, clutching books tightly to her chest. Roya's tearful eyes met Sultan's, her mouth opening in a scream. On the bed, Fahema lay in a pool of blood. The floor below was saturated with the crimson remnants of a gaping gash on each of her wrists. And the air was thick with the metallic scent of human blood. Next to the leg of the bunk rested a blood-stained razor blade.

'Call an ambulance!' Sultan screamed, looking in Farzana's direction.

'No use...' Farzana whimpered. 'She's dead. No pulse. Roya checked her neck earlier.'

Roya nodded silently, dabbing at her eyes with the corner of her scarf.

Farzana, clutching walkie-talkie radio close to her ear, suddenly jolted, as if struck by a thought. She barked at the silent group of women and children huddled on the bunk opposite, their solemn eyes fixed on the corpse. 'Come on, everyone, clear the cell! Hurry up! Take all your stuff! I'm moving you to another cell.'

She then turned to the onlookers outside the cell – women and children craning their necks for a glimpse of the tragic scene. She shouted at them to move, pushing them back from the doorway.

'She was a mother to me,' Roya said, sobbing, as she collected her books and clothes. 'The kindest human being on this earth.'

'Hurry up! I'm about to lock this cell!' Farzana yelled at her, pulling her arm. She then turned her head to Masuma, a police officer guarding the floor above, who had just arrived, breathless.

Wiping her tears, Masuma looked aghast, stealing a sideways glance at Fahema's bloody corpse, before muttering *'Allah Akbar'* under her breath. She then started to prod the stunned inmates to clear out of the cell.

Sultan helped Roya with her bags. As they walked out, she spotted Setara, who had just popped her head out of her cell, glancing with widened eyes at Farzana locking up the cell behind her.

Sultan waved at Setara, ushering the tearful Roya into Setara's cell. Times like this, Sultan thought, Setara knew better than anyone how to console tormented souls. She watched as Setara embraced Roya warmly, and carefully poured hot tea into three glass cups. With her concerned eyes fixed on Roya, Setara then retrieved a tray of *bolani* from under her bunk, which was covered with a spotless white muslin. She offered the warm snacks to Roya and Sultan, who savoured the delicious comfort food.

As Roya cautiously sipped the hot, sugary tea, she straightened her back a little and stretched her legs, appearing calmer and more composed. She gazed at the ceiling. 'Only two days left until Nowruz, and this happens. Why is God so unkind to us, taking away a beautiful being who gave nothing but love to everyone? Just a few days ago, Fahema *jaan* was sitting with others, shelling almonds and walnuts for the Nowruz *haft mewa*.' Roya shook her head in disbelief.

'She was looking very sad in the last few weeks,' Setara said softly, holding her steaming tea glass close to her lips. 'She said she had no one to go to on the day of her release. But I never thought she would kill herself.'

'How did she get the razor blade?' Sultan asked, looking in Roya's direction.

Roya, looking bewildered, exhaled deeply and shook her head. 'I honestly don't know. No one uses a razor blade in our cell.'

'If someone is determined to do something as drastic as that, she'll find a way,' Setara responded, glancing at Sultan with watery eyes. 'How did Niloofar get the Kerosene to set fire to herself?'

'Do you know where they will bury her?' Roya asked, taking another sip of hot tea.

Setara and Sultan exchanged glances, grappling with how to reveal the unsettling news to young Roya. Setara, in her tender voice, broke the news gently. 'There is a cemetery next to the prison. They will bury her there.'

'With a proper gravestone?' Roya asked, pouting her lips.

'No,' Setara replied, wiping the tears rolling down her cheeks.

'In an unmarked grave,' Sultan added, staring solemnly into the air.

Roya burst into tears. Setara, shifting to Roya's side, tried to soothe her, holding her close to her chest. 'Roya *jaan*, you can always come here before and after your lessons. I will help you with your homework and make fresh *bolani* for you. I'm a qualified teacher, you know.'

'So kind of you, Setara *jaan*,' Roya said, weeping in the warmth of Setara's chest.

'You remind me of my older daughter, Yasmin.' Setara's eyes welled up.

'Do you see your daughter at all?' Roya looked up, staring into Setara's eyes.

Setara let go of Roya and looked away, shaking her head. She then reached out for a tissue under her pillow. Wiping her eyes, she offered Roya and Sultan another round of *bolani*.

Roya took a big bite of *bolani*, pondering her thoughts. 'You know, I'd never known parental care until I met Fahema *jaan* here.' She grimaced. 'I lost both parents in the civil war. Our house in Kabul was destroyed in a rocket attack. I was then a tiny prematurely born baby struggling for survival in an incubator at a Kabul hospital. Grudgingly, my uncle and aunt adopted me. They would have gladly put me in the care of one of those shabby orphanages in Kabul had there not been pressure from my elderly grandparents. They believed I'd been a harbinger of bad luck, a curse on the family. So, I was treated harshly, blamed and beaten for everything going wrong in the household.' She sighed, holding her half-full tea glass close to her eyes, her fingers grazing its rough edges. She slowly placed the glass on the floor next to her bare feet, her eyes tracing its contours. 'We lived in Iran during those troubled Taliban years, and when our residence permits came through, my uncle decided to stay unlike his peers who had all returned to the liberated Afghanistan. He was a builder and was earning good money. Construction was a booming industry in Iran.' Roya looked up, and breathed out heavily. 'All my cousins went on to secondary school but I was kept at home to help with the housework.'

Sultan glanced at Roya, her head slightly tilted to the side, furrowing her brow. 'What happened that you end up here in prison?'

'I met Jamshid, an Afghan guy, a little older than me, two years ago and we fell in love. He asked my uncle for my hand in marriage but uncle said no. I was under-aged, he said, and the boy was far too young and jobless to provide for a family. So, we ran away together and crossed the border in the back of his friend's truck. The police caught up with us in Kabul. My uncle had reported me missing. We were both arrested. I was detained at the juvenile Detention Centre but he was sent to Pol-e-Charkhi prison. I had to undergo that wretched virginity test at the police station.' Shivering, Roya paused a little, holding and stroking the tops of her arms with both hands. 'Have you ever had to go through that?' Eyes narrowed, her gaze shifted from Sultan to Setara, who both had their heads bowed to the floor. 'They thrust two fingers inside you and twist them around a few times. The pain is excruciating. They said I was a virgin but still charged me with the intention to commit *zina*. At my trial, I was sentenced to ten years.'

'How many years did he get?' Setara asked, looking at her curiously.

'He got twelve years.' Roya cast her eyes down to the folded pink and cerise scarf she had been given as a gift at the Women's Day event, playing with its silver tassels. 'He's been told our convictions will be quashed and we will be released if he marries me. He really wants to, as do I. But his father and my uncle are not consenting to our marriage. My uncle says Jamshid has no means of supporting me and his father thinks I'm *chatal* and will never make an obedient, faithful wife. So, I'm stuck in this godforsaken place.' She looked up, her lips quivering and eyes glistening with tears. Her shoulders stiffened as if bracing against an invisible weight.

The cell door suddenly flung open and in came Farzana, teetering in her new shiny black patent stilettoes. 'Come on, hurry up,' she cried, looking in Roya's direction. 'I've been looking everywhere for you!'

Roya looked up, motionless, as if in a trance.

'You'll be sharing Cell 86 on the floor above with your new inmates Tahera, Zohra and Fariba.' Farzana stared at Roya with widened eyes and fluttering lips. 'They've started serving dinner. Move!'

Roya rose slowly to her feet, grabbing the plastic bags heaving with books and old clothes. Head bowed down, she followed Farzana out of the cell.

Sultan watched inmates filing into the visitors' hall for Fahema's *fatiha*. Fereshtah, a guard in charge of the third floor, had agreed to recite the *fatiha* – the verses of the first chapter of the Quran – though with some reluctance, as suicide is a condemned act in Islam. Bowing to pressure from peers, she had finally acquiesced to their argument that *fatiha* would not constitute a blessing for the deceased; rather, it would establish a connection for the living with God Almighty. The hall had been decorated with Fahema's numerous drawings of pious women in all-embracing, white garments and its stale smell had been softened by rose-scented candles – a gift from Shahla.

'A befitting testament to an angelic soul whose life ended so tragically,' Sultan muttered, glancing at the drawings.

Some inmates had apparently heard the guards moving Fahema's corpse out of the cell during the evening lockdown a few hours after she'd been found dead. But no one had seen how her corpse had been washed and dressed for burial.

'Have they informed her relatives?' Setara whispered to Sultan, nudging her gently in the arm.

'I don't think any family member would care to know, to be honest,' Sultan whispered back, secretly catching a glimpse of Roya, who stood opposite to them, her back slightly hunched and shoulders slumped.

Making a circle around Fereshtah, the inmates raised their hands, holding them next to each other near their faces, palms facing inwards. As Fereshtah began reciting in a low-pitched voice, '*Bismillahi Rahmani Rahim*,' the assembled crowd stared down at their hands, silently moving their lips. Some moved them more vigorously to the ebbs and flows of the Arabic verses. At the end of the recital, they ran their hands over their faces, as if cleansing them of sin with the holy verses.

Roya joined Setara and Sultan as they walked slowly in a file back to the main prison building, behind Farzana and Masuma.

'How is your new cell?' Setara broke the silence.

'Fine,' Roya sighed. 'It takes time to get used to anything new.'

'Looking forward to Nowruz and *haft mewa* tomorrow?' Setara's lips opened to a wide grin, looking in Roya's direction.

Roya nodded, quickening her pace. 'I'm late for my class,' she said and then waved a stiff-fingered hand at them and hurried up the stairs.

'I've got a ten-dollar phone credit,' Setara announced as she and Sultan settled comfortably on the floor of her cell. With her cellmates out at workshops, the pair had the space all to themselves to work through their sleuthing strategy.

'I'll pay half,' Sultan offered.

'Shall we use Niloofar's phone or mine?'

'Use Niloofar's. We have to be careful. Mustn't leave any trace of our own numbers in their phone's memory,' Sultan urged.

Setara reached under her pillow and retrieved the fully-charged phone. She scratched the phone credit card carefully, revealing the cluster of numbers beneath the silvery coating. With deliberate precision, she keyed them into the device and waited for the network to connect. After a moment, she dialled Abdullah's number and switched on the loudspeaker. A female voice answered after a few rings.

'Alo?'

'*Salaam alaikum*. Is Mr. Abdullah in?' Setara asked, her voice smooth and confident.

'Who?'

'Mr. Abdullah,' she repeated, her tone sharpening slightly.

'Who's speaking?' the woman pressed.

'I'm his cousin. Just arrived in Kabul,' Setara said, tossing in a cheeky wink and a smirk.

'We have no one here by that name. You've dialled the wrong number.'

'But he gave me this number when we last met,' Setara insisted, her tone feigning surprise. 'He told me to ring him once I was back in Kabul. He said this was the number for his boutique.'

'Boutique?' The voice on the other end bristled with scepticism. 'No. This is an estate agency. We buy, sell, and let houses and apartments. We also organise weddings and other functions.'

'Isn't this Dunya Palace?'

'Yes, but it's not a boutique.'

Looking puzzled, Setara hesitated before apologising and hanging up. She rested her head in her hands and let out a loud sigh. 'It's pointless, calling these people. I could tell she was lying. She knows Abdullah alright. Why else would she ask who I was before saying it was a wrong number?'

'But we don't know anyone who could visit the place in Kabul,' Sultan muttered. After a moment, she looked up, narrowing her eyes. 'Let's try again with my phone after the Nowruz holidays. I'll pretend I'm looking for a wedding venue, as the bridegroom's sister.'

Setara's face lit up. 'That's a good idea. Weddings are most likely to happen in spring, when the weather's just right.'

No sooner had Setara poured tea into two glass cups than Niloofar's phone rang, startling both of them. Sultan grimaced, her heart racing. 'Who could that be?' she muttered, her voice tinged with anxiety. 'Will you answer, Setara *jaan*?' Her breathing quickened as the phone continued to ring.

Biting her lower lip, Setara reluctantly picked up the call and put it on loudspeaker. A man's voice echoed through the room.

'Hello. Niloofar *jaan*? Is that you, my beauty?'

'Yes,' Setara replied, trying to mimic a young, seductive voice, matching the intonations she remembered as unique to Niloofar. 'Who's this?'

'It's Abdullah. Have you forgotten me? Where have you been,

my darling? I haven't heard from you in months. Are you okay? My assistant answered earlier when you called, sorry for the confusion.'

'It's okay, Abdullah *jaan*. I'm happy to hear your voice,' Setara responded, exchanging a perplexed glance with Sultan.

'Can I see you soon? I miss you so much. I have good news! Haji Karim, the judge presiding over your appeal, has promised to quash your conviction. But I need to see you, my darling. Believe me, you mean so much to me.'

'I can't see you, Abdullah *jaan*,' Setara said with a mischievous grin, winking at Sultan.

'You can't? Why? Don't forget what I told you last time, about the video clip I still have of you. Remember that?' Abdullah's voice grew dark, laden with menace.

'But how can I meet you, Abdullah *jaan*? I'm still here in prison.'

'I'll get Rina to bring you. My heart is yearning for you.'

'Is Rina in Kabul? I haven't seen her in a while.'

'*Wallah*, I haven't spoken to her either in a while. Let me call her. I'll ring you back. *Khoda hafez, azizum*.'

As soon as the call ended, Sultan and Setara burst into riotous laughter. Overcome with relief and glee, they leapt to their feet, throwing their arms around wildly, dancing in circles, stamping their feet in joy. The pent-up tension of the ominous call melted away as they twirled and swirled, eventually collapsing onto the floor, breathless and laughing.

Sitting up, they caught their breath and began speaking in a more composed tone. 'He was blackmailing her,' Sultan said, with a deep scowl. '*Murdagow!*'

Cell Raids

It was the first day of Nowruz, and the prison buzzed with anticipation for the celebration. The weather had turned pleasantly warm, and the inmates were eager to savour *haft mewa* served outside in the yard.

Geisha burst into Sultan's cell, visibly flustered. Panting, she pressed a hand to her chest, struggling to catch her breath. Seema and Humaira, who had been dancing to a lively Bollywood song blaring from the DVD player that Sultan had recently pinched from the African cell froze mid-movement, their curious gazes fixed on the intruder in the yellow kimono.

'Nowruz *mobarak!*' Sultan scowled, her voice laced with impatience. 'Have you forgotten? What's up? You look like you've seen a ghost.'

'I just overheard the guards on my floor talking,' Geisha replied, her voice trembling. 'They're planning to raid the cells for drugs and mobile phones. It could happen any moment now.'

'First raid since we moved into this prison, right?' Sultan tilted her head.

Geisha nodded, smoothing her yellow kimono with shaky hands.

'Will they do a body search, too?' Seema asked, casting a nervous glance at Sultan.

'No, they'll just search the cells, turning everything upside down,' Geisha said, glancing towards the door.

She had barely waved goodbye and reached for the handle when Sultan called her back. 'How is Dina?'

Geisha hesitated, her hand hovering over the door handle. Slowly, she turned back towards Sultan, her eyes glossy. 'Not good. The illness has drained her completely. We're taking turns looking after her. Bibi Gul is with her now. She can't feed herself or even go to the bathroom on her own anymore.'

'I'll come up to see her later,' Sultan said, smoothing her cropped hair with a sigh. Geisha hurried out of the cell, her kimono fluttering behind her.

Sultan turned to her wives, her face suddenly stern. 'You know where to hide the opium and *chars,* don't you?' she barked, her eyes flickering with urgency. 'Go on, quickly. Get on with it. Make sure it's well-hidden inside you. Understood?'

Seema and Humaira nodded, moving swiftly. They retrieved the drugs from a concealed hole in their mattresses. They then carefully wrapped them in a thin layer of nylon. Seema finished first in the bathroom, followed closely by Humaira.

Sultan paced the cell, her footsteps soft but hurried. Her mind raced with possibilities, each thought more frantic than the last. She perched on the edge of her bunk, her gaze distant as she nibbled on her nails. Where could she hide the mobile phones? A sudden idea struck her, sharp as a spark. She sprang to her feet, her heart pounding, and dashed towards Setara's cell. Reaching the door, she peered through the small hatch, her breath catching as she spotted Setara deep in conversation with two of her cellmates.

Pursing her lips, Sultan stepped into the cell, bowing slightly with her hand pressed over her chest. '*Salaam alaikum.* Nowruz *mobarak,*' she said warmly. 'They're handing out the *haft mewa* in the yard. Are you going down to get your share?'

Setara's cellmates lit up, children and adults exchanging joyous glances and broad smiles alike. All greeted Sultan with cheerful wishes of Nowruz *mobarak* before dashing out eagerly to join the festivities in the yard.

'Nowruz *mobarak,* Sultan *jaan,*' Setara said, her face bright with a wide grin. 'Let's follow them down.' She motioned towards the door.

'That was a fib,' Sultan admitted, her tone dropping as she leaned in closer. 'I just wanted to get rid of them so we can talk privately.'

Setara's grin faded, her brow furrowing in concern. 'What's up?' she asked, her voice quiet but wary.

'The guards are going to raid the cells any time now. We need to be prepared. They'll be looking for phones, drugs, anything illegal.'

Setara grimaced, locking eyes with Sultan. 'They did this a few times in the old prison but never here.'

'We have to hide the phones. Can you tuck them into your turban? Make sure they're all turned off.'

'I'll try. No more than three, though.'

'Fine. Mine, yours, and Niloofar's.' Sultan pulled out her own phone, handing it to Setara.

Setara retrieved her own phone and Niloofar's from under her pillow. She turned both off before checking Sultan's.

'Abdullah didn't call back.' Setara announced, glancing at Sultan.

'He must have got suspicious,' Sultan said, curling her lower lip in indifference.

'He might have found out that Niloofar isn't here anymore,' Setara murmured, narrowing her eyes.

Sultan shrugged. 'God knows. We still don't know who Rina, Abdullah's contact, is.'

Setara unfolded her voluminous turban, revealing her long, dark hair streaked with a bit of grey at the hairline. After pinning it neatly at the back, she carefully rewrapped the turban. She then tied it securely with four knots – two at the back, two at the front – tucking the three phones into each fold. She shook her head a few times, testing the security of the hidden phones.

'I'll have to get used to sleeping like this until the raid. They could come before *Fajr* prayers.'

'No, don't do that.' Sultan's voice rose slightly, her index finger pointed in warning. 'You'll make your cellmates suspicious. Keep them close, but stay alert for any noise outside. Be ready to move fast.'

The raid came unexpectedly, catching everyone off guard. The inmates had anticipated it before the *Fajr* prayers, bracing for a pre-dawn assault on their belongings. But it struck at eleven in the morning, just when most women were in classes, workshops, or meetings with lawyers and social workers. Those lounging in the yard or chatting inside their cells, some discreetly trading contraband, were ordered to vacate, leaving their possessions to the mercy of the guards.

Sultan was with Dina and Geisha when Masuma and Fereshtah stormed into the cell, barking orders to vacate.

'Don't touch her,' Sultan growled, her eyes narrowing as Masuma moved towards Dina's frail form on the bunk. 'She's too ill to move.' She threw herself over Dina protectively. 'Over my dead body!'

Masuma hesitated, exchanging a glance with Fereshtah, who was busy stripping sheets from the opposite bunk. With a nod from her colleague, Masuma relented.

'I'll leave her, but you two, out!' Masuma ordered sharply, her eyes fixed on Sultan. Sultan rose slowly, her glare never wavering as she backed towards the door. She paused in the threshold, locking eyes with Masuma, her expression a clear warning: *Don't you dare touch her.*

As Sultan and Geisha stepped into the dim corridor, they strained to catch the faint noises from the cell: the soft rustling of sheets and the occasional clatter. The air, thick with the mingling scents of chicken broth and stale sweat – a backdrop of prison life – hung heavily in the space. Tension prickled their nerves, tugging at their heartstrings.

'Dina won't last much longer. I can feel it,' Geisha whispered, her voice catching. Tears streamed down her face. She wiped them away with her sleeve in wide swaths. 'Leukaemia… just like my mother.' Her voice faltered. 'I was only ten when she died in that hospital in Mashad. I watched her take her last breath.'

Sultan shot her a side glance. *Is now the time for your drama?*

Geisha took a deep breath, shaking her head as if to dispel the memory.

Her voice dropped to a whisper. 'Then there was the fire. First, my brother's house burned down. Then ours. They blamed me.' Her tone suddenly rose, sharp and anguished, startling Sultan. 'But it wasn't me! I swear it wasn't! It was her, that wretched girl, Naheed. Her voice followed me everywhere, haunting me, tempting me to do wrong. But they didn't believe me. They beat me, starved me, and threw me out on the streets.' The words tumbled out in a torrent of sorrow and panic. Her eyes grew wide and wild, as though those painful memories clung to her like shadows she desperately wanted to escape but couldn't.

Sultan glanced at the cell door, throwing her arms up in

frustration. 'What are they doing in there? This is unbearable.' She turned her gaze towards Geisha before pacing the narrow corridor, hands clasped behind her back.

Geisha looked up, her neck craning as her eyes sought Sultan's. Sultan, now leaning against the opposite wall, absently smoothed her cropped hair.

'And you know what?' Geisha said, her voice rising, 'When I was on the run, I slept in Imam Reza's shrine, in the poor women's section, fending off all those *hajis* and *mullahs* trying to make me their *sigheh*, contract wife. And I was only fifteen!' She let out a burst of laughter that echoed down the dark corridor, the sound lingering unnervingly long in the silence.

Finally, the cell door opened, and the guards emerged empty-handed.

'You can go in now,' Masuma said, tilting her head in the direction of the cell.

When Sultan and Geisha went in, they found Dina lying on her side, facing the wall, sound asleep.

'What did you do with the *chars?*' Sultan asked, her voice cautiously low as she glanced at Geisha.

'I gave it to Bibi Gul to hide. She stashed it in her daughter's storybook, tucked away in the kids' playschool library.'

'That's reckless! Too risky. Is she mad?' Sultan glared at Geisha, frowning.

'Don't worry about it,' Geisha replied, a sly smile creeping across her lips. 'Masuma is the one supplying Dina. She searched the playgroup. Prison isn't any different from the outside world.' She perched on the edge of Dina's bed, gazing into a decorative hand-held mirror. With bright red nails, she smoothed her dark hair, tucking away stray strands from the loose bun at the back. She gasped at her reflection. 'Look at this smudge under my eyes! I look dreadful.'

Sultan shot a sideways glance at her, shaking her head. *She and her vanity!* Sultan had no patience for this nonsense today.

Clicking her tongue, Geisha wet her finger and carefully wiped the dark smudge from beneath her lower lids. Satisfied, she reached for a lipstick from the shelf overhead and painted her lips bright red. Glancing back at Sultan, who was standing by the window, she announced with a grin, 'I'll be out of here soon. The president's Nowruz amnesty edict is coming out in a week or two. Can you believe it?'

'How did you find out?'

'Masuma told me. She's heard it from *Raees Sahib*. She says they always recommend the *zina* convicts who've served half of their sentences for amnesty.' Geisha then stared into the air, hands clasped on her lap, biting her lower lip. 'Where can I go, though? Back to the *khana-e-amn?*' She shrugged her shoulders.

'Do you mean the brothel?'

'No!' Geisha burst out laughing, the sound echoing off the bare, tobacco-stained, grease-streaked walls. 'It's a shelter for the homeless and runaways. I was there a few years ago. To be honest, it's run like a prison. You're not allowed out at all, and are even forbidden to use the phone. And you are forced to pray every day.'

'From one prison to another. Is that what you want?'

'It was a long time ago.' Geisha's eyes fixated on something obscure and distant. 'I was fifteen after the ousting of the Taliban. A Hazara charity sent a coach to bring us back to Kabul from Mashad via Herat. We were wild. They couldn't contain us. Boys used to call us from the other side of the wall. We would climb the wall to spend the afternoon with them in the back streets.' Geisha chuckled loudly.

'So, I was right. It's a brothel.' Sultan smirked, watching dark clouds form a cluster in the sky. Memories of life in the Pakistani brothel run by Shaista's mother, Nasrin, the master of disguises, flooded her mind. On the surface Nasrin appeared the epitome of piety. She never failed to perform all her five daily prayers and fasting every Ramazan. She impressed everyone with her eloquence, glamour, and intoxicating beauty. In private, however, she was a whore with a heart of stone. Sultan's mind drifted to the onset of spring in Peshawar, twenty years ago, when the air was filled with the scent of apricot blossoms, jasmine and hibiscus in Nasrin's lush garden.

It was in Nasrin's lavish villa where Sultan would spend most of her time 'learning' to become a Bollywood actor, though in reality, unbeknownst to her then, her husband Sharif had loaned her to

Nasrin to groom her into prostitution. But neither Sharif, nor his side-kick Nasrin knew that Sultan and Shaista had become entwined in an intense love affair. An enthralling romance which had started with the seventeen-year-old Shaista, who had already been on the game for a couple of years, teaching the thirteen-year-old Sultan how to kiss, cuddle, seduce and give pleasure to their repulsive clients – pot-bellied middle-age men who tossed colourful, pricey worry beads, while knocking back whisky and gin.

For Sultan, as their amorous entanglement deepened, the torment of rape at the hands of these men had so magically slipped into insignificance, becoming a minor detail as compared to the immensity of her love for Shaista. The three years that followed her discovery of true love had indeed been the happiest time of her life – the only time she'd actually known what the word love meant. How painfully soon that beautiful romance ended.

Their little love nest shattered into pieces when Nasrin discovered the emerald ring. That ring had been a precious gift to her beloved Shaista for her twentieth birthday. To buy it she had saved for years the money she had stolen from her clients. It had given the sixteen-year-old Sultan enormous pleasure and pride to see Shaista wear the ring, which matched her eye colour, on her slender finger. A moment etched forever in Sultan's mind.

Nasrin's discovery of the emerald ring had brought their short-lived happiness to a tragic and disastrous end. Nasrin, interrogating her daughter about it, pressurised Shaista to reveal who had given her the expensive gift. Shaista resisted, trying to brush her mother off by telling her a lie. She told her the gift had been from a client. But Nasrin was an old hand; she wouldn't have been fooled so easily. She knew the clients would never be so generous as to give a hooker such an extortionate gift. True, those men had become richer with the war in Afghanistan. The war had been a godsend, with an abundance of American and Saudi dollars flooding their coffers in exchange for providing firearms to the Afghan Mujaheddin and essential supplies for Afghan refugees. But they weren't stupid to squander this treasure recklessly.

Exasperated at Shaista's resistance to divulge the identity of the gift-giver, Nasrin slapped her so hard that Shaista fell on her side, cracking her head on the edge of her bed. As blood gushed out of Shaista's head wound, Nasrin threw a box of tissues in her direction and locked her up in her bedroom. Having been deprived of food, Shaista could only endure three days of starvation before caving in and revealing that the gift had been from Sultan. She begged her mother to keep it to herself and not to tell Sharif. They both knew what would befall Sultan if Sharif found out about the ring.

Although Nasrin promised Shaista to conceal the truth from Sultan's husband but away from her daughter's eyes, she broke her vow. All hell broke loose when Sharif found out. He, crying obscenities, bludgeoned Sultan so hard that she couldn't get up from the floor for days. His sister Tahmina, who had never shown Sultan kindness, had heard her screams but chose to ignore them. The onslaught on her body had been so severe that to move around Sultan had to be assisted by Aziza, Sharif's maid. Sharif also banned her from seeing Shaista – Sultan's harshest punishment.

But the worst had yet to come. A few days later, Sultan heard from Aziza, who had grown empathic towards her, that Sharif had sent Shaista away to Dubai – somewhere far away and out of reach. Tormented, Sultan's strength and vigour had rapidly atrophied. To her, it was a disaster no less than an apocalypse.

One day, away from Tahmina's gaze, Sultan descended to the basement, surrounded by crates of rice and chickpeas, she consumed an overdose of the sleeping pills prescribed by her doctor for insomnia. She had yearned for death in the dark obscurity of the basement, a place where no one could find her. But Aziza, the old faithful, had discovered her curled up on the damp floor and alerted Tahmina, who rushed Sultan to the hospital. The hospital staff revived her, pumping the poison out of her tummy. But no one and nothing could have taken away the emotional torment she had been going through deep within her.

As time went by, dread and anger built up inside Sultan. She blamed her parents and Sharif for stealing her youth. Her eyes had become swollen and sore from crying, grieving the loss of her carefree days in Dehmazang's dusty streets, rejoicing in a football win with her playmates, and spotting yellow butterflies camouflaging among the marigolds that grew wild by their pond. Her laughter had now become a forgotten echo. While convalescing in the Peshawar hospital, the thought of killing Sharif, finally ridding herself of his menace once and for all, had overshadowed her mind. It was a plan that would take a decade to see through.

Geisha's shrieks of laughter jarred Sultan back to the present, snapping her out of her grim memories. She blinked, finding herself once again in the cell with Geisha still babbling about the past. 'We were thrown out of that *khana-e-amn* after they found dead babies, or… things that looked like dead babies, in the bathroom. No one could explain what they were or how they ended up there.'

Sultan frowned, unable to fully grasp what Geisha was saying. 'I'd better go to see Setara,' she muttered, smoothing down her shirt and jeans.

Geisha pouted, her voice suddenly childlike. 'Don't you want to hear the rest of my *khana-e-amn* story?'

'Another time.' Sultan forced a smile, waving as she left the cell.

As she hurried down the corridor, Geisha's words echoed in her mind, making her chuckle despite herself. *Dead babies? Or things that looked like dead babies? Bonkers.* Sultan shook her head, her thoughts darkening. *I bet she'll be back here soon after her release. She won't last a month in the outside world – whether it's a shelter or a brothel.*

When she arrived at Setara's cell, the air hit her first – a stench of dust mixed with the sour tang of sweat. 'What a pong!' she said, immediately flinging the window open. But then the sky opened, and heavy raindrops splattered onto her shirt and the carpet. Cursing, she shut the window with a loud gasp.

'Farzana and that new guard. What's her name again? The one with the peroxide hair?' Setara asked while tidying up her bed. Her face wrinkled in disgust.

'Parwana,' Sultan muttered, brushing raindrops from her sleeves.

'Yes, Parwana. She has a foul smell, that girl.' Setara forced a weak smile. 'They searched everywhere and found nothing.' Her smile quickly faded. 'I can't wait to get these phones out of my turban. They're driving me mad.'

Sultan sat cross-legged on the floor, her eyes following Setara. 'Geisha says she's getting released soon.'

Setara froze in the middle of smoothing her blanket. She turned slowly to face Sultan, her expression doubtful.

'She says she'll stay at some *khana-e-amn* or whatever it's called. Sounds fishy.'

Setara scoffed. 'She won't last there. Those places are run by fanatics. They force girls into marriages. But what choice does she have? We'll all face the same fate eventually.' Her voice softened as she sat on her bunk, her complexion turning pale.

'Not me,' Sultan said firmly. 'I'll go to Iran, get my surgery, and start a new life there.'

Setara glanced at Sultan, her lips twitching into a smile that seemed more sardonic than genuine. 'A new life, huh? Lucky you.'

Sultan felt a brief pang of irritation but brushed it aside as envy. Her eyes lingered on Setara who was now undoing the knots in her turban.

One by one, the folds came undone, and as the last knot loosened, three mobile phones fell into Setara's lap. She swiftly tucked them under her blanket, her long dark hair spilling loosely over her shoulders as if freed from the same burden. The sudden hum of voices drifted inside from the corridor – unintelligible murmurs signalling that Setara's cellmates were returning from their workshops.

Echoes of the Unseen

Setara, glancing intently at Roya, asked her to shift a little to her right so she could have a good view to sketch her profile. 'You have a beautiful face, Roya *jaan*. A small and well-sculpted nose, high cheekbones, and lips in the shape of a heart. Magnificent! Like the finest miniature portrait.'

Roya returned the compliment with a shy smile and moved slightly to the right, her eyes fixed on the cell door.

The arrival of spring – warmer air, tulips, narcissi and occasional gifts from the guards – had sparked new energy in Setara. On days when the yard wasn't crowded with screaming children, she would sit under the almond trees, her and Sultan's favourite haunt, soaking in the warmth of the sun. The towering branches, heavy with blossoms, filled her with pride for having survived yet another harsh winter – her fortieth, to be exact.

This seasonal change had rekindled her desire to draw and paint, reviving the artistic skills she'd neglected since her imprisonment five years ago. Setara now spent her days painting Herat's landscapes from memory and sketching portraits of her fellow inmates whenever her cellmates were out attending classes. Painting the almond trees was high on her list of things to do. The sketchbook, charcoal, and coloured pastels from her Women's Day gift bag had intensified her creative drive.

As she held one of the charcoals, memories of her teenage years flooded back.

'When I started drawing, there was a war raging between the communist government and the Mujaheddin, and supplies were hard to come by,' Setara told Roya, drawing the sloping curve of her forehead with her charcoal. 'I used ordinary household charcoal to draw portraits of family and neighbours.' She tapped the red box of charcoals with a smile. 'This is exactly what you need to create nice portraits. The other would break or smudge too easily. Still, my art brought so much joy to the neighbourhood in those dark days of war.'

Spring's arrival also triggered memories of her childhood in Herat. Before the wars, Setara's extended family spent Fridays and holidays at her grandparents' orchard in Gozara district. The best time was always spring, when fruit trees bloomed and the weather was just warm enough 'to shed the winter blues in your bones,' as her mother used to say. But that tradition came to an abrupt halt with the emergence of jihad and the war against the communist regime.

Her grandparents had abandoned the orchard, deeming it too dangerous. It remained out of reach for years. After the Taliban's fall, Setara and her siblings hoped to reclaim it, eager to revive childhood memories and restore the family heritage. But their hopes were dashed when they found a hostile Pashtun family living on the land, claiming ownership.

When her brother challenged their claim, the men – armed with Kalashnikovs – threatened to kill them if they didn't leave. The encounter deepened Setara's resentment towards Pashtuns, a disdain she often voiced to her Hazara and Tajik friends. 'Ignorant and culturally subnormal,' she would mutter with a wince, using harsher language among those who shared her anti-Pashtun sentiments. She wouldn't say such thing now, she thought, closing her eyes for a moment.

Setara never ventured out to Gozara again, especially after learning that much of the district had become a Taliban stronghold. To her surprise though, the man leading the terror banditry, Ghulam Yahya, was a Tajik warlord – one of her own ethnic group. He was infamously known as the 'Tajik Taliban'. He wreaked havoc across Gozara until his demise in a US raid about a year ago, to the relief of the locals. Not all of them, of course. He still had a hard core of Tajik militiamen who swore to continue his jihad.

This revelation had challenged Setara's long-held ethnic prejudices, a product of Afghanistan's civil war and the Taliban's reign. Her experience in prison, confined with women from all of Afghanistan's ethnicities, had opened her eyes to the truth: their commonalities outweighed their differences. They were all suffering, all bearing the scars of a war-ravaged society. 'War always brings out the worst in humans, no matter who they are,' she often told her cellmates. Maybe, Setara hoped, spring would truly return to Afghanistan someday. She recalled the words her mother spoke whenever she complained about their war-shattered lives: Never lose hope.

Shaking off the memories of war, Setara looked up from her sketchbook and tilted her head to the side. She reached out, gently moving Roya's face slightly to the left to get a better view. She leaned back and observed her friend's profile, smiling. 'That's perfect.' Returning to her drawing, she began sketching the delicate lines of Roya's nose and chin. 'How have you been these days, Roya *jaan*?' she asked, her tone soft as she worked. 'How are you settling into your new cell? I haven't spoken to you properly for a while now.'

Roya, her hands clasped tightly in her lap, seemed lost in thought. After a pause, she finally spoke. 'I've been busy with my studies. Someone recently donated books to the library, and I've been researching Persian poetry. Maulana's love poems. It's like he's speaking to me, describing unrequited love so perfectly.'

Setara held the unfinished portrait up at arm's length, examining the shading on the nose and chin. She murmured to herself, 'I need to darken the shades a little here.' Then, glancing back at Roya, she smiled. 'I love Maulana's poetry too. I studied it back in Herat for my thesis. I can help you with that if you'd like.'

'Thank you, Setara *jaan*. I've been lucky with books lately. Fereshtah's boss at the prison's administrative office has sent some, too.'

'Who's her boss?' Setara asked curiously, raising an eyebrow.

'I don't know her name. I haven't met her. Fereshtah has been the go-between. She says her boss is a *samunwal*, a police colonel.'

Setara didn't know anyone in the administrative section. The staff there were aloof, worked short hours, and rarely mingled with the inmates. The only time she recalled seeing them was during the prison's official opening two years ago. So, it seemed strange that a *samunwal* from that detached corner of the prison would show interest in an inmate – especially someone who had only recently arrived.

This piqued Setara's curiosity, sending her mind spiralling into old memories. She recalled the day of the prison's opening ceremony, when rows of uniformed officers had pushed the inmates back into orderly lines at the far end of the yard, clearing the way for the Minister of Women's Affairs. A short, svelte woman in a green scarf led the procession, flanked by two senior police officers: a tall, middle-aged man adorned with medals and stars – likely a general – and a short, dumpy woman with frizzy grey hair pulled back into a ponytail. Could she have been the *samunwal* Roya was talking about? Setara vividly remembered both of them standing stiffly with their feet apart and hands clasped in front of themselves.

Preparations for the opening ceremony had started right after breakfast, in the suffocating heat of Kabul's summer. The air inside the cells had been thick with the stench of stale broth and sweat. Outside, the four almond trees had begun shedding their fluffy green casings, revealing the plump, nutty fruit inside. Setara, along with fifty or so other inmates had been marched into the yard and lined up in five neat rows beneath the back wall, well away from the podium where the officials stood. The air was heavy with dust and heat, and the distant echo of guards' boots thudded ominously against the concrete walls.

When the women's minister arrived an hour later, cloaked in ceremonial splendour, a guard hurried to her car, holding up an umbrella to shield her from the scorching sun. She was trailed by an entourage of female staff, all wearing green scarves. The air buzzed with curiosity, and was punctuated by whispers and chuckles. Setara recalled the bewildered faces of the inmates, eyes wide and startled, as they watched the waves of green scarves circling the celebrity visitor. The scene had been almost comical, with Farzana – hot and sweaty – trying to explain that green symbolised the Afghan women's liberation movement. Setara had stifled a laugh at the sight of the inmates' blank stares. No one had the faintest idea what a 'movement' was and where it came from.

After cutting the ribbon to loud cheers from the green-scarfed brigade, the minister, draped in an elegant off-white silk suit, took to the podium. Speaking into a crackling microphone, she recited a poem by Saadi Shirazi, the revered Persian poet. Setara remembered how the minister's provincial accent had grated against the beauty of the verses, leaving her tight-chested and with a lump in her throat. That moment had been a sharp reminder of how far she had fallen.

That poem had once been hers to recite, one of her all-time favourites. She had earned applause for it at school events, where her clear, formidable voice had left audiences in awe. In her mind's eye, Setara could still see herself at fourteen, standing tall in her navy-blue blazer, her long dark hair tied neatly in a white ribbon, addressing hundreds of students and teachers at the morning assembly. The poem's message of human interconnectedness had resonated deeply with her then. She could still feel the pride that had swelled in her chest as she captivated the room, her voice echoing through the hall. Now, standing at the edge of this farce of a ceremony, she sighed. How cruelly fate had swept away those promising days, leaving her trapped in this desolate place, haunted by memories of a life she had once been so certain of.

Could that fourteen-year-old girl have ever imagined then that she would one day hear her favourite poem recited in a prison yard? That she, filled with ambition and dreams, would one day serve a life sentence? Back then, she had been determined to become an accomplished professor of Persian literature, aspired to make her family proud. Watching an amateur fumble through her favourite poem had been heartbreaking. It was a tragic reminder of how her teenage dreams had evaporated over the years. From that elevated pedestal, she had fallen to a pit so low.

She closed her eyes briefly, the weight of her regrets pressing against her chest. *How did I end up here?*

But then, as her fingers lightly smoothed Roya's dark, tousled hair – the strands slipping through her fingers like silk – she felt something shift. With each short stroke of the charcoal, she captured the gentle flow of Roya's hair. A smile tugged at her mouth, and her thoughts softened.

Despite everything, she had found something unexpected in this coarse, vulgar place – something almost sacred. Here, amidst the ugliness of it all, she had discovered a kindred spirit in Roya. Someone with whom she could share her thoughts, someone who appreciated the written word as deeply as she did. In this young girl, Setara had found an unlikely soulmate, a companion to explore the beauty of prose and poetry. Maybe, just maybe, there was still something worth holding onto, even in a place like this.

'You know, sometimes people are the opposite of what they seem,' Roya said thoughtfully, breaking the silence. 'Our guard Fereshtah is one of those. Stern on the outside, with a heart of gold on the inside. Her name suits her. Fereshtah, angel.'

Setara, who had never met the guard, looked up from the sketchbook. 'Is she new? I haven't seen her around.'

Roya nodded. 'Yeah, she started only a couple of weeks ago.' She shifted her legs, wincing slightly. 'Can we take a break? These pins and needles are killing me.'

'Almost done. Just bear with me for one more minute, Roya *jaan*.'

When Setara finally held up the finished portrait, she marvelled at how closely it resembled Roya, as though she had captured her spirit on paper. Roya let out a squeal of joy, the sound echoing in the cramped cell as she clapped her hands. 'Can I send it to Jamshid?' she asked, her eyes wide with excitement.

'But we are only allowed to send letters, Roya *jaan*,' Setara reminded her. The spark in Roya's eyes faded quickly. Her smile faltered.

'Hang it in your cell or the crafts workshop,' Setara offered gently. 'When I finish a few more, we can ask the prison to hold an exhibition so that everyone can see the work. It might brighten up the place a bit.' She then reached for her flask of tea and poured them each a steaming glass of her favourite Iranian blend.

Roya wrapped her hands around the cup. Her chewed nails barely grazing the glass. The sweet, comforting aroma of the tea filled the room, cutting through the cell's stuffy air.

As Setara lifted her cup, its warmth and fragrance offered a brief but welcome escape from their harsh reality.

'I don't know what to make of my new cellmates,' Roya said, taking her first tentative sip of the hot tea. 'All three are *zina* convicts. They're about my age, but they talk about sex as if it's the only thing they know.' She hesitated, her brows knitting together in discomfort before locking eyes with Setara, who was gently blowing on her tea to cool it down.

'What do you mean exactly, Roya *jaan*?' Setara asked, frowning slightly.

'They talk about men, different men they've been with, and giggle like it's some kind of joke. It's strange. They're so young, yet they talk about things I barely understand.'

Setara nodded slowly, her expression thoughtful. 'Ask them where and how they were arrested. Sometimes, the charges they carry can tell you who they really are. If they were convicted of *zina,* loitering, and drinking wine, then it's likely they're... well, like Geisha.' She paused, grimacing. 'Geisha was charged with the same things, and we all know what Geisha is.'

Roya's eyes widened in both curiosity and apprehension. Setara leaned forward. 'Just be careful around them,' she warned, raising her index finger for emphasis. 'Girls like that... they carry diseases. Don't share your drinking cup with them, and make sure you scrub the bathroom sink and shower tray before you use them.'

Roya's face dropped, as she absently traced patterns on the hard carpet with her finger. 'They say you can see it on a girl's face if she's lost her virginity. Is that true?'

'It shows,' Setara replied without hesitation, her voice firm. 'I can always tell when a girl is no longer a virgin.'

Roya groaned softly, her gaze dropping back to the floor. 'I hate it here. I just want to get out of this place, marry Jamshid, and live a proper life. I heard Geisha will be released soon. Maybe there's hope for me too, don't you think?'

Setara took a long moment before responding. She could see Roya's fragile hope simmering beneath the surface, and she didn't want to crush it entirely. Smiling gently, she met Roya's eyes. 'I'm sure you'll be released soon, Roya *jaan*. Hopefully in the next few years. Geisha is being freed because of the Nowruz *farman*, the presidential amnesty. She's served half her sentence, which is why she's eligible. Your time will come too. You just need to be patient.'

Refilling her cup with her favourite aromatic tea, Setara added after a thoughtful pause, 'And you'll see how quickly time passes here.

Before you know it, your three years will be up, and you'll be packing your bags, leaving this godforsaken place behind, my girl.'

Roya, who had fallen silent and lost in thought, stared at the floor, absently sipping her tea. After a couple of quick gulps, she wiped her mouth on her sleeve and stood to leave, clutching her portrait carefully.

'Roya *jaan*,' Setara said softly, catching her eye before she could turn away. 'Before thinking of marrying Jamshid, you need to discuss some crucial matters with him and his family. You know what I mean. His father's objections, Jamshid's ability to support a family. You can't rush into these things.'

Roya nodded, her eyes brightening with curiosity.

As she turned to go, Setara called her back again. 'Wait! Let's wrap the drawing in this.' Setara pointed to some newspaper pages she had tucked away under her bed. Carefully, Setara folded the portrait inside the newspaper and handed it back, smiling. 'It's only charcoal. It smudges easily.'

Roya beamed as she looked down at the package. 'I adore this,' she said proudly. 'I'll protect it with my life.'

After Roya left, a sigh escaped Setara. Grinding her teeth in frustration, her gaze turned towards the grimy window – the only view she had of the world beyond these walls. She rose and reached for the latch, and opened the window with a creak. A rush of fresh air swept in, carrying the scent of spring blossoms with it. Pressing her forehead against the iron bars, Setara closed her eyes, letting the warmth of the sun and the sweet breeze fill her senses.

Poor, innocent girl, she thought. *So gullible, so trusting. She doesn't see it yet, but Jamshid has no real intention of marrying her. Men like him... they use you and then vanish the moment their needs are met. He'll look for an untouched virgin when he's released while Roya is left believing in this false love.* A wave of bitterness washed over Setara. *Yet Izzuddin... khoda beyamorz, he was different. One in a million. Faithful, devoted, loyal to the end.* She smiled faintly, but the ache of his loss tugged at her.

Turning her gaze to the almond trees swaying in the spring breeze, Setara felt a flicker of joy. Their white blossoms gleamed in the sunlight. Delicate, pure. The only true beauty in this barren land. The sight of them eased the weight on her chest. She let out a quiet chuckle.

At least the almond trees don't speak. They have seen and heard everything – all our forbidden secrets – but will never betray them. They keep all of our hidden thoughts, holding them tightly within their lush branches, cherishing them in their hearts. If only men could love women with the same grace, loyalty, and endurance as the almond blossoms.

She exhaled, long and slow, as if releasing the worries that had clung to her all morning. At least for now, the almond trees stood in quiet enchantment. A reminder that even in this harsh place, beauty still bloomed.

Mary

Hazel, Esther and Hope gasped when Mary emerged from the bathroom, tall and sturdy in her traditional southern Nigerian outfit: a long sky-blue robe with a bold white motif in the front and back.

'Wow! A true Edo lady,' Hope, also from Edo but in her everyday jeans and red T-shirt, remarked.

'I want to look nice and respectable for my first meeting with the lawyer assigned to my case,' Mary said. 'Incidentally, she has been assigned by an Italian women's organisation, *Libertà Per Le Donne Afghane.*' She gave a loud chuckle.

Hope sighed staring into the distance. 'All those horrifying years in that country... did we ever know of a women's organisation who could help us? Only the blessed nuns.' A heavy silence ensued.

Mary smiled as she studied her reflection in the small mirror hung on the cell wall, running her fingers through her braided hair and smoothing it with a few drops of oil. 'I just hope this lady lawyer is as cool as yours. I hope she at least speaks English.'

'Our lawyer is from an Italian legal aid organisation as well,' Hope said. 'She took all three of us on before your arrival here. I'm sure yours will be just as good,' she added with her usual encouraging smile.

'I thought you wanted to keep this outfit untouched until your day of release. It's too good a dress for an Afghan prison,' Hazel said. 'Esther and I,' she added, chuckling, pointing at the woman next to her, 'the citizens of Uganda, like our jeans too much.'

Mary gazed intently in Hazel's direction, a mischievous glint in her eyes as she lifted the vibrant blue scarf high above her head, its fabric billowing gently in the air. 'Come on, citizen of Uganda, give me a hand with this scarf,' Mary teased, her voice light, as she playfully swayed her hips, drawing chuckles from the others. She sat comfortably on the floor, her back leaning against the edge of the bunk, and positioned herself snugly between Hazel's legs.

Hazel delicately wrapped the scarf around Mary's hair, transforming the fabric into a stylish turban.

Mary, her fists clenching and unclenching in anticipation, couldn't help but marvel at the strength and dexterity of Hazel's touch. As the scarf took shape, she hurried to see herself in the mirror. 'Perfect,' she whispered, her eyes lingering on the image in the mirror. She nodded at Hazel, a soft smile tugging at her lips as she turned her head side to side to admire the turban's symmetry.

At just under two metres, Mary loomed over the smaller Afghan inmates in Badam Bagh. Her height often gave her the vigour and stamina to survive the absurdity of Afghan prison life, not least her ten-year sentence. From her lofty vantage point, the Afghan inmates scurried, carrying trays of food, flasks of tea, and short grassy brooms. Always whispering among themselves, they appeared demure yet conspiratorial, with their oversized, unblinking stares – by far their most detestable trait – fixed on her.

Since their arrival, she and her African friends had been objects of fascination at best and ridicule at worst. Of them all, only Setara ever approached them. While the others preferred to stare and whisper, Setara brought them tea, sweetened with heaps of sugar, and served with unguarded kindness. The others, however, stole their meagre belongings – bits of bread and cheese saved from meals, and the biscuits and crisps they'd bought from the prison shop. The worst of it came when Mary's portable CD player and speaker went missing. 'Despicable,' she muttered to herself as she walked towards the meeting room on the second floor to meet the lawyer, her light brown suede Libyan slippers gliding softly against the hard floor.

Mary still couldn't grasp the madness of her sentence. Ten years for a crime with nothing but circumstantial evidence. It was hard to believe. The only 'proof' they had was her presence in a room with a group of Africans, one of whom had been caught with heroin days earlier. The trial had been brief, rushed through without a defence lawyer, and conducted in the local language. To Mary, it was a foreign tongue that felt as distant as her hopes for justice. With fingers crossed, all she could do now was pray her lawyer could help.

Her legs wobbled beneath her as she was overcome by nerves. She gripped a nearby chair for support, steadying herself just in time to greet the tall, attractive black woman approaching her with a warm grin. Muriel Chandler, tall and striking, with braided hair adorned with beads of gold and silver that softly clicked together as she moved, smiled warmly. Dressed in casual jeans and cowboy boots, she radiated warmth and confidence.

Mary grasped the lawyer's hand with both of hers, shaking it eagerly. 'I'm so happy to meet you!'

'Hey. Good to meet you too, Mary,' Muriel responded in a soft American accent. 'So, you're from Nigeria, right? Whereabouts?'

'Benin City, Edo State. Southern Nigeria.'

'Uh-huh. So, here you are, a very long way from home. How has it been here?'

'Fortunately, I'm here with three other Africans. We were all convicted of drug trafficking, but they never found any drugs. Still, we've each been given a ten-year sentence. Bizarre!'

Muriel glanced at Mary with a soft, understanding smile. 'I've gone through your case file, and I was thrilled to be able to photocopy it at the prison's central office. You're lucky. Colonel Rina, the deputy governor, has been incredibly helpful.' She turned her gaze to the stack of papers on the table, focusing on a few highlighted lines. 'You've only been to the primary court so far, which means we have a good chance of overturning your conviction on appeal. I can't make any promises, but believe me, I'll fight hard for you.'

Muriel stretched, tapping Mary's clasped hands gently, her fingers warm and steady. 'We can argue that the conviction was unsafe. You didn't have a defence lawyer to guide you, and you couldn't even understand the trial. And of course, we'll bring up the lack of evidence as a major factor.'

'I can't stand it here.' Mary stared at the grubby wall facing her, eyes welling up. 'I pray every night that this is the final page of the darkest chapter of my life. That the torment that began three years ago will end, and I'll be home with my widowed mother and my little girl.'

Muriel leaned in, her head resting in the palm of her hand, her eyes fixed on Mary. She listened with a quiet intensity. 'Tell me about it. What happened to you?'

'For three years, I've been living at the mercy of sex and drug traffickers. Nasty, vicious people. There were times I thought I'd die. They used every dirty trick to trap me like hunters circling their prey. And if they thought I was stepping out of line, they punished me, brutally.'

'Oh my God, Mary, that's horrible.' Muriel's eyes clouded with concern as she glanced at Mary's tearful eyes. 'Look, I've got another client to see at the other end of town. I'm afraid I have to go now,' she said, shifting her gaze to her watch. Straightening up, Muriel swiftly stowed her papers in her spacious shoulder bag, the weight of which sagging slightly as she hoisted it onto her shoulder. With a warm glance at Mary, she gave her shoulder a squeeze before turning on her heel. 'Don't worry, you're not alone. We're a team. I'll see you next week. Take care, Mary.' She waved and made a quick exit, her dusty cowboy boots clacking softly as she disappeared.

As Mary walked back to her cell, a surge of optimism filled her steps, but her gaze drifted to the second cell on the left. Two Afghan women worked quietly, their backs turned. One dusting, the other sweeping a threadbare carpet with a grassy broom, causing a dusty haze to float in the air. Then, something caught Mary's eye. Perched on a high shelf was her portable speaker, the unmistakable sticker of her favourite actor, Denzel Washington, staring back at her. Her breath hitched. Blood rushed to her face. Her throat tightening as she stifled a cry.

Her fists clenched at her sides as she stormed forward, her pulse pounding in her ears. In one swift motion, she snatched the CD player and speaker off the shelf. 'These are mine!' she wanted to shout, but what came out was a low, guttural growl, fierce and unrelenting.

As she prepared to leave the cell, the younger of the two women tugged violently at her hair and shrieked. Her voice rose to a piercing wail. Though Mary couldn't grasp the words, the screeching cry sent a cold wave of dread through her, making her heart race. Clutching the CD player and speaker to her chest, she rushed towards the cell door. But before she could step out, a tomboyish woman with a fierce scowl stormed out of the bathroom on the right, her eyes burning with vengeful intent. Jaws clenched, she muttered through gritted teeth.

Without a word, the woman snatched a belt from the floor. Planting her feet wide, she cracked it through the air with a sharp snap – a chilling promise of the violence to come. In an instant, she lunged at Mary, ripping off her scarf and yanking her hair with brutal force. Mary's head snapped backward, and she stumbled, gasping in pain.

'Ouch!' Mary shouted as the CD player and speaker slipped from her grip, and crashed to the floor with a sickening crack. 'Leave me alone! Get lost!' She screamed as loud as she could, hoping her cellmates would hear, but the sound was swallowed by the chaos of the moment.

The attacker shoved her to the floor, the belt biting into Mary's legs like fire with every lash.

Mary raised her arms to protect her face, her voice now hoarse with pleading. Punches and kicks rained down on her belly, each a brutal hammer blow that left her gasping for air. 'Oh my God, I'm dying. Jesus, have mercy. Please, stop!' Pain exploded in her abdomen, and suddenly she was coughing thick, metallic-tasting blood across her attacker's face.

The other Young woman grabbed the attacker's arm, shouting, 'That's enough, Sultan *jaan*. Let her go!'

Sultan jerked back with a horrified grunt, wiping her face with her sleeve and spitting on the floor.

Moments later, one of the two younger women rushed out of the cell, returning with the toothless guard.

A terse exchange followed between the guard and Sultan, whose gestures became increasingly frantic.

Mary, lying on the floor and bleeding from her mouth and nose, motioned towards the guard, pointing desperately in the direction of her cell.

The guard glanced at Mary, her face impassive as she pulled a handful of tissues from her pocket. Kneeling down, she gently lifted

Mary's shoulders, resting her head against her thigh. She wiped Mary's face and neck in silence, the tissues quickly turning crimson.

Hope burst into the cell, her face pale with terror, her breath coming in short, sharp bursts. 'What the hell happened, Mary? Talk to me, sister, please,' she urged, her voice trembling as she knelt beside Mary, gripping her hand tightly.

Mary closed her eyes, shaking her head. 'I'm bleeding too much,' she whispered, her voice raspy, each word sending fresh blood splattering from her lips.

Hope quickly wiped Mary's face and neck, her hand shaking, before calling out to Esther and Hazel, who stood frozen in the corridor.

'Get the manager,' Mary managed to say between coughs. Through her drooping eyelids, she saw Hazel and Esther, tears streaking their faces, their lips moving in silent prayer as they made the sign of the cross over their trembling chests.

'God help us. Jesus, save our sister,' they whispered in unison. Behind them, a group of guards arrived, and lifted Mary's limp body onto a stretcher. Her blood-soaked blue dress stuck to her skin as they covered her with a coarse, grey blanket. The rough fabric brushed her cheek, but all she could focus on was the unrelenting pain and Hope's steady hand on her shoulder.

'Stay with us, sister. You'll be fine. Stay with us,' Hope murmured, her voice cracking under the weight of her fear.

All three of Mary's cellmates sat morosely on their beds, their heads cast down, while they prayed in silence, when Farzana, still wearing her blood-stained uniform, appeared at the door. She motioned for them to follow her to the prison manager.

Standing in a row, Hope, Hazel, and Esther faced Shahla, who sat behind her imposing desk, clad in a sharply creased grey uniform. Her calm gaze flickered between the women as Hope described the incident in a steady voice. She explained how, alerted by the assailant's cellmate, she had rushed into the cell to find Mary lying on her side, drenched in blood. Her legs were lacerated, and her torso was covered in blood. Three inmates had stood silently by the window, one of them with blood smeared on her face and clothes.

'We know who the culprit is,' Shahla interrupted. 'It's Sultan, the prison *baashi*. The inmate in charge of keeping everyone in line. I've already questioned her. She claims Mary threatened her cellmates and she reacted too harshly.'

'Reacted?' Hazel's voice cracked, her hands trembling as tears spilled down her cheeks. 'She nearly killed Mary! She was haemorrhaging.'

Shahla nodded, rising slowly from her chair. She leant over her desk, and planted her knuckles firmly on the polished glass, her reflection wavering beneath her. 'Sultan was out of order, and she'll be punished, I assure you. We won't tolerate this.'

'Where has Mary been taken?' Esther asked, her voice barely above a whisper.

'She's at a very good hospital,' Shahla replied, straightening up. 'When I spoke to the nursing staff an hour ago, they said they were trying to stop the bleeding. They may have to operate. We'll check on her regularly.'

'Mary has a lawyer,' Hope added, her voice firmer now. 'Muriel needs to know right away. She might be able to help.'

Shahla nodded. 'I'll inform her. I've met Muriel. I'll ask her to contact the Italian charity to help cover Mary's hospital costs.'

Unbolted Doors, Unseen Miracles

'Stop following me everywhere!' Sheyda's voice cracked, raw with frustration. Her heart pounded in her chest, and her fists clenched at her sides. 'You're driving me mad! I've had enough of you. Leave me alone!' Her voice bounced off the dark walls of the corridor, loud enough to draw curious inmates from their cells.

Stooped against the cold, rough wall, Sheyda's shoulders slumped under the weight of her frustration. Her loose, flowery cotton dress clung to her damp skin, her watery gaze trailing after Wajma, stout and limping, as she hurried towards the staircase.

'What's going on?' came a voice from the left. Sheyda turned to see a middle-aged woman wiping flour-dusted hands on her apron, her warm, enquiring gaze meeting Sheyda's. Without waiting for a reply, the woman stepped forward, wrapping her soft, flour-coated arms around Sheyda in a motherly embrace. 'Come, have a cup of tea,' she coaxed, her voice gentle, like a breeze. It was the kind of embrace her mother might have given her if she had seen her in such distress.

'My name is Setara,' the woman said softly. 'I was preparing the dough for today's *bolani* when I heard you shouting.'

Inside, as Setara washed the tea cups in the small bathroom, Sheyda's eyes wandered around the cell, absorbing the mingling scents of fresh dough, spices, and faint hand lotion. The vibrant sketches pinned to the walls caught her attention, their colours bright against the drab concrete. In the far corner, shelves crammed with books stood in stark contrast to the bleakness outside.

'I love your books,' Sheyda said. 'Can I borrow one? I'd like to read the one on psychology.'

Before Setara could answer, Sheyda gestured towards the paintings. 'Are these yours?'

Setara chuckled. 'Yes, they are. Do you like them? You can tell I haven't always been a *bolani* cook. And, yes, you can borrow that book, as long as you promise to return it. I'm strict about lending my books.'

'Of course, I will,' Sheyda replied coyly, smiling as she bowed her head. Turning back to Setara's artwork, she pointed at the painting in the centre of the wall. 'They're beautiful. Are these the almond trees in the prison yard?'

Setara, now drying the cups with a small towel, nodded. 'Yes. I love those trees. You know, they blossom in the dead of winter. God's miracle.'

Sheyda stared out the window at the almond trees. 'It looks like they're losing their blossoms now,' she murmured, her voice barely above a whisper. A heavy sigh escaped her lips as her legs buckled, and she slowly sank to the floor. Her hands cradled her head as if trying to hold herself together. 'I'm losing my mind.'

Setara walked over, the rich scent of aromatic tea filling the air as she handed Sheyda a warm cup. 'I can tell from your speech that you are an educated woman, Sheyda *jaan*,' she said softly, sitting across from her. 'You seem strong-willed, resilient. So, why do you say you're losing your mind?'

Sheyda's fingers trembled around the cup as she spoke, her eyes darkening. 'I've been through such dark times… and they cling to me, suffocating me. I can't escape them. Everywhere I go, they follow.'

'Who was the woman you were screaming at?' Setara asked gently.

'Ahhh… dark times follow me like a shadow I can't escape,' Sheyda whispered, her voice raw, her eyes searching for Setara's. Leaning forward, she raised her voice slightly. 'That bitch of a policewoman, Wajma, is the reason I'm in this hellhole.' She spat. 'I'm a software engineer. I was graduated from one of Iran's top universities and now I'm rotting behind bars with that *murdagaw*, that filthy rogue.' Her fingers clenched tightly around her cup. 'I ran away from home to escape my parents' cruelty. They put me under curfews, and forbade me from marrying the love of my life.' Her breath hitched, her voice trembling with pain. 'Wajma's son and daughter-in-law found me, alone, desperate, and let me stay with them. And what does that so-called policewoman do?' Her voice cracked, her lips quivering. 'She sold me like a piece of meat. Told her police colleagues she had a pretty Hazara woman for sale. Five thousand dollars. Sure enough, the police raided their house and arrested us the next day.'

Setara nodded slowly, her brow furrowed with empathy as she took a careful sip of tea. *'Ajab...'* she said softly. 'So, she was in the police force. How despicable.'

Sheyda blew on her tea, her hands quavering as she took her first sip. She glanced up at a portrait above Setara's bunk. 'I know that girl.' Her face suddenly lit up. 'She's in the cell opposite ours. Cell 86.' She gasped, covering her mouth with her hand. 'This place gives me the shivers. As I told you, trouble follows me.'

Setara turned to look at the portrait, her expression darkening. 'That's Roya *jaan*. She's a friend of mine. I gifted her that portrait, but she returned it, saying her cell was too chaotic. She was worried it would be damaged.' She turned back to Sheyda, her face suddenly tense. Scowling, she reached across and took Sheyda's hand. 'Tell me... Has something happened to Roya *jaan*? Don't hold back. Please, Sheyda *jaan*, I need to know.'

'Nothing... nothing bad has happened to her,' Sheyda stammered, her voice wavering. 'I saw her today, leaving the cell with a stack of books. But at night... I hear things. Keys jingling, whispers, footsteps. The door unbolting.' She paused, her heartbeat loud in her ears. 'I'm a light sleeper. I hear everything.'

'Did you hear people talking? What were they saying?' Setara's voice grew sharper.

'No... just whispers, the unbolting of the door, footsteps. I wish I had the courage to look through the hatch, but I didn't want to cause alarm.' She lit a cigarette, taking a long, deep drag, the smoke curling through the air, her hands still shaking. 'I'm scared,' she whispered.

Moments later, Setara excused herself, promising to continue the conversation after she had cooked and delivered the *bolani* to her customers.

Engrossed in thought, Sheyda wandered down the stairs to the yard. Intrigued by what Setara had said earlier about the magic of the almond trees, she reached out, her fingers grazing the soft petals of the last few remaining blossoms, their delicate texture cool against her skin.

'Almond blossoms, shower me with your magic. Reveal your mystery,' she murmured, her voice a soft prayer as her eyes wandered into the depths of the branches. She found herself utterly captivated by the tender blossoms resting against the young green leaves, the air thick with their faint, sweet scent. While trouble had chased her like a shadow these past months, she had seen miracles, too.

The most overwhelming had been the revelation at the shrine of Imam Reza – the eighth Shia imam, valorous and revered, resting in Mashad, Iran. Standing beneath the vast golden dome, with her daughter by her side, Sheyda had felt an inexplicable sense of peace, as if the weight of her suffering had been momentarily lifted. Only her mother had believed her when she recounted the story of her brief stay at the shrine on her way back to Kabul with her daughter in tow.

She had been on the run before. But this time, it was her brutal husband she was fleeing. The memory of him pressing his knee into her neck, the scarf tightening around her throat, flooded her mind. The suffocating pressure, the burn of fabric against her skin. If it hadn't been for her ten-year-old son, Ali, who had punched his father with fierce, determined hands, and her four-year-old daughter, Mahtab, who bit into his arm, she would have died.

It had been a marriage arranged by her father, to a man twelve years her senior – a man of their clan, wealthy, well-respected. A marriage, they said, was blessed in heaven. But no blessing could have prepared her for the nightmare that followed.

Entering the Imam Reza burial chamber through the women's section, Sheyda waded through the throngs of frenzied female pilgrims, the air thick with the cloying scent of rose water and the sharp tang of body odour. Carrying her daughter, she elbowed her way forward, eyes fixed on the golden shrine in the centre of the chamber. Straining slightly, she reached out, her fingertips grazing the cool surface of the enormous silver padlock. The edge of her chadar, clenched between her teeth, was damp from the sweat beading on her upper lip. With her left hand, she clutched the side of the padlock, her heart pounding in her chest.

'I beg you, Imam Reza, *moin al-zoafa,*' Sheyda pleaded, her voice cracking with desperation. 'Help me unlock my path to a safe and prosperous life for myself and my children.' As if in answer to her prayer, the silver padlock gave a soft click in her hand. She gasped, her breath catching in her throat, eyes wide as the padlock loosened under her grip.

The crowd pressed against her, dozens of women all straining to touch the shrine. Gasping for air, Sheyda fought to steady herself, her body trembling as sweat and tears mingled on her flushed cheeks. 'A miracle. *Subhan Allah*,' she whispered, wiping her face with the corner of her chadar.

Elbowing her way out of the crowd, Sheyda spotted an elderly woman squatting near the wall, her eyes soft with understanding as she watched the pilgrims. '*Madar jaan*, please watch my daughter for a few moments. I need to pray.' The woman's face lit up with joy, fussing over little Mahtab as she offered her chocolates wrapped in gleaming red and gold paper. Mahtab, delighted, quickly became distracted, allowing Sheyda to slip away.

Standing in the direction of Mecca, Sheyda began to pray, her lips moving silently amidst the wails of the pilgrims. As she focused ahead, a figure emerged – a young man dressed in a long black robe, its edges lined with dazzling green. His face radiated a serene smile, and his hands reached out towards her. 'Imam Reza? *Subhan Allah*,' she whispered, her heart swelling with awe.

'My child,' the figure said, his voice soft and comforting, 'I will always protect you. Go safely.'

Overcome with emotion, Sheyda brought her trembling hands to her feverish cheeks, feeling the heat of her tears as they streamed down. 'A miracle!' she cried, her voice breaking, but her outburst was swallowed by the rhythmic whimpers of the pilgrims, still moving in hypnotic circles around the shrine.

The next day, Sheyda and Mahtab boarded the coach to Kabul, heading back to live with Sheyda's parents. Her mother had been worried sick after Sheyda's last phone call. When they arrived at her parents' house in Dasht-e-Barchi, a Hazara stronghold in Kabul, Sheyda collapsed into her mother's arms, burying her face in her chest. Her sobs came in waves, heavy and uncontrollable, as if all the fear and pain of the past months were pouring out. Mahtab stood nearby, watching silently, her wide eyes taking in everything.

Comforted by her mother's embrace, Sheyda slowly began to regain her composure, especially when her parents promised to help her file for divorce and vowed to do everything in their power to reunite her with Ali. As she and Mahtab settled into their new home, Sheyda found work as an IT officer at *New Dawn News*, a rising star in Afghanistan's media landscape. Life was beginning to look up, and Sheyda was certain this change was all thanks to Imam Reza's blessing.

But the greatest gift of all was Sahil, her most cherished miracle. A journalist at the same company, Sahil became the hero of her dreams. He was her gallant knight who seemed to have galloped into her life on a white horse just like the noble figures from the stories of her childhood.

A year later, her world was turned upside down when her parents rejected Sahil's marriage proposal. Despite him being Hazara like them, they clicked their tongues and grimaced in disapproval. 'He's not mature enough to be a proper breadwinner for a family,' they said. No matter how hard Sheyda pleaded, they refused to change their minds. Their rejection cut deeper than she had expected, and as she fought for Sahil, the walls in her home seemed to close in on her.

The more she resisted, the tighter her parents' grip became. They imposed a strict curfew, forbidding her from leaving the house in the evenings and on weekends – The only times she could see Sahil. Tensions rose in the household, the air thick with the weight of words unsaid. So, Sheyda decided to flee. One afternoon, instead of heading home, she wandered aimlessly through the streets of Karta Parwan, north of their neighbourhood, her heart racing and her breath quickening with each step. The sun hung low in the sky, casting long shadows across the narrow streets. She had no plan, no destination, just a gnawing sense of fear growing with every passing minute. The area was familiar to her; her friend Monira lived nearby. So did Sahil. But she couldn't take refuge at Monira's or Sahil's homes as both lived with their parents and numerous siblings.

Desperate, Sheyda was pondering her next move when a car pulled up beside her, the engine rumbling softly in the quiet street. A young man stepped out, his eyes scanning the area cautiously before turning to her. 'It's dangerous for a woman to be alone here at this hour,' he said, his voice low. Sheyda took a hesitant step back, but then she noticed a young woman in the passenger seat and two children in the back, their innocent faces peeking through the window.

The man introduced himself as Yousef and his wife as Simin. Their children, Yasin and Mina, were about the same ages as Sheyda's own. Seated next to the children in the back, Sheyda felt the intensity of tension inside her. The weight of everything – her children, her escape, her fear – crashed down on her, and before she could stop herself, tears streamed down her face.

Where are they now? she thought, her heart aching. *Are they missing me? Will I ever see them again?* Her sobs were quiet but relentless, shaking her body as she buried her face in her hands.

Yousef glanced at Simin, who turned around in her seat, laying a gentle hand on Sheyda's lap. 'What happened, *jaan*? Where can we take you?' Simin's voice was soft, filled with concern, but Sheyda shook her head, tears still spilling down her cheeks. 'Nowhere... I have nowhere to go,' she whispered, her voice quavering.

Simin and Yousef exchanged a glance. 'Come with us,' Yousef offered gently. 'You're most welcome in our home.'

Sheyda hesitated, her mind racing, but exhaustion and fear finally overcame her reluctance. She followed them to their house, unaware of the twist awaiting her.

When they arrived at the house, Yousef's words still echoed in her mind: *We live with my mother, Wajma...*

The flash of memory hit Sheyda like a blow to her chest. Sharp and undeniable.

The Last Almond Tree

It happened the day after Geisha left the prison. No one knew why – not even Sultan, who had been among the closest to Dina, the deceased. Why did it have to happen then and not earlier? Was it because Dina was heartbroken by Geisha's departure? Geisha, Dina's cellmate and faithful friend, had always been her crutch.

Sultan lingered at the door to Setara's cell, her hand hovering mid-air before she finally knocked. She hadn't spoken to Setara in weeks. Not since the *Mary incident.* That's how she liked to describe it – an *incident,* as if it were something that had happened beyond her control. But that wasn't how Setara saw it. Setara had taken it to heart, just like she did with everything else. Sultan drew a deep breath, the rich, appetizing scent of freshly fried *bolani* filling her lungs. Her heart pounded harder as she heard Setara's voice: 'Come in.'

Sultan rapped again, then pushed the door open slightly, leaving it ajar. She stood at the threshold, waiting, unsure of what to say.

'Who's there? Come in.' Bending to the right, Setara peeked through the gap. 'Oh, it's you,' she gasped, her tone indifferent, almost indolent. She turned back to the stove. 'Come in, Sultan *jaan,*' she eventually said.

Inside, the cell felt suffocating, the air thick with the oily heat from the heater propped up on two chairs – Setara's makeshift stove. Bending over the sizzling *bolanis,* she wiped her sweat with a greasy rag, gasping for air.

'*Salaam,* Setara *jaan,*' Sultan whispered, her voice barely audible, head downcast, shoulders hunched.

'*Salaam, jaan...* It's unbearably hot in here,' Setara replied, fanning herself with a large piece of cardboard. '*Al-hamdulillah,* it's all done now,' she added, exhaling deeply. She turned to Sultan and called out, 'Pass me that stack of foil plates behind you. I need to dish these up.'

Sultan obeyed, her fingers trembling slightly as she handed the plates to Setara. Together, they worked in silence, the only sound the hiss of sizzling oil.

'Two *bolani* on each of the small plates for the guards and inmates on the third floor,' Setara instructed, her voice more relaxed. 'Three for the Africans, and four on the rest for the guards here. And of course, one for you, one for me!' Setara giggled, her laughter cutting through the thick air.

Sultan handled each *bolani* delicately. But despite Setara's attempt at lightness, the tension between them remained, heavy and unspoken.

Minutes later, as they sat on the floor, fanning themselves with pieces of cardboard to keep cool, Sultan took a large bite of her *bolani*. Her eyes fluttered shut as the warm dough and spiced filling melted in her mouth. She chewed slowly, savouring the taste as if it were the first real food she'd had in days. 'I've been missing you and your *bolani*,' she murmured.

'Noosh-e-*jaan*,' Setara replied with a smile, pouring freshly brewed tea into two cups. Her smile faded as she looked ahead. She held Sultan's gaze as she passed her a glass of aromatic tea. 'Farzana told me Dina passed away early this morning.' The words hung heavy in the air between them. 'I know she was very ill, but it's still so sad. She also said you and the others have barricaded yourselves in her cell. Is that right?'

Sultan nodded, while chewing a mouthful of *bolani*, and placing her cup carefully on the floor to cool down. 'Bibi Gul, you know who, Dina's cellmate, the serial killer, gave us the sad news after *Fajr* prayer. We didn't want them to bury Dina in an unmarked grave next door. Respecting her wishes, we want her to be buried under the almond trees with her name chiselled on a simple tombstone. Nothing grand. That's why we've barricaded the cell, to stop them from taking her corpse. We've asked the Italian charity to cover the cost of her burial.'

'Have they said yes? The Italians, I mean. Will they call *Raees Sahib* directly? If they agree, their voice will carry more weight than yours and mine. But keep the heat in mind. A corpse will start decomposing quickly in this weather.'

'Geisha called them, spoke to their Afghan staff. You know she left yesterday. It turns out one of their staff lives in the same apartment block in Macroryan as Geisha's friend, where Geisha is staying now. You know Macroryan? It's a big Soviet-built apartment complex in east Kabul. Anyway, Geisha says the Italians are very sympathetic and will cover the cost.'

Setara shook her head, taking a long gulp of tea. 'I don't know Kabul at all,' she admitted. 'But that's good news. *Aferin!* Geisha's a master at influencing people, drawing attention and sympathy. That's what she's learned in her trade, right?' She smirked with a wink.

Sultan shrugged, finishing her tea in one gulp. 'Setara *jaan*, I sneaked out of the cell to ask you a favour. Can you make *bolani* for the ten of us for lunch and dinner? We can't leave the cell, and no one will serve us food while we hold the barricade. For the sake of our deceased sister. God bless her soul.'

Setara stared down into her cup, her fingers tracing the rim as she pondered in silence. Then, she glanced up, locking eyes with Sultan. 'Yes, I will. *Roo cheshmum!* But only if you do me a favour in return.' Her gaze sharpened, and she leaned forward. 'Take a plate of *bolani* to the three African ladies at the end of the corridor and repent for your sins.'

'Sins? What sins?' Sultan barked, her voice rising. 'Why should I? They hate me anyway.'

Setara's tone remained breezy, almost wistful. 'You know Mary, the one who lost her spleen because of you? She's gone now. Back home in Nigeria, probably overjoyed to be with her family. But her friends are still here. Still shaken. Still heartbroken. Will you do it, for my sake, at least?'

A long pause. The weight of Setara's request hung heavy in the air.

'Okay, then. I'll do it,' Sultan muttered. She hesitated, then added, 'I got my HIV test results yesterday. I'm clear, *Al-hamdulillah.*' Another pause. She glanced up. 'But I don't speak English. Will you come with me?'

Setara nodded, a triumphant smile playing at her lips.

As they rose to their feet, Setara handed the plate of *bolani* to Sultan, who smoothed the creases on her jeans before gripping the plate tightly. After checking that no guards were in sight on the second floor, they hurried down the corridor, glancing over their shoulders every few steps. The clattering of footsteps echoed faintly in the distance, but the hall was mostly empty with women either in the yard with their children or at workshops.

Before they reached the African cell, Setara grabbed Sultan's arm, her voice dropping to a whisper. 'Listen,' she said, her eyes sharp, 'I'll start by introducing you in English. I'll say you're here in remorse, apologising for what you did. I'll translate their response.'

Sultan tightened her grip on the foil plate, clenching her jaw slightly. She glanced briefly at Setara, wetting her dry lips, her stomach knotted with nerves.

Setara knocked softly on the cell door, pausing just long enough to ensure someone was inside.

'Who is it?' a voice called from within.

'Setara. *Bolani.*'

'Oh, come in, Miss Setara,' the voice replied.

'That's Miss Hope,' Setara whispered, gently nudging Sultan. Opening the door slightly, she popped her head inside, smiling. Hope was sitting on her bunk, mending something with a needle and thread. 'Good morning, Miss Hope,' Setara said, pushing the door open wider. 'We've brought your *bolani.*' She motioned for Sultan to hand over the plate, but Hope's eyes widened in shock, her mouth falling open.

The cell's warm, homely scent enveloped Sultan's senses. She enjoyed it but couldn't quite place its source. As she stepped closer, Hope gasped, covering her mouth with her hand.

'Wait… Isn't she the beast who nearly killed my sister, Mary?' Her eyes darted to Setara, her expression sharp and unforgiving.

'Yes, she is, Miss Hope,' Setara replied, her voice steady. 'She's very sorry for what she did to your sister, and she's here to ask for your… mercy.'

After a tense pause, Hope slowly stood up, her jeans rustling slightly as she straightened. She towered over Sultan, who barely reached her shoulders, but instead of filling with anger, her face softened. Stretching out her hand, she smiled warmly. 'Thank you for coming… and for bringing our *bolani*. What's your name again?'

'Miss Sultan. She doesn't speak English,' Setara answered.

Taking the plate from Sultan, Hope turned to Setara. 'Tell Miss Sultan that Mary has safely arrived in Benin City. She's recovering at home, and we hold no grudge.'

'Sorry, Miss Hope, what does that word, gerr…aj, mean?' Setara asked, her brow furrowed.

'It means… we have forgiven her. All good on our side,' Hope said with a wide grin.

Setara nodded and gently pulled on Sultan's sleeve. 'Come on,' she whispered, nodding towards the door.

Once safely back in Setara's cell, Sultan yanked Setara's arm, pulling her away from the plates of *bolani*. 'Tell me what she said,' she demanded, her voice tight with frustration. 'Now!'

Setara smirked, glancing up from the plates. 'Did you smell that coconut hand lotion in their cell? It's heavenly! Last time, they gave me some to soften my hands.'

Sultan glared at her, but Setara continued, unbothered. 'Anyway, she was pleased with your apology. All forgiven. No hard feelings.'

'You're not telling me the truth,' Sultan growled, staring into Setara's eyes. 'Didn't you see how she looked at me? She looked beastly.'

'Yes, she did at first,' Setara replied, her tone sharp now. 'You beat her friend so badly that she lost her spleen. Of course she'd glare at you! But after hearing your apology, she softened. She's a good person.'

'I'd better hurry back to the barricade,' Sultan muttered, glancing at her mobile screen. Her heart raced as she thought of what might have changed while she was gone.

'Thanks, Sultan *jaan*, for your help today,' Setara called after her, turning back to the cell's kitchen space. 'I'll start cooking the extra *bolani* now.' She glanced over her shoulder as Sultan opened the cell door. 'Let me know how you get on up there,' she said and began chopping onions, leeks, and potatoes, the sharp scent filling the air. She worked quickly, her hands kneading the dough as she focused on the task ahead.

Sultan smiled, shut the cell door and hurried up the stairs to the third floor. When she reached the barricaded cell, she tapped quietly on the door and whispered, 'Open up. It's me, Sultan.' She heard the soft patter of a child's footsteps and Bibi Gul's gruff voice barking, 'Get away from there!'

A moment later, the cardboard covering the hatch was partially removed, revealing Bibi Gul's wary eye. Muttering something under her breath, Bibi Gul cautiously opened the door, and let Sultan inside.

The stifling air hit her immediately, thick with the sour stench of bodies, sweat, and death. Her eyes fell on Dina's corpse, still clad in the threadbare red and green Kuchi dress she had worn the day of her arrest. Dina lay with her arms folded beneath her chest, as if in silent prayer, while Seema and Humaira bent over her, fanning the lifeless body with large pieces of cardboard. Sultan's stomach clenched, but she forced herself to look away.

'Open the window, for God's sake,' Sultan called out as she waded through the seven inmates perched on the beds and floor. She pushed the window open, letting a refreshing breeze sweep in. It brushed against her flushed cheeks, offering a moment of relief.

She turned back, scanning the faces around her, trying to recall their names. Apart from Sheyda, whom she'd met once in Setara's cell, the others were either vague acquaintances or complete strangers. She barely recognised three of them from the autumn riot, but their names escaped her.

'You are… can't remember your names.'

The cheeky-looking one sitting between her two friends raised her head. 'I'm Leyla, and these are my cellmates Zeinab *jaan* and Asila *jaan*. Remember us from the riot?'

Sultan nodded, pursing her lips. She then turned to the other three who sat huddled close together.

'Who are you?' Sultan asked, narrowing her eyes at the unfamiliar women.

'I'm Tahera,' said the one with light brown shoulder-length hair, hazel eyes, and a charming smile. She nodded towards her companions. 'These are my friends, Zohra *jaan* and Fariba *jaan*. We share a cell with Roya *jaan*.'

Sultan nodded, immediately recalling that Roya had been

relocated to Cell 86 over a month ago after Fahema's suicide. 'Where is Roya now?'

'She's studying in the library,' Tahera replied, a playful smile tugging at her lips. 'She's always studying.'

'Not always,' Sheyda quipped, her eyes twinkling.

All four of them giggled, their laughter quickly swelling into a cascade of mirth, their bodies shaking as they leaned on each other.

'Enough!' Sultan barked, her tone slicing through the laughter. Her gaze swept over them, her eyes hardening. 'This is serious business. We must ensure Dina is buried under the almond trees, not in an unmarked grave next door. I'm in command here, and you'll follow my lead. Understood?'

'Hear, hear!' Humaira and Seema shouted, but as soon as they caught sight of Sultan's frown, they cast their eyes down, fanning Dina's body with renewed vigour.

Sultan's phone buzzed, and she glanced at the screen. 'It's Geisha, I think,' she muttered, raising a hand for silence as she answered the call. She put it on loudspeaker. '*Salaam*, any news?' she asked, her voice tense.

'*Salaam*. Yes, good news. You won't believe it! I spoke to the Afghan staff of the Italian charity. Remember Simona from the Women's Day celebration? The manager of *Azadi Baraye Zanane Afghan*? The one who tried to hug you?' Geisha's voice broke into a loud chuckle.

Sultan stifled a chuckle of her own.

'Well, Simona has signed the papers authorising their organisation to cover the cost of Dina's burial. The Afghan staff said Simona remembered Dina well from the celebration and sends her condolences.'

'So, what has *Raees Sahib* said?'

'She needs the prison governor's approval, but let's hope it'll be granted. My friend Maryam *jaan* and I are praying for you.' Geisha hung up.

Sultan's voice softened as she stared out of the dirt-encrusted window, her gaze searching for the almond trees beyond the walls. 'Everyone knows Dina was a victim of gross injustice. How could someone who wouldn't hurt an ant be guilty of such a crime?' she murmured, her voice filled with sorrow. 'Everyone, guards and inmates alike, knew she was innocent. She was punished just for being a free-thinking Kuchi woman.'

'I never believed she was guilty of the crime she was punished for,' Bibi Gul asserted, her ever-present frown deepening. 'I once overheard *Raees Sahib* whispering to the guards, "Be kind to Dina. She's gravely ill but, above all, innocent."'

'We came here a few times to buy *chars,'* Tahera reflected, her eyes welling up. 'She was always welcoming, even when she wasn't feeling well. We loved her. That's why we're here today, to pay our respects and repay the kindness she showed us.'

Fariba and Zohra, seated beside her, laid their arms around Tahera, wiping their tears with the ends of their scarves.

Sultan jerked her head towards Seema, silently instructing her to make tea for everyone. As lunchtime approached, the group cheered when Sultan announced that Setara was making *bolani*. Meanwhile, the women perched on the beds and floor began filing and varnishing their nails, using an array of colourful polishes that Tahera and Zohra had brought with them.

'Where did you get all these beautiful nail polishes?' Humaira asked, curiosity lighting up her face.

'Keep fanning,' Sultan snapped.

Humaira sighed, shifting the piece of cardboard to her other hand. She paused, shaking out her aching arms and rubbing the stiff joints of her fingers before continuing. Soon, the fruity, tantalising scent of nail polish drifted through the cell, curling around her senses. Humaira's eyes flicked towards Sultan, wide and pleading, a faint shimmer of longing surfacing beneath the strain. Sultan's face remained impassive. Head down, Humaira tightened her grip on the tatty piece of cardboard, its edges damp and curling from the sweat of her hands. She kept on fanning, while Sultan cast her a sideways glance.

'I can take over,' Sheyda volunteered. 'I'm not into nail polish. Let her join the fun.'

Humaira cheered the loudest when Sultan finally nodded her approval. 'Just be mindful of a sudden attack,' Sultan warned, her voice dropping. 'They could storm in, just like during the last barricade downstairs.'

'The riots to restore our right to smoke. I remember it like it was yesterday,' Bibi Gul added, balancing little Shirin on her lap while helping the child drink water from a bottle.

'How exciting!' Tahera exclaimed, flashing a mischievous grin. Zohra, who was filing Humaira's nails, roared with laughter.

There was a sharp knock at the door. Sultan's ears pricked up as she stepped closer, her hand hovering over the handle. 'Who is it?' she called, her voice low with suspicion.

'It's Setara! Open up, quickly!'

Sultan and Bibi Gul pushed the bunk aside, grunting as they cleared the door. Kneeling between the door and the bunk, Sultan peeled back the corner of the cardboard covering the hatch, squinting to make sure it was Setara and not a guard impersonating her. Seeing Setara balancing two trays of *bolani*, Sultan quickly stepped back. Bibi Gul grabbed one of the trays and stepped aside, allowing Setara to enter.

Soon, they were all perched on the floor around the trays, tearing into the freshly made *bolani*. The warm, spiced bread filled the cell with an appetising scent, making the grim surroundings momentarily fade. It felt like a picnic, but the presence of Dina's corpse lying nearby was an eerie reminder of where they truly were. Seema poured hot tea for everyone, and they settled into the meal.

Once their hunger subsided, they recounted the latest news on Geisha's conversations with the Italian charity to Setara who listened with an intrigued expression, her head tilted to the side and one eyebrow raised. 'So clever of Geisha to find a way to their hearts. She's so good at softening people's hearts,' Setara said with a grin and a mischievous wink. Raucous laughter echoed off the tobacco-stained walls. Looking around, Setara's eyes landed on Tahera. 'You're new, right? And your two friends?'

'We've been here for six months now,' Tahera replied, glancing at Fariba and Zohra, who both nodded.

'We were transferred from the Mazar prison. We share a cell with Roya *jaan*,' Zohra added.

Setara's smile faltered as she cast her eyes down at her now-empty plate. Clearing her throat, she took a sip of tea, her thoughts seemingly elsewhere. 'How is Roya *jaan*? I haven't seen her for a while. I worry about her,' she murmured, her voice quieter now. 'But I'm glad to know she hasn't stopped her studies.'

'Why should you worry about her?' Tahera shifted slightly, twirling a few strands of hair around her finger, forming soft curls.

'I just do. She's so kind and caring to everyone. An angel,' Setara replied, looking up and meeting Tahera's gaze. She swallowed hard. 'She reminds me of my estranged daughter, Yasmin.'

'Mothers always worry about their children because they care about them. That's what motherhood is about. Wait until you become mothers, you'll understand,' Bibi Gul added, pulling Shirin closer and planting a loud kiss on her head. The little girl cringed, her lips pouting in surprise.

'My mother didn't care about me,' Tahera said, her voice hardening as she turned to Bibi Gul and Shirin. 'After my father died, she married a cruel man who sent me away to her parents in a desolate village in Badakhshan. The village was full of old, decrepit people hooked on opium. They got me addicted, too.' Tahera's eyes glistened with tears. 'I had to run away. That wasn't the life for me. And now look at me… locked up for *zina*. My destiny.'

Fariba and Zohra wrapped their arms around Tahera, resting their heads on her shoulders as she wiped her eyes.

'Guards outside, carrying shovels!' Sultan shouted, her voice sharp with alarm. The room fell silent as the women rushed to the window, their faces pressing against the glass.

'They're going to dig the grave under the last almond tree!' Setara's voice trembled with excitement, her grin widening as she spotted the movement below.

Before she could finish her sentence, Sultan's phone buzzed in her pocket. She pulled it out and glanced at the screen, her eyes narrowing. 'It's from Geisha, I think,' she muttered, handing the phone to Setara. 'Read it aloud.'

Setara held the phone and read the message, her voice steady but her brow furrowed. '"Have you seen the Italians yet? Miss Simona should be there by now. The prison governor has authorised Dina's burial as long as the grave is tucked away under the last almond tree and hidden from view. And no tombstone, unfortunately. I know, that's what we wanted too, but I think we should accept the deal. He has ordered the guards to keep the inmates and their children indoors while they bury Dina's body."'

Setara looked up, her gaze sweeping over the group before landing on Sultan. 'I think we should accept. We can't keep the body here any longer.'

Sultan nodded, her gaze fixed on the floor, the weight of the moment pressing down on her.

Setara replied almost immediately, reading aloud for everyone to hear: '"No, we haven't seen the Italians yet, but we are thrilled at the news. Thank you for all your efforts, Geisha *jaan*. May *Allah* accept your good deeds and grant you *sawab*."'

Tahera shot an anxious glance at Sultan. 'What will they do to us? We should go back to our cell.'

'No, we will stay as we are,' Sultan said firmly. 'Let's move away from the window.' She gently guided Tahera and Zohra towards the middle of the cell, where Bibi Gul, Setara and the others had formed a circle around Dina's body. 'When the guards arrive, we form a chain. Hold each other's arms and keep your heads down. Say nothing.'

Minutes later, there was a knock at the door. 'Open up,' a voice commanded. 'We're here to take the body for *ghusl*, the final cleansing ritual.'

Sultan gestured silently to Bibi Gul, who held her daughter's hand tightly, to open the door for the six heavyset female guards carrying a stretcher. All were unfamiliar faces. Sultan took a quick glance, then cast her eyes down, making space for Bibi Gul and Shirin to join the chain. Gripping Setara's arm beside her, Sultan saw the guards from the corner of her eye as they covered Dina's frail body with a grey blanket. Together, they heaved the emaciated corpse onto the stretcher, the blanket's edges swaying with the weight. *'Ya Allah!'* the guards cried out, their voices rising in unison. *'La ilaha ilallah,'* they chanted twice more, their voices echoing through the corridor as they motioned for Bibi Gul to close the door.

The women watched in silence, tear-streaked faces shadowed by the slanting afternoon light spilling through the barred window, as the guards bore Dina's body away for the last time.

Dina was buried in the dead of night, beneath a hazy moon that cast a dim light over the almond trees. The guards, dressed in black as per the governor's orders, moved silently through the back entrance, carrying her shrouded body to its resting place, hidden from prying eyes. No *fatiha* was held, and no tombstone would mark her grave, but every inmate knew – she lay beneath the last almond tree, where they would pause and whisper a prayer in her honour.

Cell 86

Sheyda startled Setara when she burst into her cell without knocking, her eyes wide with urgency. Setara looked up, frowning as her hand paused over the letter she was writing for Parwin Chapool, who sat cross-legged on the floor opposite her.

'*Salaam*… ahh, it's you… come in,' Setara muttered, her tone distracted. 'I'll be with you in a moment. Just finishing this letter for Parwin *jaan*.' Her eyes followed Sheyda's tall, voluptuous figure as she sat beneath the window, hugging her knees to her chest. Sheyda's long hair spilled over her arms as she rested her head on them, her expression tense.

'I'm sorry, Setara *jaan*. I've something urgent to discuss with you,' Sheyda said, her voice low.

'So, how do you want to end the letter, Parwin *jaan*?' Setara turned back to Parwin, her focus briefly shifting.

Parwin hesitated, her fingers twirling the edges of her scarf. 'Just write, "I am very sorry, *madar jaan*, for causing you so much worry. I know I have hurt you."' She swallowed hard, her voice all but a whisper. '"I dreamed of you last night. Your eyes were filled with tears."' She paused, wiping her tear-streaked cheeks. Setara reached across, wrapping Parwin's hand warmly in hers. '"I shouldn't have stolen the neighbour's TV set,"' Parwin continued, her breath uneven, '"and I should have never lied to you. Please forgive me. Your faithful daughter, Parwin."'

She let out a shaky sigh and in a swift movement glanced towards Sheyda sitting with her chin resting on her knees, on the floor, beneath the dusty window, her brow furrowed.

'You're new, right?'

Sheyda nodded but said nothing.

'I thought so… How have you been?'

Before Sheyda could respond, Setara interrupted. 'Parwin *jaan*, your letter is ready.' She handed over the letter, now tucked neatly in an envelope, while Parwin placed a few crumpled Afghani notes on the floor beside her. Setara stowed the cash discreetly in her bra and rushed to the bathroom to wash a few tea cups. When she heard Parwin asking Sheyda once again if she was alright, she poked her head out and pressed her finger to her lips. She fixed Sheyda with a sharp look, away from Parwin's prying eyes.

'Right, let's clear up here. *Khoda hafez,* Parwin *jaan,*' Setara called out, her voice firm from the sink. She stood at the bathroom door watching Parwin intently, as she lingered for a few moments, her gaze intense, as if on the verge of blurting out something – a thought hanging at the tip of her tongue.

Parwin shifted her legs awkwardly, side to side, her eyes flicking between Setara and Sheyda. But when Sheyda averted her gaze, resting her head back on her raised knees, Parwin exhaled softly and shuffled towards the door, casting one last glance at Sheyda before she left.

Setara, carrying two wet tea glasses, left the bathroom and reached for the small towel on her bunk to wipe them dry. She then hurried to the cell door, grinning as she quietly shut it behind her. 'Be very careful with her,' she said in a low voice, moving closer to Sheyda. 'Parwin's a snitch. She spends all day moving from cell to cell, collecting gossip and spreading rumours like wildfire. Loyalty and discretion mean nothing to her.'

Offering Sheyda a cup of her favourite aromatic tea and a piece of *bolani,* Setara settled on the floor across from her, sipping from her own glass. 'So, what's been bothering you?'

Sheyda sighed, rubbing her tired eyes before pressing her fingers to the sides of her nose. 'I haven't slept a wink these past few nights.' She hesitated, glancing towards the door. 'The noise in the corridor hasn't stopped. It's been constant, echoing through the walls. And the strangest part? No one else seems to hear it. It's like I'm going mad.' She exhaled sharply. 'I told one of the guards, Fereshtah, about it, hoping she would take me seriously. Instead, she laughed. Loud. Deafening. In front of Masuma.' Sheyda's voice dropped, mimicking the guard's provincial accent and her mocking tone '"You must have heard ghosts, darling. Don't go spooking others with your hallucinations."' Her lips pressed together. 'She humiliated me.'

'Is the noise still coming from Cell 86, opposite yours?'

Sheyda nodded. 'Roya *jaan* hasn't been well since yesterday. I saw her cellmate Tahera early this morning, and she said Roya's been complaining of stomach cramps and vomiting. At first, I thought the noise had to do with her being taken to the hospital or a doctor visiting her in the evening, but it kept going all through the night. Fereshtah would've said something to explain the situation, don't you think?'

'Yes, I think she would have. But then again, all kinds of things can happen here. Sometimes more sinister things. There were rumours in the previous prison that inmates were taken out for sex with the male prisoners and guards.' Setara placed her empty tea cup on the floor, immersed in thought. 'Let's visit Roya *jaan* now. I'm worried about her.'

On the way up to the third floor, Setara and Sheyda bumped into Tahera and Zohra, who were both clad in jeans and T-shirts, and sprinting. 'We're attending the art therapy class. First one ever in Badam Bagh!' Tahera cried out, as they hurried down the steps.

'Hold on a second, Tahera *jaan*,' Setara called out. 'Is Roya *jaan* back in the cell? Is she okay?'

Tahera stopped on the step below and looked up, measuring. 'She is in bed. She was sleeping when we left. She is not well. She was vomiting this morning. The guards have given her painkillers.'

Setara took a deep breath and walked up the stairs at a slow pace, her feet heavy, holding Sheyda's arm. 'It doesn't sound good, at all. Not, at all!'

'I had a strange dream early one morning.' Sheyda turned her gaze to Setara, when they reached the top of the stairs. 'I saw a train of ants moving by a stone wall. The dream was so vivid that on waking I felt itchy all over. Do you know the meaning?'

'Yes, it means there will be movements soon. A change of residence perhaps?'

'Maybe that means I will be freed soon. My second court hearing is coming up. With a bit of luck, they will quash my conviction and

I will be free!' Sheyda's face illuminated with a grin, exposing her charming dimples. However, the joy was short-lived. Soon her face dropped and a shadow crossed her expression. 'But where will I go? My parents, under the pretext of marrying me off to someone in another province, will kill me to cleanse the shame and dump my body in a dark well. I know this for sure because that's what happened to my cousin. She suddenly disappeared, and no one except her murderer knows where her body is, but everyone knows that she was murdered to cleanse the shame of *zina*.'

Staring ahead into the dark corridor, Setara held Sheyda's hand firmly. 'We all struggle with dark thoughts about what the future holds for us. None of us knows whether we will survive freedom.'

When they opened the door to Roya's cell, Setara gasped. '*Ey khoda,* Roya *jaanum,* what happened to you?'

Roya lay flat on the bed, her body limp, her face unusually gaunt and pale.

Setara's voice wavered as she knelt by Roya's bunk. Gently placing her hand on Roya's forehead, she let out a sigh of relief. 'It's cool. She has no fever, *al-hamdulillah.*' She turned to Sheyda and motioned for her to bring the electric fan closer.

'Thank God for the Italians who provided these fans,' Setara murmured, her voice soft as the fan hummed beside the bed. 'Last summer, the heat was unbearable. Some women nearly died from heat stroke.'

'Roya *jaan…*' Setara gently shook Roya's shoulder, but there was no response. Roya lay still, her sleep unnervingly deep. 'What have they given her? She's conked out, poor girl.'

'Painkillers, Tahera said,' said Sheyda.

'No, I think something stronger. Let's ask the guard. Sheyda *jaan,* can you fetch her?' Setara gestured towards Sheyda.

Parwana arrived moments later – the sharp clack of her high heels echoing down the corridor. Her peroxide-blonde hair bobbed with each step, and as she entered, a pungent wave of body odour hit her and Sheyda. Setara wrinkled her nose in discomfort, then looked up to meet Parwana's gaze.

‘What have you given this poor girl?’ Setara asked, her voice tense. ‘She seems unconscious.’

‘Painkillers for stomach cramps,’ Parwana replied, her tone flat. But then her expression darkened. Scowling, she raised her voice. ‘What do you think we’ve given her? Hallucinogenic drugs? Are you out of your mind?’

Stunned by the harsh response, Setara averted her gaze and fell silent. A moment later, she stood up, gently tugging Sheyda’s sleeve, and nodding towards the door. They quietly left the cell. Once outside, Setara’s face hardened. ‘Something fishy is going on here. A painkiller wouldn’t knock someone out like that. They’ve drugged her.’ She paused, bringing her finger to the side of her mouth, deep in thought. ‘But why?’ Her gaze met Sheyda’s, perplexed, searching.

Haunting Truth

With her phone safely concealed in her jeans pocket, Sultan waded through the crowd of inmates flanked by guards, all queuing for the visitors' hall. The prison governor had finally authorised an exhibition of Setara's charcoal portraits and pastel landscapes, with the largest, most popular, and outstanding being that of almond blossoms. Simona from the Italian charity and the deputy prison governor would officially open the exhibition.

Sultan craned her neck, peering through the gap in the half-open door. She stood on her toes, and scanned the nearly-empty room until she spotted Setara at the far end, carefully arranging the final landscapes. Dressed in a dark blue caftan and a voluminous black turban, Setara looked elegant and poised, her hands steady as she pinned the last piece to the wall.

In the centre of the display, the pastel painting of almond blossoms stole the scene. Its delicate white blooms glowed against stark, dark branches. It was stunning, a symbol of hope amid the bleakness of prison life.

'Setara *jaan*, I need to show you something,' Sultan whispered, her hand slipping the phone from her pocket. She quickly glanced over her shoulder to check for watching guards.

'I'm busy, in case you haven't noticed,' Setara muttered, not taking her eyes off the painting.

'It's only a couple of lines,' Sultan insisted, holding the phone towards her.

Setara sighed and read the message quickly, squinting. 'It's from Niloofar *jaan*,' she whispered. 'It says, "Call me." That's all.'

Just then, Farzana, newly promoted to Head Guard, flung the door open, her head held high in a commanding stance. With a sharp bark, she ordered the incoming inmates, 'Don't touch the artworks. Start from here and move around the room.' She pointed decisively to the entryway. 'When Miss Simona and Colonel Rina arrive, take your seats in the rows of chairs.'

No one noticed – at that exact moment – the sharp glances exchanged between Setara and Sultan, or the way their jaws clenched in silent recognition.

'Have you alerted the African ladies?' Setara asked Farzana, her voice sharp.

'No... This is an event for Afghans,' Farzana replied.

Setara, irritated, flicked on the fan in the centre of the hall and sprayed rose-scented air freshener, muttering under her breath about the smokers. 'This event is for everyone in Badam Bagh. I'll call them myself. This is my show, and I want them here.'

Farzana gestured for Masuma to accompany her. The guard, sweating through her thick uniform, followed Setara up the stairs towards the cells.

Sultan took a deep breath and sank into a chair in the front row, glancing at the art pieces lining the yellow-stained walls. The woman next to her whispered, pointing to the almond blossoms, '*Mashallah*, she's so talented.' Sultan grunted in agreement, not turning her head.

Moments later, the door swung open, and a short, stout woman with grey frizzy hair clipped into a ponytail, entered with Shahla. The woman's thick spectacles glinted under the light, and medals gleamed from her lapel as she surveyed the room.

Just then, Setara returned, Hope, Hazel, and Esther trailing behind her. Sultan stood, offering her seat to Setara, and gestured for the African women to sit beside her. Esther and Hazel exchanged confused glances, but Hope, dressed in a pale yellow T-shirt and black trousers, smiled sweetly, the coconut scent of her lotion lingering as she motioned for them to join her.

Simona arrived, and shook hands with Shahla and the bespectacled woman before turning to the inmates. '*Salaam be hamagi*, hello everyone!' she greeted in Persian. The hall rose to their feet, the standing ovation thunderous and unexpected.

Sultan's heart pounded as her eyes welled up. The energy in the room was palpable; she could feel it coursing through her, through all of them. It was all for Dina – for what Simona had done for her. In their eyes, Sultan saw recognition and appreciation.

Overwhelmed by the flood of emotions in the room, Simona pressed her right hand to her heart and bowed slightly, a gesture moulded to fit local customs of gratitude. Shahla welcomed the audience next, her voice a steady echo in both Persian and English, thanking Simona for all the support her Italian charity had afforded Badam Bagh prison. Then, Shahla turned towards the unassuming, modestly dressed bespectacled woman at her side. 'Colonel Rina, deputy prison governor,' she announced.

The air thickened as Colonel Rina spoke, her voice weak and raspy, cracking under the strain of her chronic cough. She smiled but there was something sharp behind it, as she addressed the crowd in Persian and hesitant English. 'We are... very happy,' she croaked, 'to open... this exhibition.' Her eyes lingered on Setara then dropped to a crumpled piece of paper in her hand. 'Such... great talent among us. Setara *jaan*, you bring so much joy to staff and... inmates. On behalf of the governor, I thank you... with all my heart.'

Sultan watched Setara put on a shy smile, glancing down at the henna tattoos that now patterned her trembling hands in delicate daisies – symbols of life in a place of such despair.

Simona's voice, thick with her charming Italian accent, broke through the tension. 'Setara *jaan*,' she said, 'we in *Azadi baraye zanane Afghan – Libertà Per Le Donne Afghane* – would like to award you the medal of brilliance, with your permission to exhibit your artwork in our office and the lobby of the Italian Embassy in Kabul. Sultan locked eyes with Setara as she slowly rose from her seat. For a moment, Setara was frozen like a painting herself, caught between joy and disbelief. Tears welled in her eyes, spilling over her cheeks as Shahla translated Simona's words. Stiffly, she walked towards Simona. She wiped her tears with one hand while the other clung to the rosette that Simona pinned to her chest, the tricolour of Italy – green, white, and red, blazing brightly against the drabness of the hall. As Simona hugged her, the room erupted in a standing ovation, but Sultan only heard the muffled beating of her own heart. 'What *Azadi* is this Italian talking about?' whispered the woman in front of Sultan, her dark red scarf framing her weathered face. She chuckled softly, her hennaed fingers flicking the edge of her sleeve. 'We are neither free in here nor out there.' She turned her head, casting a glance towards Sultan, seeking agreement.

Sultan only shook her head slowly. 'Freedom is in the mind, not the body,' she muttered under her breath, as she rose from her seat and slipped her hands into her pockets, walking out of the row without another glance back. Behind her, she heard the sharp click of someone's tongue, but she didn't care to know who it was.

Standing just outside the hall, Sultan watched through the door, her eyes narrowing as she heard Setara and Simona exchanging friendly words, all mediated by Leila, Simona's Afghan assistant. Setara's lips moved, explaining something. Technical words, perhaps – terms that Leila translated. As Setara outlined the blurb for the Italian charity's invitations meant for embassies and NGOs, Rina shuffled closer, lowering herself onto the seat beside Setara. Leaning in, Rina whispered something to Setara. Impassively, Setara, eyes cast down, mumbled a *tashakor,* thanks, before shifting her gaze to Sultan who stood frowning, legs wide apart, her arms entangled behind her. Covering her mouth, Sultan tried to stifle a sarcastic laugh, but it came out as a shy cough.

The almond trees once again provided the privacy and seclusion Sultan and Setara craved. Having lost nearly all their blossoms, the trees sheltered them from the early-May sun and the chaos of prison life in equal measure. A gentle breeze brought a calming effect, taking the edge off the tensions that had been accumulating over the past two hours – since they'd discovered the identity of the infamous Rina. It was almost like a *hijab* had been lifted, revealing just one among many repulsive beasts, ending all doubts and speculations.

'That bitch eventually showed her ugly face today,' Sultan said, her voice sharp with venom, gazing at Setara who seemed lost in thought.

'She was sweet-talking me, saying what a wonderful talent I am and that she is happy to help, whenever I need it. Her usual ploy to procure women for her repulsive clients. I felt my body going numb at that stage, a chill went through my spine. I recognised that nasty woman then. That face, the "benevolent" colonel, I had seen her before. Two years ago, at the prison's opening ceremony, chatting up the Minister for Women's Affairs. Her voice was softer then, dripping with promises for favours. We know how people like Rina have climbed ladders of power.' Setara's gaze drifted forward. 'This is only the tip of an iceberg. Somewhere beneath the surface, hidden truths churn, waiting to be pulled into the light.'

Sultan pulled her mobile out of her pocket. She dialled Niloofar's number and handed it over to Setara. 'You know her and understand her language better coming from the same province.'

After a few rings, a feeble voice answered. 'Alo?'

'Niloofar *jaan*? It's Setara. Sultan *jaan* is here too, sitting next to me… How are you, *azizum,* my dear.'

'Ah Setara *jaan*!' Niloofar's voice suddenly perked up. 'I have so far sent two long letters to you but you never replied.'

Setara and Sultan traded perplexed glances as Setara explained that she'd received none.

'Not surprisingly,' Niloofar replied. 'They don't want us to communicate with each other. But, I'm pleased to say that in none of the letters did I include the more harrowing details, things I've kept secret from everyone, even my mother. I wanted to tell you the uglier facts when I was ready to reveal all. The last few months have been tormenting… heartbreaking.'

Sultan whispered to Setara, asking her to tell Niloofar to hang up and call back. This was going to be a long call, and it would eat into Sultan's phone credit, a precious commodity in prison. On the call back, Niloofar, speaking with a slur, began telling the long-overdue tale of what had happened in the days leading up to her decision to end it all by killing herself, embracing a slow and painful death:

It all began with a prison guard whose name I've long since forgotten. She was unusually curious about my life, leaning in closer than most. When I told her my story, she wept. Real tears that slid down her cheeks, as if my misfortune were a mirror for her own hidden sorrows. She listened without interruption, absorbing every misstep, every disaster that seemed to shadow me wherever I went.

I told her how my father forced me, at fifteen, to marry an older man, his third wife, to sever my love for Sohrab, the boy I thought would save me. I lived beneath that man's roof, suffocating under the weight of his other wives and their children, who treated me like an unwelcome guest. I convinced myself that eloping with Sohrab to Mashad would mark the beginning of something new, something that could wash away the bitterness. And for a while, it did. For a while.

When money lined our pockets, happiness stretched between us like silk. But one morning, Sohrab left for Afghanistan with a shipment of perishable goods and never came back.

As the coins in my purse dwindled, so did hope. With nowhere left to turn, I boarded a coach to Herat, only to be arrested for loitering the moment I stepped off. In the interrogation room, I clung to honesty, believing it might save me. I unspooled my story to the policewoman questioning me. She seemed sympathetic, even gentle. I thought she might show compassion. Instead, she charged me with *zina*.

At my first court hearing, I received a ten-year prison sentence. Before I was transferred to Badam Bagh, I heard rumours from inmates that Sohrab, my angelic soulmate, was not an angel at all. He was a drug smuggler, caught and jailed the moment he crossed the border.

At Badam Bagh, the guard who had cried for me returned to my cell with a sliver of hope. She said *Samunwal* Rina might be able to help, might be able to get my conviction overturned at the next hearing. Rina, she claimed, had connections to a businessman named Abdullah. Abdullah knew the presiding judge, and with the right persuasion, my freedom could be bought.

A few days passed before the guard brought good news. Abdullah had agreed to meet me. His driver would come for me late one evening, she said. I wanted to believe it. I tried not to question why this meeting couldn't happen in daylight. Ten years in prison felt heavier than suspicion.

That same afternoon, the guard reappeared, her arms laden with gifts: A silk *shalwar kameez* still wrapped in crisp plastic, an Astrakhan coat lined with white fur, and gold-strapped sandals.

Lavish things, far beyond anything I had worn before. I tried them on under her watchful gaze, baffled by the extravagance.

'For Abdullah,' she explained.

The clothes felt too odd for a formal meeting to discuss my case. But I said nothing, swallowing down the unease. What other chance did I have?

I had no one else. My ties to my mother had snapped the day she gave herself to her Iranian husband and their children. Her betrayal still burned in me. My father had died not long before, and I celebrated his death. Even if he had lived, I wouldn't have gone to him. A man who sold his daughter into an abusive marriage deserved no pleas for mercy.

I was alone. If Abdullah's price for my freedom was silk and gold, I was willing to pay it.

Listening diligently to Niloofar, Sultan turned and glanced attentively around the yard to ensure no guard or squealer was around to eavesdrop on the call. Apart from a few young children on the swings, it seemed the entire prison population was indoors to escape the blazing sun. Her eyes caught sight of Dina's grave, upon which she silently recited a *fatiha* for her, then glanced briefly at Setara who had been taking notes of Niloofar's account of those fateful days in the month of *Jadi*, when the whole world came to a freezing halt.

I consider myself disastrously naïve to have even entertained the idea of an evening outing, let alone one that involved visiting a stranger. It's the stick I've beaten myself with ever since. But that night, I calmed myself with the thought that I wasn't alone. A sudden change of plan, the *samunwal sahib* herself drove me to Abdullah's office in central Kabul. I told myself that in her company, this gentle woman with her rare erudition and soft-spoken ways, I was safe. She was an anomaly in Afghanistan, someone who appeared untouchable by the grime that stained the world around us. Her presence was supposed to be a shield.

I tiptoed out of my solitary cell, perched unsteadily on high heels that weren't mine. My face felt tight under layers of makeup, the work of the same guard whose artistry transformed me into someone I barely recognised. The posh, borrowed clothes hugged my skin, and I followed the guard through the prison's back corridors to Rina's office. Her name gleamed in gold letters on a black plaque.

'Naam-e-khoda, you look stunning! Take the scarf off. Don't hide that hair under such a rag.' Rina's eyes widened behind thick glasses, round as walnuts. Her arm looped around my shoulders, tugging me closer. *'Daktar* Abdullah is an old friend. There are only a few people in this world that I trust. He is one of them.'

Through the back entrance, we left the prison. I huddled in the front seat of her white Toyota, pulling the fur-lined collar tighter around my ears. Rina was quiet as she drove through the dim streets towards Shar-e-Naw.

Abdullah's office stood at the base of a pale yellow, wedding-cake-shaped house, adorned with Roman columns, you know, those extravagant houses of people who became rich after the Taliban's fall. Its emerald-green glass façade gleamed, spotless, free of the smog and dust that coated everything else.

Rina drove through the gate and parked by marble stairs that glowed faintly under the floodlights. Abdullah, a short, heavyset man with a potbelly stretching the fabric of his coat, was waiting at the entrance. His grin was wide, flashing crooked, tobacco-stained teeth.

'Welcome, welcome, *samunwal sahib,'* he said, pumping Rina's hand with vigour. His gaze drifted towards me. Licking his lips, he wiped his mouth with thick, hairy fingers. He rolled up his sleeves, revealing forearms dense with black curls, and pulled out a set of agate worry beads. They clicked rhythmically in his hands, like the soft chime of dancers' ankle bells.

'Tea, coffee, Coke?' he offered.

Rina waved him off. 'I have to return to Badam Bagh. Call me when the meeting is over. I'll collect Niloofar *jaan.'*

When she left, Abdullah's eyes lingered. His breath, thick with raw onions and cheap beer, the kind Sohrab used to buy from

Mashad's black market, filled the space between us.

'Hot or cold drink?' he asked.

'Coke, please.'

He disappeared behind a canvas screen painted with Japanese geishas. When he returned, it was two glasses fizzing violently.

'Get comfortable. Take off your coat. The radiators are on.'

Radiators. In Kabul. I hesitated, knowing how rare that luxury was. This man was rich. I peeled the coat from my shoulders, letting my hair tumble free.

Abdullah's gaze narrowed. 'A beauty like you wasting away in jail,' he mused, tipping back in his chair, legs crossed. 'Don't worry. I know the judge overseeing your case.' He slid the Coke across the table.

'Noosh-e-jaan,' he said.

I gulped it down greedily, the cold burning my throat. I hadn't tasted Coke in months.

Dizziness crept over me. I rested my head in the corner of the sofa, sinking into a soft cushion. Through heavy lids, I glimpsed Abdullah's hairy chest pressing too close. His breath prickled against my skin. I tried to lift my arms, but the world tilted, and I fell into darkness. When I woke, I was naked beneath a thick blanket.

Across the room Abdullah sat in his chair, sipping a hot drink, fully dressed in a sharp suit.

'Get up,' he called. 'I'll drive you back.'

My clothes were gone.

'Where are my—'

'In the bathroom.' He fetched a towel from behind the geisha screen and tossed it towards me. 'Quick wash. You need to be back before dawn.' He stepped closer, his fingers brushing my cheek, faintly reeking of stale tobacco. *'Nafasum,* my breath,' he cooed. *'Wallah,* I like you… I'll see you again. Now, give me your number.'

I stared at him, blinking slowly.

'Your number,' he repeated, sharper this time.

I gave him the digits. His thumbs moved over the phone screen.

In the bathroom, I stared at the pink tiles and marble sink, the ornate bath lined with lavender, rose, and amber soaps. I scrubbed my face with shaking hands, breathing in the unfamiliar scents. A laminated card beside the soap read: '*Daktar* Abdullah Karimi, Certified Property Surveyor.'

I dressed quickly.

As dawn crept in, I slipped into the back seat of Abdullah's SUV and fell asleep. The guard's stench jolted me awake, rank sweat and unwashed fabric pressing against my face. I opened my eyes to her. The blonde guard.

The mention of the blonde evoked a knee-jerk reaction in Setara. Her head snapped up from her notebook, her eyes locking with Sultan's. 'Parwana?' she whispered, her voice barely audible, eyes widening as she searched Sultan's face. Sultan nodded.

Niloofar's voice thinned into silence, as if she were gathering broken pieces of herself. 'Yes… I think that was her name. It's strange. My memory drifts, Setara *jaan*. Like smoke. Some days I remember too much, other days nothing at all. I keep trying to claw my way out of the past, but it sticks to me.' She let out a brittle laugh that frayed at the edges. 'If you saw me now, you wouldn't know me. I look ancient, old and decrepit. I still see and hear, thank God. But everything else… everything else feels distant, like it doesn't belong to me anymore.'

'I can't imagine the weight of it, but why?' Setara's voice softened. 'To set fire to yourself… such pain, *Astaghfirullah.*'

Niloofar inhaled sharply, as if the memory seared her lungs. 'I wanted to die, Setara *jaan*. There was no hope left. Not after everything. I hated myself for being foolish, for trusting, for believing there was a way out. But more than that, I hated how the world swallowed me whole, piece by piece, and left nothing behind. Everything they did to me, from the time I was a girl, was just… one wound after another. Like I'd been marked for suffering, as if God had written it on my forehead.'

Her voice cracked, but she pressed on. 'I couldn't go quietly. I needed them to see my pain, to feel it, Setara *jaan*. To see what they did. Sometimes burning alive.' She hesitated, her voice trembling. 'Sometimes it hurts more to watch than to burn.'

Niloofar then relayed the events of the day after. She recounted her shock at finding semen on her underwear when she had undressed for a quick shower. Only then, fifteen hours later, could she sense the vile smell of the night before on her body. She said she could even smell Abdullah's repellent breath on her breasts. She had cried hysterically from an overwhelming feeling of guilt and shame – laments that went unheard and unnoticed. She had scrubbed herself as hard as she could with an abrasive loofah and soap to wash the slime off her body. She had loathed herself for being so doe-eyed and credulous, for being so easily deceived by lies, for trusting abusive people and believing their promises.

She had tried to calm her nerves by smoking the *chars* Dina, 'the kind Kuchi inmate', had shared with her. But nothing helped. Finally, the straw that broke the camel's back was a call from Abdullah, who, in his typically brazen manner, had said he wanted to see her again. He claimed he had spoken to the judge who had agreed to acquit her at her next hearing. She had screamed at him, calling him a filthy rapist. He, however, had remained silent during the tirade. When Niloofar had finished venting her rage, he had said calmly just one phrase. 'I have a video of us last night for circulation.' A cold sweat had broken out on her skin, and her heart had pounded in her chest so loudly that she worried he would hear it. She had been trapped in their sinister game with death as the only escape.

Finding a kerosene canister was easy. She had followed Parwana to the basement discreetly and when Parwana was distracted on the phone, Niloofar had snatched a canister and hid it, together with a box of matches she'd acquired from Dina, under a pile of clothes in her cell. The next day, another guard on duty had left her cell door unlocked after having alerted her of the approaching *Fajr* prayer time. An accident of fate?

Not One, Not Two, But Four

Setara sat on the floor of her cell, preparing vegetables for *bolani*, half-listening to Sheyda, who had come to visit. She could tell something was on her mind. Something she wasn't spitting out.

Sheyda took deep drags of her cigarette, speaking rapidly but absentmindedly. 'I've had two children. I know morning sickness isn't something you treat with a painkiller.'

Setara shot her a glance, wanting to ask why she was telling her this, but she let her continue.

Sheyda stubbed out her cigarette and immediately lit another. Before Setara could press her, a knock came at the cell door.

'Who's there,' Setara called out, her back to the door.

'It's Zohra *jaan*,' Sheyda said softly, gently nudging Setara.

'Tell her to come back after lunch. I'm not writing letters this morning,' Setara replied sharply.

'I want to see you about something else, please,' Zohra pleaded.

Raising her head from the chopping board, over which more bunches of leeks and onions waited to be chopped, Setara's eyes widened. 'OK, come in, Zohra *jaan*.'

As she entered the cell, dressed in a light summery blouse and long skirt, Sheyda greeted her with a warm hug. Zohra bent down to sit facing Setara on the floor below the window.

'Setara *jaan*, I can't take it anymore.' Zohra's eyes searched for Setara's gaze. 'I've reached the end of my tether.' She began to sob quietly, her tears controlled but intense.

Setara shifted closer, rubbing her hands on her apron. She wrapped her arm around Zohra, which carried a waft of onions and leaks.

'What's the matter?'

Zohra pulled out a crumpled tissue from under her sleeve and dabbed her eyes and nose. 'Please, don't tell anyone. Promise me…' Her tearful eyes met Setara's gaze.

Setara gave her a reassuring nod.

'I'm pregnant,' Zohra said, sobbing softly. 'I don't know what to do.'

'How? You've been here for how long?'

'Six months. I know, it's odd to be pregnant in a women's prison but—'

'Roya *jaan*, too, yes?' Setara said, more confirming than asking.

'Yes… she, too. But she says she is sick, which is what they've said her condition is,' Zohra said in between sobs. 'They occasionally took Tahera, Fariba, Roya and me out in a group but to separate locations. We were all told that we would be meeting men in the high echelons of the judiciary who could set us free. My cellmates don't know I'm here talking to you. They will hate me if they find out, believing that I have ruined their chances of release.'

Setara turned to Sheyda, with a slight frown on her brow. 'Did you know about this, Sheyda *jaan*?'

Sheyda nodded, casting her eyes down on the burning cigarette between her yellow-stained fingers. 'I had a hunch, yes. I wanted to tell you but I didn't want to be labelled a snitch, nor did I want to collude with any wrongdoing. For weeks I suspected something dodgy was happening in Cell 86 opposite mine.'

Setara got up to fetch three tea glasses from the bathroom. 'I suspected something odd was happening to the women in your cell, Zohra *jaan*, based on what Sheyda had previously said. But I could never put my finger on it.' Pausing momentarily from pouring the tea, she glanced at the young women seated opposite her, as if overcome by a fleeting thought. After offering tea to them, she pulled the fan closer, noticing beads of sweat forming on Zohra's forehead.

'Zohra *jaan*, what were you arrested for?' Setara asked carefully before taking a sip of the hot tea.

'*Zina*. I had run away from home. The police found me with my boyfriend at his cousin's house in Khayr Khana, not far from here.' Zohra sniffled.

'Was he arrested, too?'

'Yes, he is at Pol-e-Charkhi.'

'Are your other cellmates also pregnant?'

'Yes. All of them.' Zohra took a slow sip of her tea, her eyes cast down.

'*Ya Allah!* Not one, not two, but four pregnant women in a women's prison.' Setara gasped. 'It's Niloofar four times over,' she muttered under her breath.

'What did you say?' Zohra looked up, frowning.

Setara shook her head. 'Nothing… Something else crossed my mind. Nothing important.'

Zohra looked puzzled.

Setara just didn't trust Zohra enough. Was it because she was unknown and unfamiliar, or because she appeared fickle and unstable?

'Setara *jaan…*' Sheyda's voice wavered. 'You know about my insomnia. Well, a few nights ago, I finally gathered the nerve to peek through the hatch to see where all that noise outside my cell was coming from.' Her hands trembled as she set the glass of tea down. 'I saw four guards, each gripping the hand of an inmate. It was too dark to see their faces, but I recognised Roya. Her petite frame was unmistakable.'

Sheyda's breath caught as she paused, her eyes clouding. 'It hit me then… they were being taken to parties. It reminded me of when I worked as IT support at *New Dawn News*. The male journalists used to laugh about these rich family gatherings in Kabul where they'd have sex with Russian and Uzbek women. I still remember one of them boasting about a beautiful Russian girl, her skin scented with Chanel No 5.'

Her lips curled, eyes narrowing at the memory. 'The entire group then began mocking the guy who'd had sex with a rough-looking bandi. Answering back, the guy who was being teased said something I'll never forget. He said, "I got bored with Chanel and decided to slum it, indulge in dung for a change."'

The weight of those words hung between them like a dense and murky fog. Sheyda's voice hardened. 'The whole office exploded in laughter, Setara *jaan*. Bastards.'

Setara poured herself more tea. 'We need Sultan. She can help us work out a strategy to expose their operations. But we have to think this through carefully.' She stood up, her voice lowering as Sheyda and Zohra got up to leave. 'Keep this between us,' Setara said. 'Say nothing to no one. And I mean no one! Let's avoid being seen together, too. That will raise suspicion. Be wary of the guards, especially on the third floor. I've seen them lingering near our cells lately.'

Setara then saved their numbers in her phone before they left, her mind racing with possibilities – strategies, risks, and the dangerous unknowns that lay ahead. Glancing at the clock, she realised the urgency of her next task. 'I need to prepare the *bolani* quickly. I'll talk to Sultan after lunch and message you about the next step.'

As the door closed behind them, Setara couldn't shake the feeling of impending peril. She knew they were treading on dangerous ground. If the guards or other inmates got a whiff of their conversations, the consequences would be dire. She took a deep breath, steeling herself for the challenges ahead. The unravelling of this scandal would require caution, secrecy, and an unwavering resolve.

'We have to limit the core group to Sheyda, you, and me,' Sultan said to Setara, flicking her cigarette butt over the mesh fence in the prison yard. 'You and I will handle the planning, and decide the steps, and who gets told what. Sheyda only needs to know enough to push the plan forward. Her media contacts will be invaluable. What's happened to these inmates is shameful. This must be exposed.'

'Not all of them are victims,' Setara murmured, her voice cautious. 'You can't compare Niloofar and Roya to the likes of Tahera, Fariba, or Zohra.'

Sultan's eyes flashed with irritation. She lit another cigarette. 'You're wrong! How can you even think that?' She clicked her tongue, arms crossing tightly over her chest as she looked away from Setara. 'They've all been deceived, abused. Just like us, they're captives here. Powerless, *bekas,* abandoned, and at the mercy of our captors.'

Setara leaned back against the prison's cold exterior wall, her chin dropping to her chest. Silence stretched between them. When she spoke again, her voice was softer. 'You're right. We need to stay united.'

Sultan glanced at the almond trees. 'And we'll need the endurance of almond blossoms,' she said. 'We're facing an enemy just as harsh as Kabul's winters.'

'Should I talk to Roya?' Setara asked, her voice uncertain. 'I feel like I owe her that, after everything.'

Sultan's eyes locked on hers, smoke curling between them. 'They've already seen you in her cell. If you go again, they'll start suspecting something. We need to be smarter, understand our enemies, their fears, and vulnerabilities. They found out the weaknesses of these women and used them to trap them.'

Setara bit her bottom lip, her thoughts churning. 'I see what you mean. They must be keeping a close watch, worried someone will talk. We have to be careful around the guards, especially Parwana and the other one… the new one…' She tapped her temple, trying to remember.

'Fereshtah?' Sultan suggested, her voice cool. 'She started with Parwana.'

'Yes, that's her.'

Sultan's gaze darkened. 'I first saw her during the raid, when I was protecting Dina. Geisha was there too. I watched Masuma look at Fereshtah like a servant would her mistress. That's when I realised that Fereshtah had power. Real power. I've kept my distance ever since.'

'I believe Rina recruited both of them for her dirty work, probably promising them a hefty pay-off.'

'Murdagaw!' Sultan spat. 'These days, you can buy people for anything, no matter how unthinkable. There's lots of talk about women in the police force, how they're abused, even raped, as part of their initiation. True or not, we know how corruption seeps through everything.'

'I heard the same in Herat,' Setara murmured, her voice soft. 'My neighbour wouldn't let her daughter join the police for that reason.' She hesitated, then continued, 'We shouldn't believe every rumour, but… as my *khoda beyamorz* mother used to say, "There wouldn't be rumours, if there wasn't something to whisper about."'

'We must expose this crime,' Sultan replied sharply. 'Ask Sheyda about her media contacts. Her boyfriend's a journalist, right? We'll get Geisha to visit him or whoever he suggests, and lay it all out.'

'Shouldn't we find out more first? We don't even know how Roya got caught up in this,' Setara said.

'But we know all four of them are pregnant, and we know how they manipulated Niloofar and Zohra. That's enough. If we wait, the prison management will start sweet-talking or blackmailing the victims into silence knowing more of us are onto them.'

Sultan paused, then added with a glint in her eye, 'Get the information from Sheyda. Do it discreetly. Sketch her portrait if you have to. We can't let them catch on.'

Setara smiled, snapping her fingers. 'You've got a sharp mind, Sultan *jaan*. I knew you'd come through.'

Geisha

Makroryan was a collection of boxy apartments. Built by the Soviets in the 1980s, they bore the scars of three decades of war – conflicts that seemed never to end.

Geisha's friend Maryam, who had striking dark eyes, pouty lips, and a flair for dramatic speeches, lived in one of those apartments on the second floor with her sister, brother-in-law, and their two young children. The two had met at the *khana-e-amn* in Kabul, a shelter run by a charity for runaways, after being bussed there from Herat. Maryam, however, was lucky – her relatives in Kabul took her in, so her stay at the shelter was mercifully short.

Despite their diverging paths, Maryam and Geisha stayed connected through letters and phone calls. While Maryam earned a law degree and began working at Muriel Chandler's legal aid office near the five-star Serena Hotel in downtown Kabul, Geisha slipped further into the city's underworld.

Maryam took pride in her work. Her latest achievement – helping Muriel secure the release of the Nigerian Mary and arranging her return home – had only strengthened her resolve to push forward in her legal career.

Their loyalty always remained strong. When Geisha called Maryam, desperate to escape yet another *khana-e-amn* after her release from jail, Maryam rushed to her side. She came with her older sister and they took Geisha to their home. Though this new shelter was managed by a reputable organisation, its policies were still restrictive. Women accused of *zina* were forced to undergo virginity tests – tests performed by untrained staff, often coercive and lacking any medical accuracy. If the results were negative, they became ammunition for the courts, vilifying women who had fled their homes, seeking refuge from relatives bent on reclaiming their honour through violence and even murder.

Geisha relayed to Maryam her first experience of virginity test at a police station in Kabul, where she was raped by the policeman who conducted the test. 'It was after I ran away from the shelter that I was arrested with my boyfriend. They let him go because the bastard said I was a prostitute and that I had tried to hook him. The policeman, I still remember his ugly face and bushy moustache, told me to remove my trousers and underwear and lie down on my back on the bed behind a curtain in his office. Devouring me with his lecherous eyes, he stuck two fingers inside me, turning them clockwise and anti-clockwise, salivating over my face. He withdrew his fingers, saying I wasn't a virgin with a smirk and then dropped his trousers and raped me.'

Maryam's eyes welled up. 'You never said anything to me about it.'

'No point. I was beyond help. I was damaged.'

'Look, we will help you get a job and live a respectable life, away from harm. Muriel needs a creche assistant for the office. We have a creche for the children of the staff and clients. She is the nicest woman I have met, besides my mother and sister.'

'But I don't speak English.'

'You will learn it fast. Besides, the staff and clients are all Afghan. You will be working under the creche manager, who is a kind Afghan lady. Let me talk to Muriel about it.'

Geisha's eyes roamed around the room as she thought about the job suggestion. The idea of spending long hours cooped up in an office, surrounded by screaming children and demanding adults, made her uneasy. But she needed to earn a living, and Maryam's family couldn't support her forever. 'It's worth a try, I suppose,' she said with slight hesitation. 'Let me know what your boss says.'

Her phone buzzed suddenly, making her jump. 'It's Sultan,' she muttered, shrugging off Maryam's curious look. She answered the call, putting it on loudspeaker. Sultan's voice came through, rushed and tense.

'*Salaam!* How are you? I have to tell you this quickly. The guards are running close surveillance on us.'

'*Salaam*, Sultan *jaan*. Yes, all is good, *shukur*... What's happened? Is everyone alright?'

'Four women are pregnant. Roya, Tahera, Zohra, and Fariba.

They're in Cell 86, on the opposite wing to your previous cell.'

'What are you saying? *Ya Allah!*' Geisha whispered, her stomach tightening. Her fingers trembled as she chewed at her nails.

'They've been pimped out to elite parties, all led by that *murdagaw*, Colonel Rina, the deputy governor. We think the governor's involved too. Zohra spilled everything: How they were coerced into sleeping with men in the elite and were told these men could sway judges to get them acquitted. Remember Niloofar? The Herati who self-immolated? She told us she'd been drugged and raped. Later, they blackmailed her when she refused to see the man again. We need to expose this. Sheyda's boyfriend, Sahil Anwari, is a journalist at *New Dawn News*. I'll text you his number. *Khoda hafez.*' Sultan hung up.

Geisha sat still, the phone slipping from her hand. Her breath hitched as she lit a cigarette. The acrid smoke filled her lungs, but it did little to ease the tightening in her chest.

'Who is Sultan?' Maryam asked, her eyes wide with concern.

'An inmate. She's the prison *baashi*. Ah, this is so hard to believe…'

Maryam leaned forward, her voice trembling. 'God help us… How could something like this happen in a prison?'

A few minutes after breakfast, made up of fresh nan, cheese, *qaimaq*, and homemade carrot jam. Geisha's mobile vibrated. 'It's Sultan. She's sent Sahil's number.'

'When you speak to him, don't tell him the whole story on the phone,' Maryam warned, sipping her green tea. 'His mobile might be bugged. Just arrange a meeting somewhere safe and say you're Sheyda's friend. Has Sheyda spoken to him about any of this?'

'I don't know. But why would they bug his phone?'

'He's a journalist, right? They are always spied on. Don't ever think that there is freedom of speech here in this country. So, be careful what you say and to whom. You just wouldn't know who else is listening to your conversations.'

Geisha shifted uneasily. 'Can you speak with him, Maryam *jaan*?' Her eyes met Maryam's, pleading.

'I'll be with you, but I won't speak for you,' Maryam said softly, her tone firm. 'You know more about this than I do. You can do it, Geisha *jaan*. You'll be fine.'

Geisha's fingers hovered over the phone, her heart pounding. What if someone was listening? What if this made everything worse? She glanced at Maryam, who nodded encouragingly. There was no turning back now. Hesitantly, she dialled Sahil's number. After a few rings, a young male voice answered. 'Alo?'

'Is that Mr. Anwari?'

'Yes! Who's this?'

'I'm Sheyda's friend. Has she spoken to you about me?'

'No, I've just come back from India after a major surgery. I can't move much, while I'm recovering at home. I haven't spoken to her in a while. How is she?'

'She's alright. I need to speak to you about something important. I don't suppose we can meet now?'

'I'm on sick leave for a month, but you can contact my colleague Ajmal Saraf. I'll send you his number. Sorry I can't be of more help.'

The line went dead. Geisha put the phone down and glanced at Maryam.

Ajmal was quick to answer the call and invited Geisha and Maryam to his office at *New Dawn,* the central office in Shar-e-Naw, near the park. When they arrived, they were greeted by Nikbakht, a trainee journalist dressed in a smart black trouser suit, her dark red mesh scarf neatly pinned over her hair, showing only a short fringe. She led them to a room dominated by a large screen showing the day's news. Geisha and Maryam sank into plush white mock-leather chairs surrounded by posters of Afghanistan's landscapes and women in traditional Badakhshan and Kuchi costumes, their jewellery shimmering with turquoise and lapis lazuli.

Ajmal entered from behind a screen. His dark sunken eyes and gruff voice matched his weathered appearance. Stretching out his hand, he, in white *pirhan tunban,* eagerly shook Maryam's hand, then Geisha's, giving hers a slight squeeze. His eyes glinted as they met hers, and Geisha's stomach tightened. She cast her gaze downward, her shoulders stiffening as she tipped back in her chair, staring at her chewed, disfigured nails.

Ajmal motioned for Nikbakht to fetch tea. 'Welcome! I'm Ajmal Saraf. I'm glad Sahil referred you to me. Sorry, I don't know your full names.'

Geisha glanced at Maryam, who nodded slightly. 'My name is Nasima Ahmadi, and this is my friend Maryam Sarwari,' Geisha said. 'We're here to tell you...' She paused as she felt a sharp pinch on her thigh from Maryam – a warning. She glanced to the side, locking eyes with Maryam, unsure.

'We've heard rumours about the treatment of inmates in Badam Bagh prison,' Maryam said, her voice calm but firm. 'It's rather disturbing.'

Ajmal's expression barely changed as he leaned back in his chair. 'There were always whispers about the old prison,' he said, waving a hand dismissively. 'But since the move to the new facility, all we've heard are good things. I'm not sure where you're getting your information, but it seems far-fetched.'

'Our sources are lawyers who represent the women in court.'

'Well... they can be very biased, you see,' Ajmal said, smirking and tapping his fingers on the table. 'Some of these lawyers have dubious backgrounds. They're crooks who've forged their law degrees and are making money off desperate women. I don't trust a word they say.' He then shifted his gaze to Geisha, his voice softening. 'Miss Ahmadi... you look very familiar.'

'I've lived in this area before. A long time ago.'

'Ahh... that's it!' Ajmal snapped his fingers, grinning. 'I definitely remember seeing you in the park.'

'Occasionally, I walked my dog there. Not often though.' Distracted, Geisha glanced at Nikbakht, who returned with a tray of green and black tea in porcelain cups, accompanied by chocolate biscuits. Geisha reached for a couple of biscuits as soon as the tray was set down, biting into one and chewing slowly, savouring the taste while avoiding Ajmal's lingering stare.

'I don't recall a dog,' Ajmal said with a smirk. 'You were usually with a man. Different men.'

Geisha choked, coughing up crumbs as she reached for a glass of water, her face reddening. Nikbakht hurriedly handed her an ornate

Herati glass, and after a few sips, the coughing subsided.

Shaking her head, Geisha's voice cracked. 'I think you're confusing me with someone else.'

'Maybe, but sometimes one can't differentiate one Hazara from another.' Ajmal roared with laughter, turning to Nikbakht, whose gaze remained fixed on the wall, her jaw clenched.

'I'd like to invite both of you to my dinner party tonight at the Serena Hotel's restaurant.' Ajmal's grin widened, revealing crooked front teeth.

'Thank you for the invitation,' Maryam responded, her face solemn. 'But we're visiting our aunt and cousins this evening.'

Still grinning, Ajmal walked towards Geisha and Maryam as they stood to leave. 'Maybe next time,' he said, his hand discreetly brushing against Geisha's back before wrapping an arm around her shoulders. Geisha's pulse quickened, a wave of nausea rising as she gently moved out of his grip, stepping towards Maryam. They grabbed their handbags and said their goodbyes, hurrying into the lobby and out onto the street.

The moment they stepped into the fresh air outside, Geisha exhaled sharply, as if releasing a breath she hadn't realised she'd been holding. The sensation of Ajmal's hand still clung to her back. She rubbed her shoulders instinctively, trying to shake off the feeling.

The Big Sister

'You have the most beautiful smile, Sheyda *jaan*,' Setara exclaimed. 'Those sweet dimples! Keep smiling.' Holding a charcoal stick between her thumb and index finger, Setara began sketching Sheyda's portrait, following the plan she and Sultan had devised: to use the drawing as a pretext for finding out more about the recent incident. 'Go on… tell me. Did you speak to Roya *jaan?* What did she say?'

'Can I stop smiling now?'

Setara nodded and let out a soft laugh.

'Yes, I did,' Sheyda said, her lips curling into a cheeky smile. 'It was Fereshtah who had tricked Roya. It started innocently enough, with Fereshtah showing an interest in Persian poetry. During her breaks, she would sit with Roya on the cell floor, reading Maulana's Shams Tabrizi poems. The book was a gift from the *samunwal*. As they read, Roya confided in Fereshtah about her dreams of marrying Jamshid and having children… a normal family life.'

Sheyda's hands trembled slightly as she spoke, her voice dropping into a low whisper. 'Fereshtah… she was so cunning, Setara *jaan*. Roya never saw it coming. All those poetry readings, all those dreams of a family… it was all part of the trap. Hold on! I hear footsteps,' Sheyda whispered, pressing a finger to her lips.

It was Farzana at the door, with Sultan standing behind. 'Another portrait?' Farzana sneered. Setara and Sheyda exchanged quizzical glances. Setara's fingers tightened around the charcoal as she looked up at Farzana, unsure of how to interpret the cynical remark.

'*Samunwal sahib* asked me to tell you that your exhibition will be launched tomorrow at the Italian embassy,' Farzana announced. She's got authorisation for you to attend.'

Sultan squeezed past Farzana, entering quickly. 'Congratulations! I have a present for you.' She handed Setara a perfume bottle.

'Where did you get this from, Sultan *jaan*?' Setara gasped, her eyes glinting.

'Humaira's aunt gifted her this on her last visit. She used some of it, but there's plenty left for you to use at the exhibition.'

Setara held the bottle close, a smile spreading as she imagined wearing it at the exhibition. '*Tashakur*, Sultan *jaan*.' Tears welled up in her eyes.

'Can I try some of that?' Farzana asked with a coy smile.

Setara smiled back, offering her the bottle.

Farzana sprayed a little on her wrists and filled her lungs with the aroma, her face softening as if transported by a distant memory. 'You know who it reminds me of?' She looked up, pressing her finger to her temple. 'The Herati girl's mother… what was her name?'

'Nazia,' Setara called out, her lips curling into a triumphant, knowing smile.

'Yes… Nazia. What an elegant lady she was.' Farzana's eyes remained lifted, her gaze turning dreamy. 'Ahh… I nearly forgot.' She looked down at the poster tube in her hand, unscrewing the cap. '*Samunwal*'s younger sister will be at the exhibition tomorrow evening, too. Latifa *jaan* Wardak. She's running for parliament in next month's elections.' She pulled a rolled poster from the tube and unrolled it, revealing a close-up of a young woman's face with a strained smile. 'This is her… isn't she beautiful?'

'She doesn't look like *Samunwal Sahib* at all. I mean… she's beautiful, if not a little fierce behind that smile,' Setara remarked, pursing her lips.

'Latifa *jaan* Wardak is a real leader. She has a different mother. Her mother was the *Samunwal*'s father's second wife, a *soorati* woman from Daikundi,' Farzana explained. 'She was a Hazara, and their maid since the age of eleven. She got pregnant while in their service. So, *Samunwal*'s father married her, but only as a *sigheh*, a temporary wife, to restore her honour and dignity.'

Setara nodded, but her thoughts drifted. Women like Latifa, polished and connected, felt miles away from the prison's bleak reality. And yet, their influence crept into every corner of these walls.

'I like her makeup. Fresh and natural. No bright red lipstick or overly rouged cheeks like the other candidates,' Sheyda said, relaxing her legs and stretching them out.

'I like the way she's worn her scarf. Charming and gracious.' Setara pointed at the blue silk scarf, tied in a braid over Latifa's head.

'What's really important for a distinguished candidate like her is what she offers Afghan people. And how she can improve people's lives,' said Sultan, locking eyes with Farzana.

They all nodded in approval.

Farzana looked up, catching Setara's gaze. 'The *Samunwal* wants to introduce you to her sister tomorrow evening. Also, the Italians will be awarding Afghan women high achievers. I think *Samunwal sahib* will get an award too, for the competent and compassionate manner in which she's managed this prison.'

Setara forced a smile, glancing at Sultan who was standing feet apart with her hands clasped behind her, gazing into the distance. Each word from Farzana felt like another weight on Setara's chest, her jaw tightening as she forced her voice to stay light. 'She certainly deserves praise,' Setara replied, her tone thick with forced flattery. She then fixed her gaze on Sheyda, who was nodding eagerly.

'Aferin, Samunwal Sahib!' Sultan turned her head towards Setara, smiling with a satisfied nod.

'*Samunwal* has instructed the guards to pin her sister's posters around the prison along with a detailed description of their family heritage, how her benevolent father has moulded her into a leader, her unique attributes, and what she will do if elected. She believes it will be inspirational for the women here,' Farzana said, locking eyes with Sultan.

'We can also help you with it,' Sultan said with an eager voice.

Smiling, Farzana promised she would inform them when the writing was completed. On her way out, she stopped and turned back to Setara, who had been trying hard to keep a straight face.

'Perhaps you can review the text before it is printed and displayed, checking for any inaccuracies. What do you think?'

Setara kept her smile tight as Farzana spoke, but inside, her mind raced. Helping with Latifa's poster might be an opportunity or a trap. She nodded, hoping her enthusiasm sounded convincing. 'Definitely. I'm ready to help anytime.'

When Setara, Sultan and Sheyda were on their own, they burst into raucous laughter, tears soaking their cheeks.

'*Samunwal*'s praises reminded me of "Teacher Taraki" billboards during the communist era,' Setara said, a glint in her eye. 'Taraki was president, but he only lasted a year before his rival Amin suffocated him in his sleep. His image was everywhere. Marketplaces, shops, hospitals. Always looking at us with that twinkle in his eyes.' She stood up, giving a mock military salute. 'Teacher Taraki, the compassionate father of our nation, the protector of the workers' and peasants' revolution!'

'*Aferin* to us for our wonderful playacting.' Sheyda raised her right hand in a clenched fist, grinning.

As their laughter subsided, a sombre look passed between them. Setara's grin faded, her mind drifting back to Roya. 'That's exactly how we should be with them,' she said quietly, her tone shifting. 'I had this dreadful vision the other day… of them transferring Roya and the others to another prison. It reminded me of your dream about the migrating ants.'

Sheyda sat on the floor, facing Setara and Sultan, her smile restrained.

Setara, fixing her gaze on Sheyda's almond-shaped eyes adorned with long dark eyelashes, began sketching. 'Have you seen Tahera or Fariba?'

'Yes, they came to my cell, asking for a lighter. But before I could say anything, Parwana called them to the art therapy class. I could see the bump on Tahera's belly, but nothing was showing on Fariba's,' Sheyda replied, her voice lowering as she spoke.

Setara's hand paused, her charcoal hovering above the paper. 'Do you know for sure they're pregnant?'

Sheyda's voice wavered as she swore on Sahil's life. Tears brimmed at the edges of her eyes, but she blinked them away, trying to stay composed.

Setara put the charcoal and sketchbook down on the floor and gave Sheyda a hug. The warmth of their closeness settled the moment, though a hint of urgency crept into Setara's voice. 'I wasn't doubting you, *azizum*, my dear,' she said softly.

Sultan leaned in. 'We have to get the full story. If there are any gaps, the media won't take us seriously,' she said. 'They'll throw the whole case out. Try to get them to spell out exactly what happened to them.'

'I can't imagine it's vastly different from Zohra's predicament.'

Setara rose to her feet to fetch three tea glasses.

A Twist of Fate

After seeing her sister and her family off early in the morning – they were travelling to Charikar, a town north of Kabul, to stay with their aunt for a few days – Maryam began preparing breakfast. Geisha's mobile rang, but she was fast asleep. Maryam glanced at the screen, frowning at the unknown caller.

'Mysterious caller,' she muttered, raising her eyebrows. The phone stopped ringing after a few seconds, only to start again minutes later. Tea was brewing in the large teapot on the burner and fresh bread was neatly arranged in the basket beside white cheese, *qaimaq* and plum jam. Maryam hesitated. The call was probably from someone at the prison, but it might be urgent. She tapped her index finger on the table, pondering.

'Geisha *jaan*... Geisha *jaan*' Maryam called out. 'Breakfast is ready, and your phone is ringing. Someone's calling you!' Hearing no response – no yawns, no bed creaking – she walked over to the bedroom she had been sharing with Geisha since she moved from the *khana-e-amn*. She found Geisha sleeping on her front, her head buried under the pillow. Maryam shook her shoulder gently and called her name a few times until she heard a muffled groan. 'Come on, Geisha *jaan*... Time to get up.'

Geisha sat up slowly, yawning. 'Why the rush?' she said, rubbing her eyes, and stretched. 'I'm so tired from yesterday's meeting with that *murdagaw*. That *harami* drained every ounce of energy out of me.'

'*Beshak jaanum*,' Maryam replied. 'You handled it well, though. You used your discretion with that repulsive so-called journalist and didn't reveal too much.'

'He knew I was a hooker, didn't he?'

'But you skilfully deflected his questions. I had to keep a straight face when you said you'd walked your dog in the park, knowing full well you're petrified of dogs.'

They met each other's gaze and burst into laughter. Maryam paused as the faint sound of a ringing phone came from the dining room. She hurried to fetch it, handing it to Geisha, who answered it on the loudspeaker.

'Is that you, Geisha *jaan*?' a soft, friendly female voice spoke.

'Yes, who's this?' Geisha said, exchanging quizzical glances with Maryam.

'Nikbakht. Remember me from yesterday at *New Dawn News?* I tried your number earlier, but couldn't get through. Are you alright?'

'Yes, I'm fine, *shukur*. How are you?' Geisha's eyes widened, staring at Maryam who pressed her finger to her lips in a gesture of caution.

'Can we meet somewhere? I have something important to discuss with you. Six o'clock?'

Maryam nodded and scribbled "Istanbul Café, near Makroryan" on a piece of paper, passing it to Geisha. They exchanged a knowing glance. It was a place neither had been before, but it offered anonymity. Somewhere they wouldn't be recognised, or followed. Geisha agreed, and they set the meeting there.

When Nikbakht entered the café, dressed similarly to her and Maryam, Geisha couldn't help but wonder whether it was intentional – that all three of them wore plain, indistinguishable clothes. Or had the loose-fitting, long-sleeved, ankle-length cotton dress – sometimes plain, sometimes embroidered – along with the long cotton or mesh scarves that covered them from head to belly, become the uniform of a young generation of urban Afghan women? A quiet replacement for the *burqa* their mothers and grandmothers once wore? The soft cotton that brushed against her skin was a far cry from the suffocating *burqa* her mother had worn, but the weight of expectation still lingered. Geisha wasn't sure if the shift had been empowering or if it was just another layer of social control. The cotton scarves were lighter, yes, but was there really more freedom in this new uniform?

Geisha and Maryam waved at Nikbakht from the gallery as she walked towards them.

The family section, where they had been directed, was designated for women – whether on their own or accompanied by men. The logic behind the segregation, as their elders often explained to curious young women, was to protect them from the sinful male gaze. Geisha, however, saw it differently. To her, it was more about protecting men from committing sin by fantasising about women who were *haram*, forbidden to them. But wasn't that something men were generally encouraged to do, even praised for, in their circles?

The smell of grilled meat wafted through the air, mingling with the scent of fresh bread and spices. The hum of quiet conversations floated through the gallery, a low murmur broken only by the occasional clink of crockery and the whining of restless children.

Nikbakht ordered a kebab wrap and *ayran*, a Turkish yoghurt drink. Geisha and Maryam, having already eaten a generous portion of *ghaboli palow* left by Maryam's sister, ordered black tea.

'First of all, I want you to know that I detest Ajmal and how he behaved towards you yesterday,' Nikbakht said. 'Working under his supervision as a trainee journalist has been a nightmare. I hate his guts. He's a *lochak* through and through, and an incurable liar.' Nikbakht paused for breath, exhaling deeply as if shedding the weight of her disdain. 'He's never hidden his hatred towards our Hazara colleagues: ridiculing their work, mocking their looks, calling them names behind their backs. And he does all that without any consideration for me. He knows my mother is a Hazara. Once, he called me a "corrected Hazara" because my father was a Pashtun. Detestable!'

Geisha nodded silently, her thoughts racing as she tried to imagine the weight of Nikbakht's discontent. The venom in her voice was hard to ignore, and Geisha could sense how deeply the prejudice had cut.

Nikbakht paused as the waitress brought their orders. She took a gulp from the *ayran* before rummaging through her bag. Her hands fumbled through the contents, her brow furrowed in frustration. She let out a sharp sigh, and leaned back in her chair. 'I thought I had put the cigarettes in my bag, but I can't see them.' She then grabbed her bag and emptied the entire contents onto the table, shaking it vigorously, her fingers trembling as her frustration mounted. No cigarettes. She leaned back in her chair again, her cheeks flushed, leaving her handbag upside down on the table, its contents spilling out like fragments of her scattered thoughts. Crossing her arms over her chest, she sighed, gazing into the distance. 'These days I don't know what I'm doing.'

Geisha pulled a packet from her small bag and lit a cigarette for Nikbakht, who took a deep drag, then blew a thick cloud of smoke into the air. Geisha flicked the match again, watching as the flame slowly devoured the wood. She inhaled the scent deeply, almost savouring it. 'There was this wretched girl called Naheed in Mashad,' she said, 'her voice like nails on a chalk board. She followed me everywhere, commanding and controlling me. If I disobeyed her orders, she would scorn me, beat me on the head, and scratch my face.'

Geisha paused, the memories thickening her voice. She wiped the tears rolling down her cheeks, inhaling slowly. 'My siblings were horrified when they saw my wounded face one day. Naheed was wicked. She told me to set places she considered evil-stricken, like my father's and elder brother's houses, on fire.'

Maryam pulled her chair closer and wrapped her arm around Geisha's shoulders, squeezing gently. They locked eyes.

'You see,' Geisha said, 'Naheed knew that both of them had molested me from a young age.' She lit another match, watching the flame eagerly. 'I had to do it… but, *astaghfirullah,* I couldn't deny it. I loved the intoxicating aroma. The way the heat kissed my skin. The searing flames that danced as if they were alive.'

'So, what did your father and brother do?' Nikbakht asked, her eyes wide as she stared at Geisha.

'They threw me out with nothing but a loaf of bread, a chunk of cheese, and a few pieces of walnut. I had no one to defend me. My mother was dead, and my sisters were too timid to stand up to my father and brother. So, I took refuge in the Imam Reza holy shrine. Imam Reza was my only protector.'

Nikbakht blinked rapidly, her gaze darting nervously between Geisha and Maryam. Her fingers fidgeted with the edge of her scarf, as if bracing for whatever truth might come next.

Maryam glanced between the two of them, then took a breath. Clearing her throat gently, she leaned forward, fingers curling around the edge of the table as she locked gaze with Nikbakht. 'As you heard yesterday, Nikbakht *jaan*, we have something urgent to expose.' Maryam leaned closer, her voice low but firm. 'Four women have been forced into prostitution at Badam Bagh prison. All four are pregnant.'

She paused, sipping her tea as Nikbakht's wide eyes followed her every movement. 'We believe it's part of a larger trafficking ring.' Maryam let the words settle. 'Run by none other than the prison's governor and deputy governor.' Setting down her glass, Maryam's voice steadied. 'My boss, Muriel, knows this story inside out. She's defended dozens of Afghan trafficking victims over the years. It often starts with local, forced prostitution. Once young people are hooked on drugs, they become dependent on their captors. And that's when they're trafficked to rich Arab countries.'

Maryam turned to Geisha, who nodded quietly, her gaze steady. 'They've been exploiting these inmates, forcing them into sex with the political elite,' Maryam said. 'It's a scandal that's about to blow wide open.' She leaned back, her gaze on Nikbakht. 'Can you help us?'

'I'd very much like to help. I know a journalist, Simin *jaan* Afzali, a seasoned professional, who works at the rival media company, *Khawar News*. I think she would be just the person you are looking for.'

'Excellent!' Maryam's eyes sparkled.

Geisha smiled in approval, her eyes meeting Maryam's joyful gaze.

Marriage Made in Heaven

Setara changed her mind about going to the Italian embassy multiple times while she was showering. The warm water and the subtle scent of the hand-made olive soap she'd purchased from Farzana did little to soothe her swirling thoughts. Back in her cell, she glanced down, fingers tracing the soft fabric of the towel wrapped around her shoulders. The embassy, the guests… it felt like stepping into a world not meant for her. What would they see when they looked at her?

Later, as Sheyda styled her hair with a hairdryer and round brush borrowed from the hairdressing workshop, her doubts resurfaced. She had never been to a place like that. She didn't know anyone there. She had no idea how to fraternise with people of a higher class and calibre. The very thought of mingling with sophisticated strangers made her stomach churn.

'Here you go.' Sheyda passed the large hand-held mirror to Setara. 'Do you like the twists and curls in your hair?'

'*Naam-e-khoda!* I love them. Many thanks, Sheyda *jaan*.' Setara's gaze lingered on her reflection, the unfamiliar woman in the mirror watching her like a stranger. The excitement shimmered faintly, but beneath it lay something else – a tugging whisper she couldn't ignore.

'But, Sheyda *jaan…*' Setara's voice softened, resignation curling around its edges. 'This isn't me. I don't want to go. Something feels… off. It's not my place.' Her eyes, weighed down by the gentle slope of her lower lids, met Sheyda's in the mirror. The flicker of doubt passed between them, silent but heavy.

Sheyda gave Setara's shoulder a gentle squeeze, her smile unwavering. 'They'll be charmed by you, Setara *jaan*. Trust me.' She tilted her head, catching Setara's eye in the mirror as her tone turned resolute. 'It's your exhibition, after all. The Italian ambassador has officially invited you. This is your moment. With your irresistible allure and erudition, you'll outwit them all. Just be yourself. Now, let me do your make-up.'

'No...' Setara shook her head, scowling. 'Just a bit of kohl will do. What shall I wear?'

'Guess what... your friend Hope has lent you a beautiful lilac kaftan. It's in my cell. I've washed and ironed it for you. You should wear it with your white mesh scarf, and drape it loosely over your hair.'

'Sheyda *jaan*, you're a gem of a friend.' Setara's tearful gaze met Sheyda's smiling eyes in the mirror.

'Don't forget the perfume, Setara *jaan*. The one from Sultan.' Sheyda said, leaning in.

'I haven't forgotten! So kind of her. She can be generous. Well, only sometimes.'

An hour later, Farzana arrived in her summer uniform and red patent stilettos to escort Setara to the van parked at the prison's back entrance. Setara's heart pounded in her throat. It wasn't so much the anxiety of leaving the prison that unsettled her. Rather, it was the sharp, jarring sound of the handcuffs and ankle cuffs jingling in Farzana's hands. The sound alone sent her pulse racing, pulling her back to the day of her arrest, when a cruel Herati policeman yanked her by her hair while another handcuffed her, all the while screaming obscenities.

Setara's eyes met Farzana's, her heart sinking. A chill ran through her, but she extended her arms, swallowing her pride. Her heart heavy, she cringed as Farzana locked the handcuffs around her wrists with a definitive click. Kneeling, Farzana attached the ankle cuffs with practiced, impersonal movements. Then, as if to soften the weight of her actions, she offered a faint smile. 'You look very beautiful and stylish today. And your aroma... it's mesmeric, Setara *jaan*. The *setara,* the star of the show. Living up to your name!'

Was Setara supposed to smile and thank Farzana for her compliment? For the clumsy attempt to soften the torment? Or was she to shrug it all off and pretend she wasn't offended at being taken out like a common criminal? But that's exactly what she had been reduced to. Not once had anyone paused to question her predicament. Instead, they'd done the unthinkable. They had mutilated her life by sowing hatred in her daughters' hearts, severing her from the two beautiful souls she'd nurtured with her body and spirit. Not a single one of them, not even the revered judge nor the lowly guard, possessed a grain of fairness or compassion.

'Damn you,' Setara muttered under her breath, as the cold metal of the cuffs dug into her wrists and ankles. With heavy, chained feet, she followed Farzana to the waiting van.

'*Samunwal Sahib,* welcome!' Mr. Enrico Rossellini, the Italian ambassador said joyfully. 'It's an honour to meet you.' An attractive middle-aged man of medium height, clad in a dark suit and silk tie, Mr. Rossellini warmly shook hands with Rina, who was plainly dressed in a frumpy black dress and a sequined grey scarf.

Bowing slightly with her right hand on her heart, Rina responded in her croaky voice, while adjusting her thick spectacles. 'The honour is mine, Your Excellency. May I introduce Mrs. Setara Aryan, our celebrated artist.'

'Mrs. Aryan, I am so delighted you accepted my invitation. We couldn't have launched the exhibition of your magnificent artworks without you.'

Setara smiled and shook the ambassador's hand, inhaling deeply as she took in the lush embassy garden hidden behind sandbags, blast walls, and razor wire. A gentle evening breeze swept through the gathering, where waiters nimbly carried trays of cold drinks to mingling guests.

When Mr. Rossellini ushered Rina into the heart of the party, introducing her to his noble guests, Setara turned to Farzana, who was wobbling slightly due to her red stilettos. 'May I have a drink? My throat is dry.'

Farzana nodded and called a waiter over, who then presented a tray, balanced elegantly on his fingertips, of red and white wine and fizzy orange drinks.

Setara, standing on the fringes of the party, gazed into the crowd clinking their wine glasses. She reached out for a glass of fizzy orange with a shaky hand, spilling a bit onto the glistening silver tray. Apologising profusely to the Chinese-looking waiter, she took a sip, the bubbles tickling her nose, then a larger gulp. Beads of sweat forming on her upper lip and forehead.

'*Salaam,* Setara *jaan*!' called a familiar voice.

Setara turned and gasped with joy. It was Simona. Exhilarated, she set her glass on a nearby table and drew Simona into a warm hug, her eyes welling up. 'Simona *jaan*, what a pleasure to see you.'

'Let's go indoors. I want you to be the first to view the exhibition. We'll open the doors to others in about twenty minutes.' Holding Setara's hand, Simona led the way in her red silk banquet dress with Farzana trailing closely behind. As they passed a large fan that sent Simona's dress fluttering gracefully, Simona ushered Setara into a dimly lit dining room. The ceiling carvings and framed oil paintings glowed under spotlights, each piece exuding an aura of grandeur.

Before Setara could take in the ornate paintings, Simona pulled her onward, Farzana in tow, into an adjoining room illuminated by bright ceiling lights and spotlights. Setara's eyes widened as she took in her own creations – portraits and landscapes framed and mounted neatly on all four walls.

Setara marvelled at the lavishness surrounding her. The polished floors and flamboyant furnishings contrasted starkly with the barren, stale confines of the cell where her creativity had struggled to survive. Here, her art was celebrated. There, it had been a solitary escape. A sense of pride began to swell within her, the kind she hadn't felt since high school, when she recited Persian poetry to the cheers of young and old audiences alike. At the centre stood her masterpiece: a depiction of almond trees, radiating under Kabul's sun.

Her trance was broken when the door creaked open. Leila, Simona's assistant, entered, followed by a middle-aged Afghan man with sunken eyes and protruding lips dressed in a smart suit. Setara recognised Leila from the prison exhibition a few weeks ago. After a warm greeting, Leila introduced the man as Ajmal Saraf, a senior reporter from *New Dawn News*.

Hearing the name, Setara froze, her breath catching in her throat. A chill ran down her spine as she faced the scoundrel who had insulted and harassed Geisha. The room seemed to close around her.

Ajmal, holding Simona's hand, bowed to kiss it. 'It's an honour to meet you, Mrs. Rossellini.'

'Oh, so sorry, I'm not Mrs. Rossellini,' Simona chuckled loudly.

Leila, stifling a laugh, explained, 'The gentleman asked me to take him to the exhibition organiser. So, I did.'

Ajmal shifted on his feet, clearing his throat. He cast his eyes down as he held a hand over his mouth. 'And you are?' he asked, looking up with a feigned grin.

'Simona Curti, Head of *Libertà Per le Donne Afghane,* an Italian charity.'

'Nice to meet you, Miss Curti. I'd like to interview you as the patron of this magnificent Afghan art exhibition. We're also writing a tribute to His Excellency Mohammad Kamal, the Mayor of Kabul, *Samunwal Sahib* Rina Wardak, and her sister Miss Latifa, the promising parliamentary candidate. I'd love a quote from you.'

Simona smiled politely. 'Mr. Saraf, I'm the organiser. Mr. Rossellini is the patron. Perhaps we can talk after the launch, just before dinner?'

Ajmal nodded, his jaw clenched and eyes blinking rapidly.

'Please meet the artist, Mrs. Setara Aryan,' Simona said, smiling and glancing in Setara's direction. 'It is in her honour we're launching this exhibition.'

Glancing sideways at Setara, Ajmal coughed into his hand. 'I don't want to bother you any longer. Let's leave it until later.' As he turned to leave, he paused. 'I understand you're granting the *samunwal* an award, correct?'

'Mr. Rossellini is awarding Afghan women high achievers tonight, but I'm not sure who they are.'

Just then, a man in a dark suit and glasses walked in, catching Ajmal's attention. With a knotted brow, Ajmal listened as the man whispered something in his ear. His scowl deepened. 'Please excuse me. The Mayor has just arrived,' he muttered before leaving the hall in haste, leaving everyone bewildered.

Moments later, the hall was brimming with art enthusiasts. Some hovered around the portraits, their eyes fixed on Roya's likeness to a Bollywood star, while others admired the almond trees in Setara's landscapes. A hush fell over the room as Mr. Rossellini welcomed all present, including the Mayor of Kabul – a short, balding man clad in caramel-toned silk *pirhan tunban* and a light brown *chapan* draped from his shoulders. Three tall, fierce-looking men in dark suits and earpieces stood behind him, their dark glasses fixed straight ahead.

As a part of the exhibition's official launch, Mr. Rossellini called Setara forward and handed her a silver figure of a woman in traditional Afghan dress, holding a gold star above her head, 'for her remarkable talent'. He also commended *Samunwal* Rina and General Rahimi for their work at the prison, as well as Rina's efforts to unlock its prisoners' potentials.

The audience responded with enthusiastic applause. Mr. Rossellini looked in the direction of Rina's sister, who was dressed in an oversized olive-green dress and matching scarf, and concluded his speech by wishing her well in the upcoming parliamentary elections.

Returning to her place in the front row, Setara clutched the silver figure tightly, while watching five younger women, all dressed in elegant suits, each receive an accolade for their contributions to Afghan literature, poetry, humanitarian aid, and medical relief. When the launch concluded, Setara noticed Ajmal and the mayor in an intense conversation in a corner. As she approached, she overheard Ajmal's low voice, almost a whisper, say: 'Listen to me, no one in their right mind would believe the word of a prostitute. Don't waste your energy on a cheap hooker.' Setara's pulse quickened. She immediately turned away, heading towards Farzana.

Farzana motioned for Setara that it was time to leave.

'We have to be back by 9 pm,' she whispered.

As Setara said her goodbyes to Simona, she couldn't help but notice a short man with agate worry beads holding Latifa Wardak closely. His fingers traced the beads rhythmically as he leaned in to kiss Latifa just below her earlobe. Setara felt a pang of embarrassment mixed with a sharp sting of anger. She turned back to Simona, pretending she hadn't noticed. The awkwardness of the scene hung heavily in the air.

The full moon shone gloriously, its light washing over the landscape as Setara's ankle cuffs clanked with every heavy footstep on the short walk to the prison van. Seated behind its bars as the van's door slammed shut, Farzana, starry-eyed, began chatting about the event and 'the beautiful people' who were in attendance. 'And wasn't it romantic to see Latifa *jaan* Wardak with her future husband, *Daktar Sahib* Abdullah Karimi? He owns the largest estate agency in Afghanistan… *Samunwal Sahib* says it's a match made in heaven.'

Setara tipped her head back against the hard seat, holding her breath as the truth dawned on her. Rina's future brother-in-law was the ponce who had raped Niloofar. The blackmailer who drove her to set herself on fire. The deputy prison governor, who had called his marriage to her sister 'a match made in heaven' all the while procuring young inmates for him.

Tearing Down the Veil

Simin, in her mid-thirties and clad in a smart, peach-coloured Punjabi-style *shalwar kameez*, took a pinch of raisins from the turquoise-blue bowl in the centre of the table. She watched Geisha hurriedly shutting the window to keep out the whirling sand. Outside, a storm raged, turning the world into a searing sea of orange and brown. Sycamore trees were barely visible, their branches thrashing in a frenzy as sand lashed against the glass.

'Judgment day,' Geisha remarked, casting a bewildered glance out the window at the empty street.

Simin removed her large scarf, releasing long, dark, silky hair. She took a hearty sip of green tea. 'Have you heard from your friends in Badam Bagh recently?'

'Yes, they're delighted about our meeting today,' said Geisha. 'They are praying that you can publish an article that will shake the entire corrupt establishment. You're our only hope to expose these crimes.'

Simin nodded, looking over her notes. 'Let me recap what you've told me so far... Four inmates have become pregnant, all victims of a trafficking ring led by the prison governor and his deputy. The victims were drugged and taken out of prison by guards for sex with the elite in government and the judiciary, with the promise that these men would attempt to release them. How does it sound to you?' Simin looked up, her gaze questioning.

'I don't like the phrase "taken out of prison for sex with the elite". It sounds like the women consented. We know they didn't. They couldn't have, being drugged like that,' Geisha snapped, frowning.

Simin's expression softened. 'You're right. We need to be careful with words. We'll make it clear they were coerced and had no choice, especially under those circumstances.'

Maryam leaned forward, her voice steady. 'Yes, they were convicted of *zina*, but they were duped into thinking they could secure an early release. Drugged so they'd be complicit. That's not consent.'

'Okay…' Simin paused for a while, pondering. 'Okay, I see your point. I'll change that.'

'Excellent!' Geisha said, clapping. Then turning her gaze to Maryam who smiled and nodded.

'You should also say something about how Niloofar, without mentioning her name, set fire to herself after she was blackmailed by the man who raped her,' Maryam said, glancing back at Simin. 'And how about mentioning that the man who raped Niloofar after drugging her is the future brother-in-law of the deputy prison governor?' Maryam added.

'I don't think we should give personal details yet. Naming individuals could lead to legal complications,' Simin said, locking eyes with Maryam. 'What we need to do is push the authorities to investigate. This is about the abuse of defenceless women by a corrupt prison management,' she said after a pause, then turning to Geisha. 'We can hand over the details to investigators later. With parliamentary and presidential elections approaching, the men in charge will want to be "Mr. Clean". You've chosen the perfect moment to expose this scandal.'

Geisha topped up everyone's tea glass with freshly brewed green tea. 'When will you publish this?'

'I'll have to speak to my editor. I know he will be thrilled to publish it. He is always looking for stories to expose the endemic corruption in this country.'

'Who is he?' Maryam asked.

'*Daktar Sahib* Hashmat.'

'Yes!' Maryam chuckled. 'He would be, wouldn't he? He is Yousefzai's political opponent. But is he "Mr. Clean"?'

'I haven't heard anyone bad-mouthing him,' Simin said, gazing out of the window. 'Ah, thank God, the storm has subsided,' she gasped, smiling.

'I heard he made his wealth through drug smuggling and arms racketeering during the civil war. He's not very clean, is he?' Maryam pressed on.

'Nor is anyone heading any of our institutions, my friend,' Simin sneered. 'We have to cling to "my enemy's enemy" principle. That's how things roll here.'

Witch Hunt

Sultan stood beside Farzana in Shahla's office, her eyes drawn to the large, empty desk where the flag of the Islamic Republic of Afghanistan stood prominently.

'Why has *Raees Sahib* called me? Do you know? Where is she?'

Farzana cleared her throat and looked away into the distance. 'She didn't say. She'll be here soon. Be patient.'

When Shahla eventually entered, she wasn't alone. A tall, bearded man in uniform followed her. He was a commanding figure with three gold stars on his shoulders and a stern expression that demanded obedience. Upon entering, he removed his cap, tucking it under his left arm. Farzana immediately stood to attention as he greeted them with a silent nod before taking a seat at the side of the desk. Shahla took her seat behind it, her expression unreadable as she nodded to him.

She broke the silence. 'General *Sahib* Sharifi has asked me to call this meeting. General *Sahib*?'

'*Sepas, Raees Sahib,*' he replied, his eyes fixed on Shahla. 'We have had complaints from government officials and politicians who claim they have been receiving nuisance calls from inmates in this prison. Some even allege blackmail. And we all know blackmailing is a crime punishable by a hefty prison sentence.'

His gaze turned sharply to Sultan. '*Baashi Sahib,* have you heard anything? You are, after all, our eyes and ears here.'

Sultan shifted slightly, her fingers tightening at her sides. 'No, nothing of the kind,' she said. 'Mobile phones are banned in prison.'

'Yes, we know phones are banned, but we also know many inmates use them in secret,' General Rahimi responded with a smirk, his voice rising slightly. His eyes darted to Sultan.

Shahla turned to Sultan, head tilted to the side. 'Sultan *jaan*?'

Sultan's heart pounded as she kept her head down, her mind

racing for the right words. She had to say something, anything. 'A few inmates had phones in the past,' she finally murmured, 'but after the last search, all were confiscated.' She shot a glance at Farzana, who remained motionless, her eyes fixed ahead, avoiding everyone's gaze.

The General's gaze fixed intently on Sultan, lingering for a few seconds. 'Can *Baashi Sahib* enlighten us about the inmate named Zohra Ashrafi?'

Sultan nodded, eyes cast down. 'Yes, I know her.'

'Anything else?' His voice sliced through the silence, sharp and commanding. A heavy pause followed. Sultan felt the weight of his gaze.

'She's a troublemaker.' General Rahimi broke the silence, shifting his gaze from Sultan to Shahla. 'She'll be transferred soon. Until then, keep an eye on her. *Baashi Sahib?*'

Sultan nodded, her gaze still on the floor.

'I expect regular reports on troublemakers like her.' General Rahimi placed his cap on his head with measured care. After nodding to Shahla, who stood at attention, he left the room.

Sultan looked up at Shahla as Farzana relaxed her shoulders.

'*Raees Sahib,* I don't think the inmate General *Sahib* mentioned is a troublemaker,' Farzana said, glancing at Shahla before looking briefly at Sultan. 'I've heard nothing to that effect from the guards on her floor.'

'Let's keep an eye on her until she's transferred to Welayat.' Shahla shut her large notebook, dropping her signature gold pen on the glass-top desk with a loud click.

'Welayat?' Sultan winced slightly. '*Raees Sahib,* that's a terrible place.'

'That's what happens to inmates who create a nuisance,' Shahla blurted, raising her index finger, pointing at Sultan. 'Welayat's strict regime serves as both punishment and warning. Make sure the others understand that.'

It was lunchtime when Sultan left Shahla's office. When she got to her cell, Seema held out Sultan's phone. 'Your phone was buzzing.'

Sultan threw a glance at the screen before sliding it into her jeans pocket. The cell was hot and stuffy despite the fan and open window. The midday sun beat down mercilessly, and the walls radiated heat with no breeze in sight.

In their cell at the far end of the corridor, Sultan found Setara and her cellmates eating lunch – rice and white beans in tomato sauce, accompanied by cucumber, tomato, onion, and lemon slices. '*Salaam*, Sultan *jaan*,' Setara called with a grin. 'Come and join us.'

'I'm not hungry. Shall we talk about the portrait after lunch? Same spot?' Instead of waiting for a reply, Sultan strode out of the cell.

Setara turned, sketchbook in hand, as Sultan's voice came from behind her: 'Let's sit in the shade of the almond tree.'

Smiling, Setara fanned herself with a piece of cardboard as they settled under the tree with the same threadbare blanket as always spread beneath them. The almond trees were now lush with dark green, serrated leaves, their shade a welcome relief from the blazing sun. Amidst the leaves hung almonds still in their fluffy, velvet casings, protecting the raw fruit from inside the harsh elements of summer.

'We used to eat raw almonds in Herat when I was a child.' Setara said, lifting her gaze.

'So did we here in Kabul,' Sultan replied, examining a branch. 'But they're too hard now. We should've picked them two months ago when they were soft enough to chew.' She dug out her phone wrapped in brown paper, and passed it to Setara. 'There's a message from Geisha, I think.'

Setara, sitting cross-legged, rested the sketchbook against her knees, then carefully unwrapped the phone, her gaze darting to her sides. A group of rowdy children played on the swings nearby, their mothers watching intently. Shielding the screen with her cupped hands, she read the message in a hushed voice. 'Yes, it is from her.' Setara squinted. 'She says: "The mayor of Kabul has resigned after an anonymous call from a young woman who accused him of rape and sexual abuse. Hehehe... another *lochak* exposed. We've found a good journalist, a woman from *Khawar News,* to write the story. Will keep you informed."'

Setara buried the phone back in her skirt and picked up a piece of charcoal, pretending to sketch Sultan's portrait.

'I get it now,' Sultan said, clicking her fingers. 'So, that's what today's meeting with General Rahimi was all about! *Murdagaw.* And I'm starting to wonder if that cell raid a few months ago was no accident either. It happened after our call to Abdullah, didn't it?

'What happened? What do you mean?' Setara looked up from her sketchbook, dropping the charcoal onto the paper.

'Sharifi said some government officials and politicians had complained about blackmail calls from Badam Bagh inmates. He mentioned Zohra as a suspected troublemaker and said he plans to transfer her to Welayat. *Harami,'* Sultan groaned, clenching her jaw. Locking gazes with Setara, she raised her voice a notch. 'Remember the call you made to Abdullah on Niloofar's phone? He must have had his suspicions then and told Rina, which is what sent her into a panic. Hence the cell raid to find the phone.'

'Ey khoda, yes, I get it now… it's all becoming clearer now.' Setara gasped. Her charcoal-stained hands shot up to her flushed cheeks, leaving dark streaks across her skin. 'Oh, I forgot to tell you and Geisha…' her voice tailed off, her fingers tapping against her lips. 'At the exhibition, I saw that *lochak* reporter… What was his name again?'

'Ajmal? By the way, you have smeared your face with charcoal.' Sultan said with a quiet chuckle.

'Oh, no!' Setara wiped her face with the edge of her sleeve. 'Has it gone?' She smiled, as Sultan nodded reassuringly.

'Yes,' Setara said, going back to Sultan's question, 'Ajmal.' She nodded slowly. 'The mayor called him over before the launch. When he hurried to meet him he looked anxious. Later, I saw them in a corner, deep in conversation. I moved closer and heard Ajmal whispering, trying to reassure the mayor… telling him not to worry because no one would believe a prostitute's word.'

'Do you think they were talking about Zohra?' Sultan's voice trembled slightly.

Setara's brow furrowed. 'I'm not sure. I've kept my distance from her to avoid suspicion. But Sheyda has seen her and recorded her account, which I've shared with Geisha. I don't recall any mention of the mayor, though. Should we ask Sheyda to warn her?'

'No.' Sultan's eyes narrowed. 'Tell Geisha about what General Rahimi said today. We'll update her if Zohra's transfer goes through. That transfer could actually work in our favour. Another piece of evidence against General Rahimi and Rina. We need to play our cards right. They're panicking because they know they're in deep shit and any minute now they'll be exposed, too.'

Setara set the sketch book and charcoal aside. She let out a loud sigh, resting her head on her arms after she wrapped them around her knees. She glanced at Sultan, whose resolve and steady confidence gave her a glimmer of hope – a sense of dependability in the chaos.

Welayat

'Setara *jaan*, I need your help.' Roya sobbed, her face flooded with tears, eyes sore and bloodshot. '*Raees Sahib* wants to transfer me to Welayat. You know how horrible it is, crawling with cockroaches and rats.'

Setara passed a box of tissues across the floor to Roya. 'What? Why you? Do you know when?'

Roya shrugged, locking eyes with Setara. 'Farzana said today after lunch.'

'Roya *jaan*, I've been so worried about you, but I lost all contact. I heard Zohra's account of the last few months, but I haven't heard yours yet. What happened?'

'I couldn't talk to you before because Fereshtah and Parwana were watching me like hawks, every minute of the day. But today, they've been transferred to Welayat, too. That's why I could come to see you.'

'Let's have tea and *bolani*.' Setara hugged Roya, kissing her tear-streaked face before getting up to fetch a small plate of *bolani*. After Pouring them their favourite aromatic tea from the flask that never left her, Setara glanced at Roya, who now sat lost in thought, wincing, as she bit her nails, her breathing shallow and rapid. Although hidden under a loose dress, Setara still noticed the bulge in Roya's tummy. She looked gaunt, with dark circles under her eyes and sallow skin. Missing the youthful glow that had shone so brightly in her portrait.

'Roya *jaan*, you look anaemic. Do you know what that is?' Setara said as she handed Roya a glass of tea and a plate of *bolani*.

Roya shook her head, blowing on the tea glass to cool it down. 'Right now, I want to die. Can't you see, Setara *jaan*? My life is over. What hope do I have to cling to? What could I do with an illegitimate baby? Where could I go? Jamshid and his family would never accept me.'

Setara leaned forward, narrowing her eyes. 'Who is the baby's father?'

'I wish I knew his name.' Roya closed her eyes, frowning and shaking her head as if in a trance. 'All I recall from that delirium is lying naked on a large bed in a high-ceilinged room. He was short, bald on top, wearing an elegant silk *chapan,* standing over me and looking down.' Tears welled up in her eyes. 'It's all so bizarre, looking back on the last few months.' She exhaled, glancing down at the dried blood on the corner of her thumb nail. 'It started with a blasted headache,' she said in a voice hardly louder than a whisper. 'I asked Parwana for aspirin, and she gave me two tablets at lunch, then another two later in the afternoon. My head began to spin, my vision blurred, and I collapsed on the bed. I remember waking up in the dark. My eyes were open, but everything was hazy. I saw shadows moving around the cell, heard footsteps, clothes rustling, the cell door slamming, chains clanking. I couldn't tell where I was.'

She paused, sipping the hot tea gently. As she moved to place the glass on the floor, it slipped from her unsteady fingers and fell. Tea splashed across the floor, scalding her toes.

'Akh!' she cried out, clutching her foot.

Setara leapt to her feet, quickly fetched a wet rag, and then gently pressed it against Roya's burnt toes.

Roya exhaled deeply, closing her eyes for a moment. Her fingers found the wet cloth and held it. Then, quietly, she began to speak. Her voice trembled.

'I remember the man in the *chapan*... petting me, coaxing me.' She swallowed hard. '"I know you like it, darling. I'll be gentle,"' she said, mimicking his voice with hollow detachment. 'Then I felt his weight... felt him inside me. It ached. I cried. He pressed a pungent handkerchief over my nose, and I blacked out again.' She took a deep, shuddering breath and stared into Setara's eyes.

Setara, however, knew there was a powerful backstory that Roya wasn't letting on. 'There was more to it though, right?' She looked up, meeting Roya's swollen eyes, resting her fisted hand under her chin. 'You received those expensive gifts from an anonymous senior officer who you believed was an erudite devotee of Persian poetry.

Do you recall that?'

Roya buried her face between her knees. 'That's how they captured my heart,' she murmured, her voice muffled. 'Fereshtah would spend hours listening to me. She heard it all: my frustration with this unjust sentence, my dream of studying Persian literature, and my fading hope of ever marrying Jamshid. One day, she told me that she and her boss, a *samunwal,* she never said her name, could help me win my appeal. She said her boss was close to the mayor of Kabul and could pull some strings with the presiding judge. I was flabbergasted. Who wouldn't be?' Roya looked up, her eyes wide.

'Did Fereshtah tell you, before that first night you were taken out, that you'd be meeting the mayor?'

'Not directly. She always spoke in this guarded, coded way. She once hinted that her boss would discuss it with the mayor and "take it from there."'

'I've seen the mayor, Roya *jaan*. He fits your description of the man who raped you that night. How cunning they were, to deceive you so ruthlessly and keep you in the dark for so long.' Setara's voice softened. 'So, what happened when you woke up the next day?'

'I can't remember the time, but I woke up alone and panicked. I kept seeing demonic figures creeping towards me, their arms outstretched and mouths open with long black tongues coming out. I screamed. Fereshtah burst in, cradling the back of my neck and putting a glass of water to my lips, slowly pouring it down my throat. Then she gave me more tablets, and I fell asleep again.'

'What about your other cellmates?' Setara asked after taking a gulp of the now lukewarm tea.

'I could hear them, but I never saw them to speak to. I only spoke to Fereshtah once, in the late afternoon the day after that dreadful night. She told me to take a shower and helped me undress. I freaked out when I saw drops of blood and smelled something pungent on my underpants. She consoled me, saying, "It's from last night. You were unwell." I felt so confused. When I asked her who the man in the *chapan* was, she said that image must have come to me in a dream.' Sniffling, Roya blew her nose into a tissue.

'Did they take you there again?'

'No... or maybe they did... I don't know.' Roya furrowed her brow. She took a bite of the *bolani* and left the rest, her gaze distant.

'Roya *jaan*, don't worry yourself. We're here for you.' Setara set her tea glass down and embraced Roya's fragile body, giving her a firm, comforting squeeze.

'Setara *jaan*, do you have Geisha's number? I need to call her urgently.'

'What for? Is it something I can help with?' Setara asked, meeting Roya's curious gaze. 'Geisha's started a new job, so she's often unavailable.'

'I know Geisha's aborted pregnancies in the past. Remember her stories of dead foetuses in the bathroom?'

'I'm not sure what she said was real or just a hallucination. I wouldn't put too much faith in Geisha's words. I know of women in Herat who used knitting needles, but I wouldn't recommend that. It's dangerous. Look...' Setara looked up to the cell's murky ceiling. '*Subhan Allah*, Roya *jaan*, a life is a life. Do you really want to end the life of another of God's creature?'

Roya's face softened, her eyes filling with tears. 'No,' she replied gently.

A frantic pounding on the door startled them both. Zohra burst inside, her hair tangled and wild, her eyes wide with panic. Pale and dishevelled, she looked as if she'd seen a ghost. She let out a shriek so piercing that Roya winced and covered her ears. Zohra tore at her own hair and clawed at her face, leaving angry red welts as tears streamed down her cheeks. '*Ya Allah, ya Allah!*' she cried. 'They'll kill us! That bastard, the prison governor, it's all his doing. He's terrified I'll expose him. Yes, that's their plan. To bury us away, make us disappear. They'll kill us in Welayat, out of sight.'

Setara jumped up, grabbing Zohra's hands to stop her from hurting herself. But Zohra shoved her so hard she stumbled backwards onto the floor. Suddenly, the door burst open. Farzana stormed in, flanked by two unfamiliar guards. They seized Zohra, pinned her arms, and neck-locked her before slapping on the handcuffs. Zohra's screams echoed through the cell and down the corridor as they dragged her out.

'There is a new jar of tablets in your lockers,' Setara overheard

Farzana mutter to the guards.

'They'll drug her now,' Setara said softly, settling herself beside Roya. 'That's how they control us. Have you seen Nafisa, the inmate on the first floor, lately? I knew her back in Pol-e-Charkhi. She was a fierce woman. She'd killed her mother-in-law after years of brutal abuse. Now, she's a ghost, staring at everyone with empty eyes.'

The cell door swung open again, and Sultan, with her usual stern expression, stepped in, followed by a breathless Sheyda.

'What's going on?' Sheyda's voice trembled. 'I just saw the guards dragging Zohra to Cell 86. I ran into Sultan on the way. She'd heard the commotion.'

Their eyes fell on Roya, huddled in a corner with her knees tucked tightly against her chest, her arms wrapped around her legs.

'What happened to you?' Sheyda whispered, stunned.

It was a balmy day but Roya was cold, shivering. Her hollow gaze drifted towards the barred window. Dark clouds had gathered, blocking out the sun, and a faint light struggled to filter through layers of grime on the glass.

'They'll all be transferred to Welayat after lunch,' Setara murmured, standing to rinse the cups and saucers in the tiny, cramped bathroom in the corner of the cell.

Meanwhile, Sheyda reached under her sleeve, pulling out a small bundle. 'I've brought some saffron for you, Setara *jaan*.'

'*Shukur,* Sheyda *jaan*. Add a pinch to the tea in the flask,' Setara replied with a nod.

As she dried the crockery with a small towel, Setara's voice lowered. 'Zohra was hysterical when she found out about their transfer. She was lashing out at the whole world. I think the drugs they've been giving them has messed their minds up, *bel-kul!*' She glanced around cautiously before adding, 'Zohra suspects it's all orchestrated by the governor. He fears her exposing him. She wasn't explicit but reading between the lines. She meant he's the one who raped her.'

'Keep your voice down,' Sultan quickly cut in, her voice a whisper. Her eyes briefly met Roya's half-opened ones. 'You should all go to Welayat without making a fuss. Their days are numbered. I promise you.'

From the Ashes of Time

'*Salaam,* I'm Asila Ashrafi, Zohra *jaan*'s sister,' announced the voice over the phone. Geisha gasped, her hand tightening around the phone, now slick with sweat.

The timing couldn't have been worse – she was in the middle of reading a story to toddlers at Muriel Chandler's office creche when the phone first rang. She knew Zohra from Badam Bagh but little else, certainly not that she had a sister. To her, Zohra was just another shadow drifting through the prison corridors. And now, suddenly, her sister was on the line. How had this stranger found her, let alone obtain her number? Could she be one of Ajmal's cronies aiming to ensnare her? A string of previous nuisance calls, including one with a phony job offer, had made her wary.

'*Salaam,*' Geisha replied, her voice cautious but steady, masking her rising doubts. 'Excuse me, have we met? I don't recall your name.'

'You know Zohra *jaan*, don't you? I got your number from her cellmate. She's in Welayat now.'

The mention of Welayat lent a layer of authenticity to Asila's claim. Just yesterday, Setara had texted her about the transfer of Cell 86 inmates to Welayat – *out of sight, out of mind,* she'd said. It was a grim reality: Zohra, along with Roya, Tahera, and Fariba, now enduring the harsh conditions of that ancient, crumbling prison.

Following Maryam's advice, Geisha decided to meet Zohra's sister at a neutral location. Istanbul Café came to mind as a safe, inconspicuous choice, the only venue she could think of that didn't attract attention. Conveniently, Asila was staying with relatives nearby and agreed to the location.

A petite figure in a long black embroidered dress under a *burqa* stepped into Istanbul Café. She lifted the *burqa* at the double doors, uncovering her face. Her eyes scanned the room. From the ground floor, packed with men, mostly from nearby offices, to the gallery above, where women and children filled the family section. Ascending the stairs, she gasped.

Maryam gently pinched Geisha's thigh. 'I think that's her,' she whispered.

Geisha glanced at Maryam, shaking her head. 'Can't imagine Zohra's sister in a *burqa*.'

'I think it's her.' Maryam waved at the forlorn stranger, who responded with a cautious smile and a tentative nod.

Geisha approached her, arms stiff and hands clenched. '*Salaam*. Are you Asila?'

The woman nodded, and Geisha invited her to their secluded table by the window.

Once seated, Asila's gaze drifted to the menu. 'Adana Kebab... sounds appetising with yoghurt. I'm very hungry. I haven't eaten since yesterday evening.' Her voice trembled, her hazel eyes welling with tears.

Maryam quickly called the waitress and ordered Adana Kebab, a few cold mezzes, flatbread, and a bottle of *ayran*.

'I went to see Zohra's lawyer at her NGO office in Karta Chahar,' Asila began, her voice faltering as she clutched her black mesh scarf, the fabric snagging on her trembling fingers. 'The office was packed with people clamouring to see one of the few lawyers. Together, we went to Welayat. We waited outside the front door for what felt like hours. The stench of sewage was just unbearable.'

Asila glanced over her shoulder, scanning the nearby tables. Seeing no one close by, she let out a shaky sigh of relief. She leaned in, and whispered, 'When they brought her, we could only see her through a tiny peephole barely the size of my face.' Tears streamed down her face. 'I only arrived from Ghazni two days ago. This city feels like a labyrinth. Cold, loud, and full of strangers. Even Zohra seemed like a stranger to me. Scruffy, distant, her eyes darting like a cornered animal. She couldn't hear me, couldn't even understand. She's lost her mind.' Asila covered her mouth with the scarf, muffling her sobs, her shoulders quivering with each stifled breath.

Geisha reached across the table, gripping Asila's hand, which was cold as ice despite the summer heat. 'We heard about Zohra *jaan*'s tragic state from friends at Badam Bagh. We believe the *murdagaw* General Rahimi, the prison governor, raped her and that's what's shattered her. But also—'

'No!' Asila interrupted, shaking her head vehemently, her voice breaking slightly. 'She's been drugged! Let's get the facts right. That's the only reason for her state of mind. Let's be clear!'

Geisha turned her gaze to Maryam who had been following the conversation silently. She then turned to Asila again. 'Asila *jaan*, she and the others were drugged before being taken out of the prison. I know it's painful to imagine your younger sister being raped by some *lochak* of a man, but that's the harsh reality. Did you know she's pregnant?'

Asila nodded, her eyes cast down, her lower lip trembling. 'I know, that's why I've come all the way from Ghazni with my brother-in-law, both of us praying we wouldn't encounter a Taliban checkpoint, who are still active in our area, during the long journey in his old, rickety car.'

Maryam leaned in, trying to catch Asila's eye. 'When was the last time you saw Zohra?'

Asila began to cough, quickly spitting into a tissue. When the waitress arrived with their order, she turned her gaze to the wall, taking a long gulp of *ayran* before biting into the yogurt-soaked kebab wrapped in layers of flatbread. She paused, resting her head in her hands. 'Ten years ago… no, twelve. We're a tragic family.' Her voice wavered. 'I'm ten years older than Zohra. I practically raised her. Our mother was stretched thin with six other children, and my father's butcher shop barely brought in enough to get by.'

She met Maryam's gaze, her face taut. 'Please, I beg you… don't misjudge us. We are poor but honourable.' She pushed her plate with less than half a kebab remaining, to the centre of the table, wincing. 'I can't eat anymore,' she said tersely, turning her gaze to the wall, arms folded tightly across her chest.

Clearing her throat, Asila glanced up at the ceiling, eyes clouded as she sank into the weight of dark memories. 'Everything went sour when Zohra ran off with a Tajik boy from the neighbourhood, fighting against my father's decision to marry her off to an older man from our clan, a Pashtun. She was only fifteen.' She paused, her voice breaking. 'Our father never forgave her. He filed a missing report, but she was never found while he was alive. He died last year, and I began searching for her. I've never married, thanks to the disgrace of it all. My older sister was the lucky one. She married a compassionate man before disaster struck.'

Asila's lips curved into a faint smile, though it quickly faded. 'A few months ago, I heard from the Tajik boy's grandmother. His only relative left in Ghazni. She said the police had arrested them both not long after they moved in with his cousin here in Kabul. In Khayr Khana, where the Tajiks from Panjshir live.' Asila paused to sip water, then continued, 'I had no idea where they had taken her until one day, my phone rang. It was her, my baby sister! We cried through most of the call, and though she was in prison, a dark, cold, and lonely place, I was overjoyed to find her. But prison... it's no place for a decent girl.' She shook her head, clicking her tongue.

'What are you planning to do now?' Maryam asked, her eyes wide with curiosity.

'I'm not literate. I need an attorney to draft a legal testimony for me, an official condemnation of my sister's treatment in that godforsaken place.' Asila's eyes sparked with sudden determination as she met Maryam's. 'But I don't want Zohra's lawyer for this. I need someone independent from all these political entanglements and ethnic loyalties. It's these divisions that have cursed us for so many years, ruined our country's decency. Can you suggest anyone?'

'Muriel?' Geisha glanced at Maryam, who nodded.

'Yes, we know just the lawyer. Muriel Chandler. She's American but knows our laws and can navigate the maze of our system. I work as a junior lawyer at her office, so I can translate for you.' Maryam's voice was steady with confidence, making it clear Muriel was no ordinary lawyer but one who was compassionate and could truly help.

'Please, take me to Mrs. Muriel.'

Public Unveiling

'It's out! It's out! *Khawar News* published the article today with a quote from a member of parliament. We're exhilarated!'

Geisha's early morning message buzzed onto Setara's screen. Setara jumped up, hugging Sultan, who wasn't one for embraces but made an exception this time. Speaking in whispers and grinning from ear to ear, Setara told Sultan that Geisha would text the article in pieces during her tea break. 'I'll write it all down so we can share it with Sheyda too,' she added.

Sultan pressed her lips together, a shadow crossing her face. 'Good news, but it's the reaction that worries me. What if they find out about us? The warlord mafiosi are ruthless. They'd want revenge,' she murmured, her voice trembling slightly.

'Geisha and Maryam kept all names out, and the journalist promised to keep personal details hidden.'

'Journalist?' Sultan chuckled dryly. 'And you believe in their promises?' With that, Sultan left Setara's cell, her words leaving Setara in deep thought.

Later in the day, Setara fetched her sketchbook and box of charcoals. She and Sultan walked to their usual spot, spreading the familiar, threadbare blanket under the almond trees.

'Let me sketch your profile,' Setara said with a secret smile, glancing around to ensure they weren't being watched. Other than three women with children near the entrance to the prison block, the courtyard was empty. A refreshing breeze cut through the summer heat, making the air feel lighter.

Holding her charcoal, Setara traced lines on her sketchbook as she read aloud from Geisha's texts, each line stirring her resolve. 'Geisha says it's made the front page. The title reads: *Sex Abuse Allegations in Badam Bagh Prison*. The article opens: "*Khawar News* has become aware of four pregnancies among inmates in Badam Bagh, all incarcerated for a year or more. Witnesses report that these women were taken out for sex by prison guards, often drugged to ensure compliance. Allegedly, the prison governor and his deputy were both involved. *Khawar News* obtained an affidavit from a family member of one victim, stating that hallucinogens caused severe mental health issues in all four women. One inmate, under intense pressure, resorted to self-immolation. Readers may remember the recent resignation of Kabul's mayor amid accusations of sexual misconduct. Could he be implicated here, too? The public deserves answers. *Khawar News* urges a thorough government investigation and justice for these human rights violations. Mrs. Shaima Qureishi, the Farah Province MP and Chair of the Parliamentary Committee for Gender Equality, called the allegations 'damning' and emphasised the urgency of an inquiry." What do you think?' Setara asked, holding up her sketchbook.

'Personally,' she continued, 'I think they did the best they could, given the circumstances. And, as you said, what's crucial is how people react.'

'It's hugely watered down,' Sultan replied, scowling. 'But I get it, probably a legal compromise. Mark my words, the warlords won't let this slide. These people will kill to keep their privileges. If I were the journalist who wrote this, I'd be worried. And let's hope we're never called on to give statements in an investigation.'

Just then, Setara's phone vibrated. It was Geisha calling, wanting to know their thoughts on the article.

'It's good, Geisha *jaan*,' Setara replied, shielding the phone with her sketchbook. 'We're sure it'll rattle a few cages. *Shukur* for all your hard work! And it's amazing that Niloofar spoke to the reporter. But we're anxious about the reaction from those whose cages are rattled by this.'

'There's nothing to worry about, Setara *jaan*,' Geisha reassured her, her voice brimming with excitement. 'The important thing is that these people can no longer hide behind their fake reputations. And I'm telling you, Niloofar was fierce! She's even willing to cooperate with an official investigation. The reporter's just as bold. She told me the former mayor called her this morning, threatening to sue if they dragged his name into the scandal. He's claiming to be a "pious Muslim, a family man devoted to his wife and children, who's never failed in his *Haj* and *Zakat* duties as a devout man,"' Geisha added, breaking into laughter.

'Has anyone else contacted the reporter?' Sultan asked, her voice tense.

'Not that I know of. Akh, sorry, yes, I nearly forgot. Someone from the national TV channel. Can't remember his name. Not sure exactly what he wanted. Something about setting up interviews with the "brave ladies" who have exposed the crime.' Geisha's voice softened as she prepared to hang up. 'I'll be eager to hear what happens next on your end. Must go now.'

Geisha's last words gripped both Setara and Sultan. Frowning, they exchanged anxious glances as they walked back to their cells at a slow pace.

It had been a week since the publication of the article, yet nothing seemed to have shifted within the prison. The guards passed Sultan in the corridors with indifferent eyes, no telling glance or lifted eyebrow. Not a single word slipped from their lips. Until one day, her phone rang.

The sharp trill of the ringtone sliced through the silence in the cell. She froze, her breath catching. It had to be Geisha. It had to be news. Heart pounding, she began to frantically search for the phone, her mind racing. Humaira joined in, diving under the bed, rifling through shoes and plastic bags. The tension mounted until, at last, Humaira pulled out what they were looking for.

It was Geisha, with news that sent a chill up Sultan's spine: the President had appointed a parliamentary committee to investigate the allegations of rape and sexual assaults in the prison. They planned to interview everyone named, including witnesses.

'They're finally doing something,' Geisha's voice buzzed with excitement. She relayed that Simin had said the committee would interview all witnesses, inmates, and prison staff. But at Welayat, not Badam Bagh.

'Inmates, too? Why Welayat?' Sultan's voice shook as her fingers tightened around the mobile. 'Don't they want to see where these women were drugged and smuggled out in the dead of night? Idiots!'

Geisha continued, explaining that arrangements were underway to interview Niloofar at her home in Herat given her inability to travel due to her disabilities. Then she added, 'Here's something to ponder on: Parwana and Fereshtah have been sacked. Just ahead of the investigation.' She chuckled darkly.

'They won't find them now. They could be anywhere.' Sultan hung up, wincing. Fury burned within her, threatening to spill over. She had to leave the cell. She didn't want her wives to see her on the verge of breaking.

'Have you heard?' Sultan burst into Setara's cell. 'Parwana and Fereshtah have been sacked.'

Setara looked catatonic, as if she'd been electrified.

Sultan shook her by the shoulders. 'Are you okay? Answer me!'
'It's all happening. Soon they'll be coming after us.' Setara's face had drained of colour, her eyes locking onto Sultan's with a blank stare.

'What's the matter with you?' asked Sultan. 'You look... odd.'

'The anonymous caller Geisha mentioned last week really unnerved me,' Setara said, her voice catching in gasps. 'I'm tired of it all. You know what? I'm scared. Very scared.' She paused, her hands trembling slightly. 'Last night, when everyone was sound asleep, I saw shadows hovering near the door. A few days ago when I was alone in the cell, I heard knocks on the door, but when I called out to them to come in, there was nothing. No one.' She swallowed hard, glancing up at the ceiling. 'Only God knows how I have been suffering these last few days. I couldn't sleep again last night, terrified of what they'll do to us.'

'Me, too.' Sultan paused, sitting across from Setara on the floor, lost in thought.

Setara broke the silence, her voice dropping to a whisper. 'I had a nightmare last night. I woke up, shivering. It was a warning, I'm sure of it.' She raised her voice slightly. 'I saw myself wandering around our old house in Herat, calling out to Izzuddin. *Khoda beyamorz.*' Her fingers caught on to the edge of her sleeve, pulling out a loose thread, her eyes cast downward. 'I told him I was running from people who wanted to hang me for a crime I hadn't committed. My cellmates woke me up I was whimpering so loudly. Let's pray our identities stay hidden.' She looked up, hands raised, tear-filled eyes fixed on the ceiling. '*Ya Allah*, please help us, have mercy on us.'

'I always pray for us, day and night. But listen,' Sultan continued in a whisper, leaning in, 'Geisha says a parliamentary committee has been appointed to investigate. So why were Parwana and Fereshtah sacked before the investigation even began?' She winked, her lips curling into a half smile.

Setara scoffed. 'I can't help being cynical about this, either. It's obvious, isn't it? They know too much. They've probably been kidnapped to keep their mouths shut. For all we know, they've already been taken across the border into Pakistan.'

Niloofar

Propped up in bed, Niloofar faced her daily struggle with mealtime. Her stiff elbows, wrists, and deformed fingers resisted her efforts, but she refused to give up, insisting her aunt, Khala Farida, not feed her. She was determined to live. Saliva slipped down her chin as she chewed her first bite of breakfast. 'Dirty! Messy!' she muttered, scowling as she wiped her mouth with an abrasive brush of her sleeve.

In moments like this, despair crept in, stirring dark thoughts of ending her pain and pathos once and for all. But each time, she shook them off with a short, painful walk – unaided – through her aunt's pomegranate orchard. Past the curtained window that greeted her each morning, she would taste life beyond her bed – her prison.

Recently, she had begged her aunt to keep that window open, to let in the warm breeze and the occasional butterfly and ladybird, to see the baby pomegranates ripen through her tearful eyes, to smell the geraniums, to hear the buzzing of the bees. 'Let me breathe. Let me live,' she'd cried, her voice cracking. Then she fell silent, guilt setting in as her aunt, wrapped tightly in her Herati *chadar*, cowered into the corner.

Niloofar avoided mirrors. Catching her reflection made her flinch, each glimpse ushering in a wave of tension that clenched her muscles, leaving her body trembling. Her uneven eyes – one bulging, the other half-closed and twitching with nerves – along with the crinkled, rough skin surrounding her mouth and thinning hair, stray strands escaping from the scarf she wore to hide her bald patches, all pointed to a self she barely recognised. Yet she couldn't escape the world's unrelenting reflections. She saw herself mirrored in her aunt's eyes, shrinking beneath the pity softening her gaze.

The once-praised beauty who had captivated Sohrab, the most sought-after young man in Herat, was now marred, her skin taut and fractured with deep scars. Her eyes, which had once sparked with warmth, charm and defiance, had become haunted pools of sorrow, a relentless reminder of the flames that had reduced her life to ashes. Yet beneath the pain and disfigurement, a tiny ember of her former self flickered – A stubborn remnant she clung to, hoping it might one day burn brighter, if only for herself.

Her tea was heavy with sugar, just as she liked it; the sweetness brought memories of her childhood, of a mother who'd left abruptly when she was ten and only returned after the flames had crippled her. But she bore no grudges – not anymore. She'd let the past burn away in the same flames that scarred her six months ago. These months of solitude had become a sanctuary, a place to reflect and to soliloquise. In the darkness of her room, with its single window shut tight against the world, she had embraced silence.

That was winter. With the coming of spring and then summer, she, like the world on the other side of the window, had turned a new leaf. She felt a new energy budding within her – a faint warmth spreading through her limbs, like sunlight breaking through frost. And she wanted to nurture it, to let it take root and flourish.

Still questions haunted her, gnawing at her core: Would she ever marry like her classmates? Bear children? Live surrounded by people who loved her? And would she ever know a life free from the captivity of pain? Though the prison service had mercifully rescinded her term, but captivity was not confined to those dark, pungent cells with unyielding metal bars. It was also this defaced, mutilated body – A prison she could never escape.

When she heard the doorbell, she hurriedly pulled her scarf over the lower half of her face. This piece of cloth had become a refuge from the gaze of strangers for some time now. She knew who it was. It was Mrs. Karimi, Herat's one-and-only female prosecutor. Short, stout, and teetering on her clunky platform shoes, Mrs. Karimi had become Herat's 'lady of steel' – a prosecutor lauded with awards from both Afghan and American dignitaries. Mrs. Karimi had been sent by the delegation investigating Badam Bagh's sex abuse scandal to interview Niloofar whose disabilities prevented her from travelling to Kabul.

She heard *Khala* Farida showing their visitor into the lounge where Niloofar, clad in a loose, unshapely black dress with sleeves extending beyond her fingers, the kind sold to pregnant women in Herat's bazaar, sat with a shawl on her shoulders and a blanket on her lap.

'*Salaam ghandool.*' The Prosecutor's lips opened to a shallow chuckle, pointing at the blanket on Niloofar's lap. 'How's your health, *jaan*? Are you feeling cold in this heat?'

'Niloofar *jaan* is much better now. *Shukur*,' Niloofar's aunt chimed in. 'Would you like tea?' she asked, while her eyes flickered down, unwilling to meet the Prosecutor's gaze.

'Can she talk?' Mrs. Karimi offered a withering glance at her.

'Yes, of course, she can!' Khala Farida said, wincing, before she disappeared into the kitchen at the far corner of the corridor. The distant clink of a teapot echoed down the hall.

Mrs. Karimi grunted as she stood with her arms folded across her chest. She then slammed the door shut with a finality that left the room in a tense silence.

Draped in a black suit with a green Herati silk shawl, Mrs. Karimi sat down on the comfortable chair opposite. She glanced at Niloofar's face, lips pursed. She pulled out a notebook, jotting something down. After a long pause, her gaze shifted to the window. 'A pomegranate orchard. Soon you'll have baskets of that heavenly fruit. Lucky girl!' Her tone was cold, dismissive.

The door creaked open, and Mrs. Karimi turned to Khala Farida, who was carrying a tray with tea and sugar. 'Two heaped spoons, please,' she instructed, barely looking up. 'Please leave us, and close the door quietly behind you. *Shukur*.'

Khala Farida cast a narrowed glance at Mrs. Karimi's back, a disdainful look Niloofar had rarely seen on her gentle aunt.

'Call me if you need me,' Khala Farida said with a slight edge as she exited.

Watching Khala Farida leave, Mrs. Karimi raised her eyebrows, her gaze sharpening as she turned back to Niloofar. Wincing at her first sip, she placed the glass on the side table with a sigh, shaking her head. 'Lukewarm tea.' Then, fixing her eyes on Niloofar, she continued, 'So, tell me. Why did you do it?' Her stern tone echoed in the room.

'Do what?'

'You know what I mean. Don't play clever with me, girl. Why did you burn yourself? Why did you ruin your future?'

'I had no future. I wanted to die, but not quietly. I wanted the world to know how I suffered.'

Mrs. Karimi's frown deepened, her pen poised. 'So you think you've achieved what you wanted?' she sneered, her voice cutting.

'Are you here to interview or insult me?' Niloofar's throat tightened, a painful lump forming. She coughed into her scarf, her eyes filling with tears.

With a worried glance, Mrs. Karimi poured water from a jug into a small glass and offered it to Niloofar, who shook her head vigorously, avoiding eye contact.

Taking a deep breath, Mrs. Karimi set the glass back on the side table and cleared her throat. 'Let's be civil here, please. All I am doing, *azizum,* is trying to make sense of the events you were embroiled in.'

'Well, let me enlighten you,' Niloofar replied, her voice trembling. 'I was tricked by the guards and the deputy governor, who told me that a man named Abdullah, Kabul's wealthiest and most influential businessman, would use his connection with the judge to secure my release.' She paused, swallowing hard. 'They took me to a palatial house on a leafy street in Kabul and left me with that monster. He drugged me and… raped me.' She swallowed once more and continued. 'The next day he demanded to see me again. When I refused, he threatened to post a video he claimed to have secretly filmed of me… in the nude… on social media.'

'If you were unconscious the whole time, as you claim, how could you know he'd raped you?' Mrs. Karimi pressed, her pen hovering above the page.

'I opened my eyes for a moment, caught in a haze, and saw him, naked, on top of me, on the sofa.' Niloofar's voice wavered, thin and brittle. 'And then later, the stench… the stains on my underpants.' She gasped, her eyes shutting tightly as a shudder ran through her, the horror still fresh in her mind.

Mrs. Karimi's tone remained cold. 'You might have seen him in a dream. And as for the stain, that could have been from an infection. Just a normal discharge.'

Niloofar's tears spilled over. She cast her head down, shoulders shaking as she wiped her eyes with the corner of her scarf. 'I knew you wouldn't believe me. You're looking for a scapegoat, and who better than me? A cripple with no connections in the elite, no strings to pull.'

'Look, *ghandool,* I'm only trying to establish the facts.' Mrs. Karimi cast a fleeting glance at her, as if already rehearsing her departure.

'I want justice. This man hasn't just violated my body. He's destroyed my soul. What have I got left to live for? He's taken everything from me, yet he's free in Kabul, free to do this again to other girls, other women. Can't you, as a senior lawyer and a woman, understand my meaning, feel my anguish?' Niloofar's head dropped as she gazed at her long sleeves, her words trembling with grief.

Mrs. Karimi set down her pen, folding her arms across her chest as she leaned back, her gaze drifting into the distance. 'I hear you, *azizum,*' she said softly, nodding as her eyes returned to search Niloofar's face.

The bell rang, a distant male voice speaking with Khala Farida at the door.

'It's Kazim, my driver. I have to go.' Mrs. Karimi jolted slightly, glancing at her watch as she rose.

Khala Farida, *chadar* wrapped tight, announced the driver's arrival.

Mrs. Karimi flinched, then turned to her with a wink, as she walked out. 'Don't forget me when you harvest your pomegranates, *khala jaan.*'

A Victory Sweet but Tainted

On her way to find Setara, Sultan caught sight of Farzana through the glass wall of the meeting room. She paused, pressing her forehead to the glass for a closer look. Farzana's hair was unusually unkempt, her eyes cast downward as if she were drowning in troubled thoughts. She looked beside herself. An unyielding pillar in her police uniform – sometimes softened by shiny patent stilettos – Farzana's gaze was usually steely, her demeanour unsparing. But now, that formidable stature had collapsed. Her shoulders sagged, and her once-proud posture had folded into a hunch. Her fierce eyes, now red-rimmed and wet, glistened under the harsh fluorescent lights.

Suddenly, Farzana looked up. Her shaky hand motioned for Sultan to enter. 'I'm ruined, Sultan *jaan*,' she cried out.

Jaan? Sultan blinked. Farzana – of all people – had never used such an endearment. Not to her.

'I've resigned,' Farzana whispered hoarsely. Her voice was frayed, half disbelief, half despair. 'My career is in tatters. I'm finished.' She ran her index finger sharply across her neck in a swift, final gesture.

Although Sultan suspected Farzana's resignation was related to the Badam Bagh sex abuse scandal, she never imagined Farzana herself might be directly implicated. Eager and wary, Sultan felt compelled to find out what had driven her to this point after so many years of service – especially after her recent promotion to Head Guard.

Pre-election rumours had rippled through every corner of the country when the investigation's final report was released, naming the prison governor and his deputy as the masterminds behind the scandal. Both resigned swiftly, vanishing from public sight. Parwana and Fereshtah had been erased from all records, as though they'd never existed. According to Geisha and Maryam, the fallout reached far beyond the prison walls; even prominent politicians and hopeful parliamentary candidates had slipped away from view. Among them was Latifa Wardak, her once-bright future now in shambles. Her fiancé, Abdullah, had fled to Dubai, safely beyond the reach of Afghan law, and word on the street was that Latifa would soon follow.

'But why you?' Sultan demanded, eyes locked on Farzana, who sat at the table, her frame deflated, her elbows pressing onto the hard wood as she hid her face in her hands.

Farzana's lips twisted into a bitter smile. A chuckle escaped her but it quickly turned into hysterical laughter. Her eyes were hollow. 'Guess who's the new governor now?' She let out a short, harsh laugh, shaking her head.

'Raees Sahib?' Sultan guessed, shocked.

'Yes.' Farzana's voice cracked. 'She told me that despite my innocence, and years of loyal service, mind you, as Head Guard I was guilty of failing my responsibilities. "You should have been more vigilant," she said.' Farzana threw her arms up, her voice rising. 'How could I have known? The entire operation was orchestrated from above! Why didn't *she* speak up?'

'Maybe she sensed something was wrong but was too scared to confront it.' Sultan responded in a subdued voice. 'She's new, after all.'

Farzana's gaze sharpened, her voice dropping to a murmur. 'New? She's sly! No one knows her like I do.' She leaned in, her voice barely above a whisper. 'Did you know she's been visiting the Italian ambassador? Of course you wouldn't.' Her voice grew colder. 'It's been going on for months. I arranged her private transport myself.' Her lips curled with disdain. 'Ever wondered where she got that gold pen? Those silk scarves? You think her salary covers that?'

Sultan felt a chill run through her. Farzana's revelations hung thick in the air.

'At least you know you had nothing to do with the rape and abuse of inmates,' Sultan said gently. 'We've always regarded you as a friend and confidant. Even during the times you reprimanded us harshly, none of us spoke ill of you.'

Farzana nodded, a slow, resigned look crossing her face. 'You know… I believe it was meant to be,' she replied, sitting up straighter, her voice steadier. 'My resignation. Maybe it was God almighty pulling me out before I was tarnished with the same brush.' She crossed her legs, dabbing her eyes with the cuff of her shirt. *'Khodaya shukur.'* She raised her hands to the grubby, tobacco-stained ceiling, as tears trickled down her face.

Sultan glanced towards the corridor where she heard footsteps approaching.

Setara appeared with her cellmates and their children. She froze briefly in the doorway, her eyes meeting Sultan's in confusion. After a moment, she murmured something to the others and pointed to the floor below. A few other inmates joined, and Setara, still looking puzzled, gave a small wave to Sultan and Farzana before following the others down the stairs.

Oblivious to the goings-on outside the meeting room, Farzana leaned closer, lowering her voice. 'I was present for most of the delegation's interviews with the women from Cell 86. The things I heard…' she trailed off, shaking her head slowly. 'I wouldn't wish that suffering on my worst enemy.'

Sultan's voice dropped. 'Was Niloofar there, too?'

'No. They interviewed her in Herat. I know nothing about what happened there.' Farzana straightened, tying her hair into a ponytail. Her expression hardened. 'Tahera, Fariba, and Zohra…' Her voice trembled as she paused, swallowing hard. 'They're all certifiably insane now, *bel-kul!*. That's what the psychiatrist said. They had been given ketamine repeatedly, a hallucinogenic tranquiliser. It's destroyed their minds completely.' A grim shadow crossed her face as she hesitated. 'The men responsible… not a single name was mentioned in the report. All we know is they're powerful figures in government and business. But it doesn't end with them. This is all run by a network of *lochaks*. Shaming or jailing a few won't touch the dozens, maybe hundreds, still involved.'

Sultan leaned forward, choosing her words carefully. 'Have you heard of anyone threatened by the ringleaders?' she asked, hoping to gauge the danger facing herself, Setara and others who had collaborated in exposing the scandal.

Farzana nodded, her expression dark. 'Masuma told me she'd received several death threats in text messages. She's resigned from her post and is petrified to leave home. One message read something like, "We know who colluded with you. Their time will come." That's all I know.'

'Why Masuma? Mind you, that doesn't surprise me. The culprits must have targeted her because she was clean,' Sultan muttered under her breath, a lump forming in her throat.

'Only *Allah* knows the truth. But what about those poor girls? Disgraceful! What will happen to their babies?' Farzana clicked her tongue. 'I think the drug has damaged the foetus, too.' She shook her head, her tone sharpening. 'And guess who raped that poor girl, Zohra. The governor! Can you believe it? Remember that meeting he held with us?' Farzana let out a loud, sarcastic laugh, her bitterness palpable.

'What about Roya?'

'She was the only one still sane. She had two interviews. I sat in on the first. I think they've struck a deal, an early release if she keeps quiet.' Farzana sneered. 'And as for those repulsive whores, Parwana and Fereshtah, the ones who orchestrated this... they've vanished. Someone's protecting them.'

'The former mayor of Kabul?' Sultan asked with a sly grin.

'Maybe. New additions to his harem.' Farzana chuckled, her mood lifting slightly. 'But here's what gets me,' she said, furrowing her brow. 'Who tipped off *Khawar News?* I've thought about it long and hard, but I still can't work it out.'

'Divine intervention.' Sultan winked, and they both burst into laughter.

A knock interrupted them. Farzana craned her neck, peering through the glass to see who it was. 'Ah yes... it's Samira, the new Head Guard. I have to go.' She stood, gathering a small pile of books, clothing, and her signature red patent stilettos from the floor. As she made her way to the door, she paused, her gaze roving over the room – her old stomping ground, now a memory. She took a deep breath, her voice barely audible. 'I never thought it would end like this. Sultan *jaan*, forgive me if I ever wronged you or caused you grief.'

Sultan's green eyes softened with a smile. 'Go safely and proudly. All forgiven, even that time you confiscated my first mobile phone.' She let out a loud chuckle.

Farzana's lips quivered, her eyes glistening as she blew a soft kiss. She took another steadying breath, shoulders shaking slightly, and then walked through the door for the last time.

'Congratulations!' Setara yelled as she, Sultan and Sheyda sat, away from the curious eyes of the new guards on their same old threadbare blanket under the familiar almond tree. With only an hour left until the evening lockdown, the sun dipped below the horizon, casting a warm glow over the rugged mountains.

'We did it!' Setara announced, her voice brimming with pride. 'The beasts have resigned and been stripped of their ranks.'

Sultan and Sheyda clapped their hands, their joy subdued to avoid drawing attention from a small group of inmates queuing for dinner outside the kitchen.

'But they're not behind bars, where they belong,' Sultan replied, a chill in her voice. 'They can sneak back into the system whenever they like. Justice still hasn't been served, my friends.' She pulled her phone from her pocket, turning to Setara. 'A message came through earlier. I think it's from Geisha.'

'Let me see.' Setara wiped the grime off the phone's small screen with her sleeve. 'Not one message, there are twenty of them,' she murmured, scrolling down, her eyes narrowing. She froze after reading the first few, putting the phone down on her lap, and taking a deep breath.

'What do they say?' Sultan pressed, her eyes fixed on Setara's face, now drained of colour.

'They're death threats. Anonymous. They all say: "We know who you are. You dirty slut. We're coming for you, wherever you are."'

Sultan gasped. 'I knew this would happen. Who squealed?' She turned her gaze sharply to Sheyda.

'Me?' Sheyda's voice trembled. 'I'm not a snitch, I swear on Imam Reza and my children's lives, Sultan *jaan*! Believe me! It wasn't me.'

Sultan folded her arms, staring into blank space, lost in thought. 'Roya. It has to be her. The conniving floozy!'

'Roya?' Setara shot back, defensive. 'She barely knew if she was coming or going, totally out of her mind. What are you saying?

Besides, we were so careful when she visited that last day. None of us mentioned *Khawar News,* not even hinted how they found out.'

'Wait.' Sheyda's voice softened. 'No, we weren't so careful. Sultan *jaan*, remember what you said? "Their days are numbered."'

Sultan's face went slack. Her hands shot up, covering her ears as if to block out the words. Her eyes widened. 'Damn it... I did.' Her head shook in disbelief, horror etching into her features. 'She tricked us. Played the helpless, innocent act perfectly.' Sultan's voice dropped, heavy with anger. 'Farzana told me. Roya wasn't just sane, she was sharp enough to cut deals with the right people.' She paused, letting the weight of the revelation settle. 'Farzana suspects she got out early. Silence bought her freedom. Or worse, she walked away with more than that.' Sultan's jaw clenched. 'Maybe they rewarded her for giving up our names.'

Sultan's eyes locked with Setara's, rage smouldering beneath the glassy surface.

'What else did Farzana say?' Setara asked.

'She's resigned.'

'Resigned?' Setara shook her head in disbelief. 'Why? Was she implicated?'

'No,' Sultan replied. '*Raees Sahib* had admonished her, accusing her of "failing her duties as Head Guard." And guess what...' Sultan smiled with her usual slyness. Then leaning in, she revealed, 'Farzana said the Italian ambassador is screwing *Raees Sahib*. Those silk scarves and that gold pen she's flaunted were gifts he's given her. Things she can never afford on her salary.' Sultan's voice dropped to a whisper. 'And she's been promoted to governor. So, her powerful connections run far deeper than we thought.'

Sultan's gaze lingered on Setara, her eyes narrowing, brow furrowed. 'Her promotion is just another perk of powerful friends. Don't you think so? And as long as money and influence talk, the cycle goes on.'

'No way!' Setara let out a disbelieving laugh. 'She's married with children.'

'Don't be so naïve. They all have secrets. They're not the ones locked up for *zina*, are they? No, these cells are reserved for the likes of us.'

Sheyda sighed, her voice quiet. 'Who can you trust or believe anymore?'

Setara's face stiffened. 'And Parwana? Fereshtah?'

'Vanished. They've disappeared without a trace.'

Setara sighed, a shadow of resignation crossing her face. 'Victory, however sweet, always comes at a cost.' She smiled faintly, yet her eyes held a hardened determination.

As the light dimmed, they walked back to their cells, their steps heavy, slowed by the weight of their uncertain future. The victory they'd once celebrated now seemed fragile, a thin veil over a system that remained unshaken. For every name exposed, countless others lurked in the shadows. They had faced darkness to reach this point, but knew they'd need far more than luck to survive what lay ahead.

And so, as they disappeared into the fading light, Setara clung to a fragile hope that one day, their sacrifices might spark a fire capable of burning through the shadows that haunted them, even if that day remained painfully out of reach.

Epilogue

Niloofar's fire set the silence ablaze.
Sultan carried it in her rage.
Setara, in her charcoal portraits.
Others carried it in silence, in bruises,
in names they no longer spoke aloud.

The fire passed between them.
It caught on with Sheyda and Geisha, too.
It did not consume everything.
It chose what to remember.
The prison still stands.
In Taliban's Kabul.
The blossoms still come.
And the fire remains –
not wild now, but steady, in every Afghan woman.
Burning to bear witness.

Glossary

Dari and Arabic words and their English equivalents

Aferin	Well done, bravo
Ajab	Wonder, wonderful, amazing, astonishment
Al-hamdulillah	Thank God
Anbagh	A co-wife in a polygamous marriage
Andiwal	A mate
Astaghfirullah	God forgive
Azadi	Freedom
Azan	Muslim call to prayer
Aziz	Dear
Azizum	My dear
Baad marriage	A method of settlement of debt or compensation for a crime, whereby a woman from the debtor's/perpetrator's family is given to the creditor's/victim's family as a bride.
Baashi	Chief
Bacha	Boy, son
Bacha be-adab	Rude boy
Bacha posh	She who wears boy's clothes
Bandi	A prisoner
Banjan rumi	Tomato
Bekas	Helpless, destitute
Bel-kul	Totally, entirely, wholly
Bismillahi Rahmani Rahim	In the Name of God, the most Gracious, the most Merciful.
Beshak	Without a doubt
Bibi	Lady, a noblewoman
Bolani	A popular street-food snack in Afghanistan: flat bread fried with a vegetable filling.

Burqa	A long, loose garment covering a woman's body from head to feet, including the face.
Chadar	A large piece of cloth that is wrapped around the head and body leaving only the face.
Chapan	A traditional Afghan long, loose-fitting coat.
Chars	Cannabis
Charsi	Cannabis user
Chatal	Trash, rubbish
Churis	Bangles, bracelets
Daktar	Doctor
Doogh	Yoghurt drink
Ey Khoda	Oh, God
Farman	Edict, order
Ghaboli Palow	Afghan rice dish
Ghandool	Sweetie
Gum shoo	Get lost
Haft mewa	Seven fruits, fruit and nut delicacy served at Nowruz.
Haj	Muslim pilgrimage to Mecca
Haji	Title for man who has made the pilgrimage to Mecca.
Halalah marriage	Marriage to dissolve the triple divorce.
Harami	A bastard, illegitimate child
Jaan	Life, darling, a term of endearment.
Jaanum	My dear
Jadi	Afghan month equivalent to 22 December-20 January.
Kachal	Bald
Khala	Aunty
Khana	House, home
Khana-e-amn	Safe house
Khoda	God
Khoda beyamorz	God forgive her/him
Khoda hafez	Goodbye
Khodaya shukur	Thank God
Khosh amadi	Welcome
Kuchi	Nomadic

Kunduzi	From Kunduz, a northern province of Afghanistan.
Kussi	Whore, harlot
La ilaha ilallah	There is no god but God
Lochak	Scoundrel
Madar	Mother
Mahram	A legitimate male companion for women.
Maman	A title for Nigerian brothel madams.
Maqbool	Popular, pretty, approved
Mashallah	What God has willed – usually used for praise.
Moin al-zoafa	Protector of the poor
Mujaheddin	Islamic warriors
Mullah	Muslim preacher
Murdagaw	Pimp
Nafasum	My breath, the air I breathe – a loving term.
Naam-e-khoda	In God's name
Nikah	Islamic marriage, matrimony, wedlock
Noosh-e-*jaan*	May your soul be nourished, bon appetite
Nowruz	Afghan New Year
Nowruz mobarak	Afghan Happy New Year greetings.
Pirhan Tunban	Tunic shirt and baggy pants for men.
Qaimaq	Afghan clotted cream
Qandool	Sweetie, term of endearment
Raees	Chief, boss, manager
Roo cheshmum	Literally means 'on my eyes; at your service'.
Sahib	Master/mistress, owner
Salaam	Hello, greeting
Salaam alaikum	Peace be upon you (meaning in Arabic) – a formal greeting.
Sawab	Spiritual reward
Sepas	Thanks, gratitude
Shalwar Kameez	Punjabi tunic and matching trousers.
Shukur	Gratitude, thankful
Shukur-e-khoda	Thank God
Sigheh	Temporary marriage contract
Sobh bakhayr	Good morning

Soorati	Temporary wife
Subhan Allah	Glory be to God
Tashakur	Thanks
Ummat al-Muslimin	The Muslim nation
Wallah	Swear to God
Ya Allah	Oh, God
Yaar	Friend
Zakat	One of five pillars of Islam, giving to the needy

'The women in this novel blaze with defiance and resilience. A powerful testament to the refusal to be silenced against all the odds.'
—**Lillie Razvi Toon**, project manager at Untold Narratives, co-editor of *My Dear Kabul: A Year in the Life of an Afghan Women's Writing Group*

'Afghanistan is the worst country in the world to be a woman. This novel exposes the hardship many women face there but also their quiet dissent, resilience and solidarity... Mandana's deep knowledge of the country breathes life into this moving novel which is inspired by true events!'
—**Baroness Fiona Hodgson of Abinger**, CBE, and fellow campaigner for the rights of Afghan women.

'In 2010, Mandana Hendessi was working for an international NGO and supported Afghan women at risk from gender-based violence before she volunteered in a Kabul women's prison. The women she met in Badam Bagh appear as unforgettable characters in her debut novel, *The Almond Garden of Kabul*. Inmates are puzzled by the self-immolation of a young prisoner. Illiterate but resourceful Sultan, who dresses and acts like a man – she is saving up for a sex change operation in Iran after her release – investigates. *The Almond Garden of Kabul* is based on real events. Its portrayal of Afghan women defies western stereotypes of the boundaries gender in a patriarchal religious society.'
—**Malu Halasa**, editor of The Markaz Review, author of *Mother of All Pigs*